An entrancing and prismatic debut novel by Christine Lai, set in a near future fraught with ecological collapse, *Landscapes* brilliantly explores memory, empathy, preservation, and art as an instrument for recollection and renewal.

In the English countryside—decimated by heat and drought—Penelope archives what remains of an estate's once notable collection. As she catalogues the library's contents, she keeps a diary of her final months in the dilapidated country house that has been her home for two decades and a refuge for those who have been displaced by disasters. Out of necessity, Penelope and her partner, Aidan, have sold the house and its scheduled demolition marks the pressing deadline for completing the archive. But with it also comes the impending return of Aidan's brother, Julian, at whose hands Penelope suffered during a brief but violent relationship twenty-two years before. As Julian's visit looms, Penelope finds herself unable to suppress the past, and she clings to art as a means of understanding, of survival, and of reckoning.

Recalling the works of Rachel Cusk and Kazuo Ishiguro, *Landscapes* is an elegiac and spellbinding blend of narrative, essay, and diary that reinvents the country house novel for our age of catastrophe, and announces the arrival of an extraordinarily gifted new writer.

Praise for *Landscapes*

"Gentle and wise, intimate and atmospheric, elegant and impressionistic, at the center of *Landscapes* is a question that is almost always on my mind now. What do we do with art, with beauty, in a time of crisis and collapse?"
AMINA CAIN, AUTHOR OF *A HORSE AT NIGHT* & *INDELICACY*

"Christine Lai's *Landscapes* is a haunting archive of the long-gone, the broken, and the soon-to-be-lost—a study in disintegration—but also, simultaneously, a heady page-turner about beauty and community and, through these, hope. A startling and beautiful debut."
DANIELLE DUTTON, AUTHOR OF *MARGARET THE FIRST* & *SPRAWL*

"In deft movements triangulating possession, loss, and memory, Lai's meditative accounting of lives and culture in violent displacement and ruination feels like a witnessing of our probable path through the years ahead, in which all may be uncertain but the human will to repair and rebuild."
PITCHAYA SUDBANTHAD, AUTHOR OF *BANGKOK WAKES TO RAIN*

"A marvelous, deeply intelligent novel about art, and ruins, and loss—and the stubborn, beautiful human urge to never give up. Christine Lai's *Landscapes* shimmers in the mind's eye, long after the last page has been turned. Wonderful."
STEVEN PRICE, AUTHOR OF *LAMPEDUSA*

"This is a novel engaged in inventive, intelligent, challenging conversation with the literature of the past, while presenting a clear-eyed and prescient vision of the future. Lai writes gorgeously of transience and decay, capturing the aesthetic ecstasy and redemptive power of art while interrogating its role in a crumbling and unjust world. A bold and rewarding debut."
KIM FU, AUTHOR OF *LESSER KNOWN MONSTERS OF THE 21ST CENTURY*

"An exquisite debut about art and desire, love and deceit, reminiscent of A.S. Byatt in its richly researched and deeply compelling story and prose."
LEE HENDERSON, AUTHOR OF *DISINTEGRATION IN FOUR PARTS*

"In an apocalyptic future that feels eerily familiar in its prescience, two characters, their pasts woven together and marked by an act of unspeakable violence, make their way back together across space and time, their memories mediated through observations about art, music and architecture… *Landscapes* is a propulsive read that teems with tension and pathos. With captivating and crystalline prose, Lai weaves art criticism, feminist theory and epistolary writing to maximum effect, the result a work that is haunting, prismatic and utterly engrossing. Stunningly brilliant and intricately observed, Landscapes is an astonishing debut."
JASMINE SEALY, AUTHOR OF *THE ISLAND OF FORGETTING*

"A powerful meditation on the aliveness of art, and the myriad ways in which our most meaningful experiences coalesce in the world of things. Set in a world falling to ruin, Lai deftly conjures a prismatic lens through which the consequences of obsession and neglect can be viewed. An elegant novel with an urgent undertow, *Landscapes* is a potent reminder of what it means to be a custodian: of the planet, of our own creations, and of each other. An impressive debut from a singular voice, *Landscapes* is a rewarding read—as resonant and tonally rich as the works by Turner that haunt its core."

AISLINN HUNTER, AUTHOR OF *THE CERTAINTIES*

"Lai captures the intersectionality of art, feminism, and environmentalism in this moving debut novel... Though the themes of this book are complex, Christine Lai's writing does not over-complicate the art. *Landscapes* is beautiful, provocative, and accessible. It will remind you that destruction is rarely the end and that we all must continue forward."

SAMANTHA HUI, *INDEPENDENT BOOK REVIEW*

"Lai debuts with an intelligent narrative of an archivist living and working in the English countryside in a near future wracked by climate change... Alongside Penelope's trauma, thoughtfully developed ekphrases show how violence against women has not only been banalized, but positively coded in the tradition of Western painting. The text is an elegant assembly of such descriptions, along with catalogue entries, excerpts from Penelope's journal, and sections written from Julian's perspective. Sebald fans should take note."

PUBLISHERS WEEKLY

"[*Landscapes*] builds an electric undercurrent of doom. In cool, sinewy prose, this astute and timely novel explores the roles of beauty, art, and passion in a time of survival."

KIRKUS REVIEWS

"A celebration of co-creation at its best. Christine Lai chronicles the days of the end in a subdued manner. She makes sure we know that we all have something at stake in the climate crisis, and we can continue to reach towards each other in the end."

TAY JONES, WHITE WHALE BOOKSTORE

"This exceptional, atmospheric book is anchored in the equally atmospheric landscape paintings of Turner. Inventive in form, it moves between diary, catalog, critique, and narrative as it tells the story of a woman in a ruined near future slowly letting go of the life she knew, while being haunted by an attack she suffered years ago. It's a book with so many layers it requires a rereading, or two, to appreciate all it holds. Have your phone or tablet at the ready as you'll want to reference the many artworks mentioned."
ALANA HALEY, SCHULER BOOKS

"Catastrophes are also quiet. Climate change will also change our hearts & minds. In what might be my favorite novel on the topic, [Lai] uses the dissolution of previously grand English estate & the grumbling mental & emotional resolve of its archivist to explore the experiences and emotions of decay and disintegration. Art. Politics. A love triangle involving brothers. There is also great depth to this story beneath the big impacts of rising sea levels. A truly brilliant novel."
JOSH COOK, PORTER SQUARE BOOKS

"Told through diary entries and catalog notes *Landscapes* by Christine Lai a powerful debut novel about memory, empathy, art, loss, and climate change."
CAITLIN BAKER, ISLAND BOOKS

"Beautiful writing…"
PERCY SUTTON, BOOKS ON THE SQUARE

"I am very excited for everyone else to read Christine Lai's pastoral novel that blends narrative, diary, and essay while exploring memory and our connection to art objects against a backdrop of an old mansion in the dying English countryside."
CHARLENE CHOW, FLYING BOOKS

Two Dollar Radio
Books too loud to Ignore

WHO WE ARE Two Dollar Radio is a family-run outfit dedicated to reaffirming the cultural and artistic spirit of the publishing industry. We aim to do this by presenting bold works of literary merit, each book, individually and collectively, providing a sonic progression that we believe to be too loud to ignore.

TwoDollarRadio.com

Proudly based in
Columbus
OHIO

 @TwoDollarRadio

 @TwoDollarRadio

 /TwoDollarRadio

Love the
PLANET?

So do we.

Printed on Rolland Enviro.
This paper contains 100% post-consumer fiber, is manufactured using renewable energy - Biogas and processed chlorine free.

 100%   PCF   BIO GAS° ENERGY   PERMANENT

SOME RECOMMENDED LOCATIONS FOR READING:
Pretty much anywhere because books are portable and the perfect technology!

COVER PHOTOS⇢ BACKGROUND: *Woman Viewing Abstract Art* by Alvin Nee/
Unsplash; CENTER: English Lake Scenery, Illustrated with a series of coloured plates
from drawings by A. F. Lydon/British Library/Unsplash. **DESIGN**⇢ Eric Obenauf.

Two Dollar Radio would like to acknowledge that the land where we live and work is the contemporary territory of multiple Indigenous Nations.

for Diccon

What is ultimately most important about *durée* for me is the way it crystallizes into a shape, a form, an image, a metaphor.

Louise Bourgeois

landscapes

A NOVEL

Christine Lai

Two Dollar Radio
Books too loud to ignore

PROLOGUE

Throughout his long career, the nineteenth-century English painter J. M. W. Turner returned repeatedly to the Ehrenbreitstein Fortress, in the German town of Koblenz. For centuries, a fortified edifice stood on the site that overlooks the confluence of two great rivers, the Mosel and the Rhine. Ehrenbreitstein was once a Roman military fort; the home of a holy relic; a symbol of successive regimes of power; and the target of countless attacks. During the Napoleonic Wars, the Prussian defenders lost Ehrenbreitstein to the French army, who destroyed it ahead of their retreat. The fortress lay in this state of devastation when Turner first encountered it on his tour of the Rhineland.

On his subsequent visits to the region, he would have seen the rebuilt, grander structure. Yet in his sketches, watercolors, and one major oil painting, Turner depicted not the forbidding battlements of the reconstructed Ehrenbreitstein, but the wreckage of the old fortress, standing defiantly atop the cliffs. It was as if the painter's eyes overleapt the newly built form and his gaze continued to be held by the ruins of the half-demolished structure, poised on the threshold between collapse and renewal.

ONE

SEPTEMBER

SEPTEMBER 1

I picture myself standing in the midst of a ruin. All around me there are mildewed canvases, rolled up crudely or crammed into drawers. The edges of the papers, mouse-eaten or worm-eaten, fall into heaps of dust.

As I work through the disorderly archive and chip away at the mountain of responsibilities, my mind is drawn back to this image of Turner's studio, left in a state of Pompeii-like destruction after the painter's death. That same atmosphere of decay permeates the Library in which I spend my mornings. On better days, disorder is forestalled, and there is only the linearity of the catalogue and the neat collection of books and objects. On days of anxiety, such as today, I find myself stranded in the wreckage. The dust that has gathered in the corners, the moldy papers, the shelves that bend under the weight of books and archival boxes, all these seem to be advancing toward me, millimeter by millimeter, until they overwhelm me.

SEPTEMBER 2

A calmer start to the day. A thin column of sunlight shines down from above. Elsewhere, the Library's underground storage space is illuminated by a solar-powered lamp that is recharged daily on the desiccated lawn. I write by the light of this lamp and a pile of books serves as my desk.

Before I sat down to write, I spent some time admiring the flowers I keep in secret. The earthquake five years ago resulted in an irreparable crack down one wall of the Library. But plants have forced their way through the fissure and have begun to sprout in the space where books were once stored. Even now, as aridness eats through the outside world, the weeds and flowers that have flourished in the aftermath of disaster are protected by the shadows and nourished by the water from the broken pipe. I have not told anyone about this pipe, not even Aidan, as it would be fixed immediately, depriving the flowers of their sole source of water. This spot of green is the only place where I allow water to drip away unchecked; these flowers the only luxury I permit myself to keep in these days of want and longing.

It has been almost three years since it rained in this part of England. First came the floods, then came the droughts. Here at Mornington Hall, the one-thousand-acre parkland is parched, and the remaining leaves crumble between my fingers. Parts of the earth lie fractured, creating intricate webbing that spreads out like dark veins. I never thought I'd miss the cold, wet air on rainy days. We now count in milliliters, careful not to exceed the amount of water the government has allotted to the house. The small bottles Aidan and I pass between us are not merely tools of survival, but also mementoes of a past that recedes further and further with each passing month.

A nature diary composed over the past decade would read like a catalogue of losses. There was a time when catastrophe seemed far away. We glided through the seasons confident that each calendar year would yield the same degree of heat and cold, the same blossoms and migrating birds. Then change became visible. In aerial photographs, the earth, cracked, burnt, and striated by the lines of industry, resembled a painting, and some saw beauty.

Nothing is certain, they continued to say. *We'll see, we'll see.* We have seen, yet the debates have intensified and some persist in believing the sky to be unchanging, the only immutable thing in a world of fluid truths.

Yesterday, I agonized over what to do with the boxes of newspapers I had collected at one point, news articles that detailed the progressive deterioration of the world we knew. I felt obliged, as an archivist, to keep a physical copy of everything, as though the collecting and preserving of these words could somehow stave off disaster. But a few months ago, during yet another heat wave that killed human and non-human animals alike, I stopped collecting the news. For the first time, archiving seemed futile. The heat encased us like a cocoon and we re-emerged into the melting world with fewer illusions about the future.

This morning, after confirming that the cedar tree I have loved for so long is indeed beyond saving, I started using the archived newspapers for packaging.

SEPTEMBER 3

I left my childhood home and came here to Mornington Hall twenty-two years ago, at the start of my research fellowship. But now, in less than a year, this house, too, will be gone. The Long Gallery with its view of the park; the Conservatory with its surviving plants; the Library with its white columns—all these are to be demolished in about seven months.

Mornington, in its old age, has endured countless cycles of change and reinvention. It was once an aristocratic estate, a school, a hospital, and for a period of time after the Second World War, a cow shed and pigeon coop. When Aidan's family purchased the estate decades ago, they restored it to its former self as a symbol of long-lost refinement.

We have now entered another phase of disrepair. The house has been falling apart for years. Rainstorms have inundated rooms; heat has dried and cracked the paint and plaster. Some days, Mornington seems uncommonly fragile. Pipes burst, windows break, and parts of the façade peel away in the wind. Since I first moved in with Aidan, we have attempted to avert decay by daily care, by the physical work of cleaning and mending, saving the house one piece at a time, and accommodating as many travelers as possible in the rooms that remain intact.

People once spoke of *Ruinenlust*, of the picturesque and melancholy beauty of abandoned buildings. On one occasion, Aidan joked that Mornington resembles the Villa Savoye, which had fallen into a state of complete dilapidation, filled with the stench of urine and excrement, its white walls smeared with graffiti. Even in that soiled state, Villa Savoye was still considered beautiful by some. But here, we know only the exhaustion of having to keep the house from collapsing.

The structural damage caused by the earthquake compromised much of the underground storage system in the Library. The robotic arms are broken, and we have to climb down a ladder to access the lower storage level. The flood from the burst pipes also damaged the collection. We have sold most of the valuable pieces to finance the repairs, including Turner's *A View on the Seine*, once the gem of the house. Some artworks have gone to the national archives and museums; others to private collectors.

The items that remain in the Library do not have high market value: the books and objects that have sustained significant damage from the flood, and the ephemera I added during my time here. Before Mornington is dismantled, most of these artifacts must be reorganized and re-catalogued for potential online sale. Some items will be discarded. Others we might add to our own collection, which we will take with us when we leave in the spring. I also wish to keep a record of the objects that I find evocative, with a description of their physical states as they exist now, in my hands. This, then, has been my main task since early August: the building of an archive of remains.

Also in seven months: Julian's scheduled return to Mornington, to visit the house one last time. And I will see, for the first time in twenty-two years, the man who forced himself upon me in the unbearable summer heat. I still remember the cries of the nightjar that evening, and the agitated glimmer of the lamp that arced over the painting of death hanging on the wall.

PHOTOGRAPHS
Twelve black-and-white photographs, measuring 27 x 35 cm, depicting Mornington Hall, *ca.* 1920. Unbound, held in brown archival box. Photographer unknown. Toning and wear along the edges. Imperfections due to moisture.

SEPTEMBER 12
The house in the photographs both is and is not the house I know. The first photo in the series shows the front façade. At the start of my fellowship, I first beheld this view in person: the pale stone, the central dome, and the long path lined with stretches of uncut grass. I remember how a breeze moved through the grass as I walked by, so that the undulating fields resembled a green sea bearing the barge that was Mornington.

The next photo shows the main entrance, flanked by Corinthian columns, with a marble frieze and intricate stone garlands above. When I reached the front door that first day, I found it wide open. My eyes scanned the colors in the vestibule—the black-and-white marble of the floor; the bronze of the sweeping staircase; and the pale-green panels on the walls. The house was silent and pristine, as if it had never known human habitation. An administrative assistant came out to greet me and led me to the Round Gallery, where I was asked to wait.

She told me that the quiet was to be enjoyed while it lasted, because the renovations were to begin in a few days' time. A new glasshouse was to be erected in the garden, and many rooms to be modernized, at the behest of the new owner, Julian.

Next in the box is a photo of the Round Gallery, an octagonal space topped with a dome and sky-lit through a glass oculus. Inside the semi-circular apses were marble statues of Roman gods; on the walls were some of the best paintings in the house.

On that first day, I tried to take a closer look at the Constable, but it was hung rather high up. As I stood on tiptoes to examine the landscape of a rural scene, a gust of wind blew in through the open front door, bringing with it a spiral of loose sheets of paper that spun around the gallery before the gust died down and the sheets settled on the floor. That was when I first met Aidan. He ran in after the papers with a stack of sheets in his hands. I still remember the warmth of his extended hand, which I held lightly in mine.

I wanted to welcome you when you arrived, he said, but I lost track of time. This place is temporarily in my charge.

He picked up the papers, covered with architectural sketches, and led me into the Hall, which was modeled on the atrium of a Roman villa. There were twenty fluted alabaster columns, with Corinthian capitals, standing on the patterned marble floor. A skylight lit the space from above. Gilded plaster ornaments filled the voids between antique statues and urns.

I know it's a lot to take in at first, Aidan said. But these great houses are never what they seem. You see the faded silk wallpaper? I've been told to get rid of that. I also need to replace that tapestry. The moths got to it.

In the nineteenth century, I later read, Mornington Hall was famed for its seamless transition from interior to exterior, so that the man-made and the natural were interlaced in complete harmony. Large doors and windows opened onto the veranda lined with plants, beyond which were the flower beds and the velvety lawns, all replicated in the mirrors of the Long Gallery. Wallpaper was covered with trellises of roses, and ceilings painted with clouds and stars. The first owner, who had commissioned the building of the house to showcase his sugar wealth, held parties regularly. One party, mimicking a famous fête hosted at Carlton House by the spendthrift Prince Regent, featured an actual stream that coursed through the Dining Hall, stocked with goldfish and lined with real banks of moss and grass.

I sometimes wonder what Turner, the son of a barber, felt when he first stepped into Mornington. I wonder if he felt the same sense of unease that I, the daughter of a gardener, felt— still feel—when I came to this seat of opulence, the opulence that would not have allowed room for someone like me. I find greater comfort in the house's current state of dereliction. It seems more honest, more aligned with the rest of the world.

SEPTEMBER 15

Tonight, a simple dinner of vegetable soup and roasted potatoes. Aidan has just returned from a work trip, to survey a potential construction site. We decided to use candles at dinner, for the ambience, and the candlelight created haloes around the faces gathered at the table so that, for a brief while, we resembled the subjects of a painting. Aidan had on blue denim this evening, with the orange sweater that I knitted for him three years ago. The colors recall a Poussin painting, even though I don't think he ever captured a scene by candlelight.

When I first stood before Poussin's *The Abduction of the Sabine Women*, I was seduced by the intense colors. The ultramarine appeared to exert a physical force that leapt out of the frame and into the space of the gallery so that I was pinned to the spot, unable to move or avert my gaze. I was so transfixed by that blue that I nearly overlooked the violent nature of the subject.

The painting, completed in 1633–34, originally belonged to the French ambassador to Rome; then it passed to Cardinal Richelieu in Paris, where it stayed in several palatial residences before it was sold to a collector in Rotterdam. In the late eighteenth century it arrived in England, where it was housed for over a hundred years at the magnificent Stourhead. A few decades at Doughty House, in Richmond, followed, before the painting entered a museum collection in New York.

I try to imagine what the residents and visitors at Stourhead or Doughty—grand estates like Mornington—would have thought of *The Abduction of the Sabine Women*. I picture a party at Stourhead in the late nineteenth century, in the heyday of the English country house. All the elegantly dressed guests, wine glasses in hand, are scattered around the drawing room furnished with Chippendale cabinets and lined with Persian rugs. Outside the curtained windows: the sculpted gardens and the Wiltshire Downs beyond.

The male guests have returned from a hunt, the female guests from a walk in the gardens. The butler enters with drinks and hors d'oeuvres on a silver platter. The men discuss banking and the state of their companies in distant lands. They discuss art, for they are all collectors. Someone gestures to the Poussin, and the owner, proud of the acquisition, shares the details of the auction and the moments of anxiety when the painting was nearly lost to the other bidder, followed by the eventual relief and triumph. The female guests join in the collective admiration of the masterpiece illumined by the chandelier. They comment on the composition, on Poussin's expert rendering of ancient architecture.

Only one person turns away from the painting, an older woman, the sister of the owner of the estate, who is herself a collector and has written a few essays on art. She stands at the window and her gaze is drawn to the scenery outside, scarcely visible in the waning twilight.

A gong sounds. The butler announces that dinner is served. The group proceeds to the dining room. But the woman remains standing at the window. She looks at the Poussin through its reflection in the glass, its colors slightly dulled. As she studies the image of the abducted Sabine women superimposed on the layered landscape outside—on the woods emptied of a few more living beings after each hunt, on the remnants of the unsightly thickets that were burned, on the folly that was torn down after she herself, barely fifteen, was assaulted in its stony interior—as she contemplates all this, she understands, not for the first time, the true cost of all this beauty.

OBJECT
Claude glass, *ca.* 1800, small convex mirror, with dark tinted glass. Approximately 10 cm in diameter. Circular bronze case, covered with leather; interior lined with silk. Cover scratched; mirror bears mark of mended fracture. Named for the French painter Claude Lorrain. Used by artists and landscape viewers to reflect the view or make tonal adjustments for painting.

SEPTEMBER 21
Last week, while the solar panels were being repaired, a toolbox was accidentally dropped onto the central dome of the Round Gallery. The stained glass shattered. Thankfully no one was in the vicinity when it happened, but I cut my fingers as I helped clean up the multicolored glass fragments scattered across the floor.

I can't believe this happened, Aidan said. They should have been more cautious. No, it was my fault. I should have supervised more closely.

It'll be okay—I say this to him often.

That beautiful stained glass, he said in a low voice.

I know. But we can't fix that.

Over the years, pieces of the house have slipped away from our hands, one by one, and loss has become commonplace. When we first began selling off the artworks in the Round Gallery, I grieved for the paintings. They left gaps on the walls, patches of brilliant color that contrasted with the ashen parts faded by sunlight. Each time I experience a sense of loss, I tell myself that none of this was mine to begin with, and none of it was as important as it seemed.

We cleared the broken glass, then Aidan, with the help of two of the men who have been staying with us, blocked off the Round Gallery using wooden planks taken from the empty bedrooms on the upper levels.

The money from the sale of the last batch of paintings has given us funds for repairs and a new backup generator. In order to conserve energy and better insulate the areas that are frequently used, Aidan and his colleagues from the architectural firm constructed plexiglass partitions to separate the living quarters from the disused rooms.

But at times, I still like to venture into those blocked-off areas, in spite of the cold. I'm particularly fond of the room at the top of the three-story southeast pavilion that extends outward from the front of the house. The roof of the pavilion collapsed years ago, during a season of storms. Initially, we panicked. But Aidan grew fond of that wound in the ceiling; he said it reminded him of the oculus at the Pantheon.

We adapted to the new space, just as the room itself adapted to the opening in the roof, taking in all the elements of the outside world. Birdsong, when it still existed, entered through the opening. Dust entered, and sometimes the smell of distant smoke could also be detected. Vines grew, puddles formed, and dead leaves carpeted the floor. When it rained, a column of water would materialize in the middle of the room.

The rain left dark streaks down the whole length of the walls and exposed the wormlike pipes. The colors of the walls changed, year by year. The blue faded into mottled green, and the green gradually became yellow. Dampness also created pockets of air bubbles in the damaged wallpaper.

Sometimes, when the sun shines directly into the room, a column of light appears. I like to set up a desk in this column, so that the sunlight envelops me. It is here, in the middle of this interior landscape, that I write today.

SEPTEMBER 22

The house is quiet. There are twenty-one people staying with us right now. During the day, most of them are on the main floor of the central block, the *corps de logis*, which stretches from the Dining Hall on the northern end, through the Long Gallery and Conservatory, to the Green Writing Room, which has been converted into an office where I spend half of my days, overseeing the management of the house and grounds. Next to the Green Writing Room are the doors to the Library.

Aidan has been spending most of his time in the studio on the upper level, which faces west, offering a view of the sweeping vista designed by Capability Brown. All the larger bedrooms next to ours are currently occupied, and these, too, face the parkland. The group of younger travelers have little interest in such a view, perhaps not wanting to be reminded of all that had been destroyed. They have, instead, set up tents in the Hall. In the evenings, the tents glow from within when the inhabitants read or chat by the camping lanterns.

The northeast pavilion, which forms its own self-contained three-story block, has been repurposed to accommodate most of the other travelers. Some of them stay with us for as long as a year; others, mere days. Most stay for about a month before they move on to their next destination or to government housing. It is for them that we strive to keep the house intact. I call them travelers because not all of them are refugees. They are also not wanderers, for they have destinations, even if the gates might be closed to them. In all cases, though, they are bodies in transition, moving toward an uncertain future.

The plan to take in travelers was partly to do with my own internal shifts, and partly to do with Aidan's work, his emergency shelter built using salvaged wood and construction waste. That summer when I accompanied him to the refugee camp near the Mediterranean was a pivotal point, and I think about it occasionally. When we returned from that trip, I applied for a non-profit license for Mornington. After the final residency program ended twelve years ago, and the artists departed, we refurbished the bedrooms and posted announcements online. We settled into a rhythm of preparing, welcoming, sending off, and reorganizing. This, then, became the work of my life.

The trip to the camp also marked the end of my academic career. Up until then, I had continued to apply for research positions, with little success, even as my belief in the efficacy of intellectual work was waning. At the refugee camp, it shocked and shamed me to realize that all of my research could not tell me what to do when money ran out, when the earth ceased to produce food. Ideas and theories could no longer hold together the disparate parts of the world. I rarely think back on my sojourn in academia. I cannot bear to remember the yearning for accomplishment, for prestige. The blindness of it all. I have retained the love of art, of Turner, disentangled from the obsession with accolades. This love sustains me, however naïve it might appear from the standpoint of scholarship. Looking back now, I doubt whether it was really knowledge I possessed, and not a very selective, rarefied view of the world.

In recent months, I have gotten to know two of the travelers, since both of them are staying at Mornington on a long-term basis. Miranda is here with her husband, Carlos, a carpenter, who has been working in the village nearby. Before coming here they lived in Spain, where Miranda taught English and ran an online shop selling cross-stitch and embroidery kits. The heat forced them to migrate north.

Celia is a painter. She stayed here years ago for one of the residency programs; I had invited her here after seeing some of her evocative pieces at a small gallery in London. She too had studied at the Slade, though she was a few years ahead of me. Her portraits of strangers and loved ones exude a deep sense of pathos, as though they offered a narrative about the subject, despite not presenting a single fact about them. She has painted Mornington too, but never in its entirety, only in parts—a column, a cornice, or a door handle, rendered in muted, autumnal tones.

Today Celia asked if she could paint my portrait. She has painted many of the people she met during her travels. Having never sat for an artist, I have no concept of what exactly I have agreed to do. But it was difficult to refuse her. Whenever I speak to her, I get the sense that she is someone who has surmounted untold obstacles, someone whose seeming fragility belies great resilience.

BOOK

Cicero, *De Oratore*. Published by B. et Gul Noyes, 1839. Chipped spine edge. Tan leather boards with moderate wear. Marbled endpapers, water-stained. Binding loose, but all contents intact. Significant foxing throughout.

SEPTEMBER 26

I first came across *De Oratore* by chance, at an art exhibition in which the artist referenced Cicero's tale of the poet Simonides, who was able to recollect the exact location of all those who had perished in a disaster by retracing the architectural space. The art of memory thus involves forming visual placeholders for objects, people, or ideas, and depositing them into an imaginary building erected in the mind.

Two houses serve as my memory palaces—Mornington Hall and the house I shared with Dad for the first three decades of my life. The latter was the same as countless such houses in the many boroughs of London. White doors flanked by white columns, with brick walls and small bay windows overlooking a tiny garden. Dad was proud of the fact that our house blended seamlessly into the neighborhood, without any details that stood out or drew attention. But I wished we had a mint-green door, which I have seen on a similar building in an adjacent street.

When I started university, I moved into the refurbished lower ground level, which used to be my mother's dance studio and storage space. After she left us, when I was a few months old, Dad discarded most of her belongings, and the space remained empty. As soon as I moved in, I cleared away the dust and detritus, and lined the walls with pictures. I remember the few pieces by friends, all of which I lost in the flood: an oil painting of a glass vase filled with peonies; a portrait of a London street; pencil sketches of abstract shapes and lines. I also displayed copies of the artworks I have loved at one time or another, many of which I still keep with me. There was Rodin's *The Cathedral*, with two stone hands turned toward one another, holding an empty space between them. Those hands intrigued me, and I always wondered whether they were on the verge of touch or separation. As a response to the Rodin, I pinned a postcard of Louise Bourgeois's *10 am is When You Come to Me*, consisting of twenty etchings of red, pink, and brown hands overlapping or clasping one another—a portrayal of friendship, of art as a meeting of hands. Below this was a black-and-white photograph of Joseph Cornell in his studio, hemmed in by pictures and miscellany.

I recall the thrill of being surrounded by these images. I remember how it felt to be captivated and confused by them, to be at a complete loss for words.

On the wall next to my desk was a framed print of Turner's 1845 *Norham Castle, Sunrise*, the first painting I ever loved. I settled on Turner as my subject of study because of that painting. At a certain point, I wanted to spend my life in that landscape. By using a technique that he had perfected in watercolor, Turner applied thin layers of translucent paint which rendered everything luminous and diaphanous, the radiant forms blending into one another and melting into golden light. But the painting's radiance belies its dark core, the ghostly blue ruins of Norham Castle, once the site of battles and death. This is what I love in Turner—the way violence is embedded in a gleaming landscape.

Next to *Norham Castle, Sunrise* I had pinned postcard reproductions of Turner's marine disasters and stormy seas. I wrote my thesis on his works all those years ago, seated next to the images. During those research days, it was as though I, like Turner, had strapped myself to the mast of a ship in the middle of the storm and witnessed the raging of the sea and the tumultuous waves that swallowed the untethered human bodies. If I studied the disaster paintings long enough, I would experience the sensation of being thrown upon the wild waves, along with those frail human forms entangled in the white crests, their arms reaching out desperately for the chance to evade death.

Those images accompanied me during one of my most intense intervals of waiting. After I finished the doctoral program in art history, I spent a long stretch of time waiting. There were days when I would wake up early in the morning, then, after finding no replies to any of my applications, I would go back to bed and sleep until the afternoon, then attempt to continue writing in the garden. I waited for the desired response that never arrived. At the time, I found it ironic that I was named after the wife of Odysseus, the woman who waited. I learned that the only way to wait was to cancel out all thoughts of time until the days melted into one another. There is a boundary beyond which one ceases to believe that waiting will yield anything except the passing of minutes and hours. The only things that remained clear were the pictures on the wall.

All in good time, Dad used to say to me. He would bring tea down to my room, and we would have our evening chat in the little sitting area.

It took me ages to get my job at Kew, he said. You must be patient.

I am patient, or I think I am. But how long do I have to be patient for?

I know the situation is difficult, Dad said. I honestly can't say how well I would do if I were in your position. But I was patient, and then something came along and you take the opportunity, and more opportunities will come from that. You'll see.

I'm not sure about that anymore. Maybe art... I mean, maybe something other than art, maybe I should have done that instead. You know, all those classmates who went into useful, pragmatic disciplines? Those classmates are somewhere else.

Where are they?

Well, we never kept in touch, so I don't know exactly. But that's not the point. The point is... well, I can't remember what the point is, but it doesn't matter. Can we please, please stop talking about this?

Dad would gently pat me on the shoulder when I felt hopeless. Be patient, Penny, he would say to me. Something will come along. You'll see.

Dad was the only one who called me Penny. I have not heard that name since he passed away.

I got the sense that he never knew how to react to my despondency. But there were times when he accepted my frustration, times when he said, I know, dear, how unfair the system is. None of us know what will happen. But no matter. You will find something.

What Dad had hoped would happen never happened, and the world became what it is. But I did receive the three-month research fellowship that brought me to Mornington Hall, and to Turner's *A View on the Seine*.

I knew that the painter himself had stayed in the house for a period of time, when he was a young artist who had received patronage from the original owner of the estate. In an unfinished watercolor, Turner depicted the Library at Mornington, with its mahogany desks and shelves of leather-bound books. Another drawing shows bookcases and armchairs bathed in diagonal lines of sunlight. The Library underwent extensive renovations before I arrived, so the space I saw was no longer what it was in Turner's days.

As I had feared, the work on this archive, the handling of these artifacts and images, means sliding slowly into memories. Or rather, I feel as if I'm standing inside a tank, and the memories are rising higher and higher until one day, they will tip over the edge and I will drown.

BOOK
Aby Warburg, *Bilderatlas Mnemosyne*. Published in 2020 by Hatje Cantz, as a companion to the exhibition at the Haus der Kulturen der Welt in Berlin. Elephant folio. Volume contains facsimiles of the sixty-three panels of Warburg's monumental "image atlas," composed of reproductions of paintings, sculptures, old photographs, books, newspapers, magazines,

tapestries, playing cards, and postage stamps. In fair condition—
except for a ripped copy of panel no. 77.

SEPTEMBER 30

Today I cleaned an unconventional portrait of Aidan's family. It
was covered in dust and the paint was flaking off. The picture
showed Mornington Hall as seen from the garden, with Aidan,
Julian, and their parents looking toward the house, their backs to
the viewer, their faces unseen.

Twenty-two years ago, while waiting for the result of my
application for the Mornington fellowship, I developed a sort
of obsession with the family in the portrait. I dove into a frenzy
of fact-finding and image-collecting, though it is unclear to me
now why I was intrigued by them in the first place.

At the time, one of the few connections I discovered between
myself and the family was through Toby, a former classmate of
mine at the Slade. When he was around twelve, he had attended
the same school as Julian, though Julian was older. I contacted
Toby, who divulged very little at first, except that he had known
Julian well at one point. I pressed him for more details. It was
not until after the acceptance letter for the fellowship arrived
that I received Toby's response, in which he related an incident
that occurred during Julian's final year at the school.

That spring, Toby explained, it rained relentlessly, so the
students stayed in the school building more than usual. After
classes, many of them would gather in the library. One day,
someone took an object that belonged to Julian, and a confrontation ensued. It was something Julian made, Toby recalled,
a little building made out of paper and wooden sticks. The other
boy mocked him and tore it to bits.

"Before the tutors arrived," Toby wrote in the email, "Julian
jumped on the boy. He beat him with his bare hands. It was
shocking. I called Julian's name but he didn't seem to hear me.

He held the other boy down, and fed him punch after punch. Blood streamed out of the boy's gums and nose. I stood there watching with the other students until the adults intercepted. The wooden floorboards of the library were stained with blood, I remember that very clearly. Julian never talked about that day. We went on like nothing happened. He transferred to another school the following year. I don't know if that had anything to do with the incident. I never saw him again."

After reading Toby's email that day, I visited the Victoria and Albert Museum to look at the stone effigies in the Cast Courts. The museum also served as a memory palace at various points in my life. There was a time, when I was about six and I had an argument with Dad during one of our visits, I hid in the galleries for an hour before being discovered. Later, I fell in love in a room full of Raphaels, when Michael, a classmate at college, had kissed me. The ceramics gallery on the top floor was a sanctuary where I worked my way through the subsequent heartbreak. One corner of the museum offered a great view of the cityscape, and there I sat for the whole afternoon after I received the acceptance letter for graduate studies. In the Cast Courts, I found inspiration for the doctoral project. In the shadows of the truncated Trajan's Column, among the statues and effigies, I grasped the importance of darkness in Turner's works. Everyone was enthralled by the light in Turner, but I wanted to explore the shadows. Even in the brightest landscapes—like *Norham Castle, Sunrise*—there was chaos and darkness in which one might detect the artist's wish to paint an entirely different sort of picture. The darkness of battles and empires; the dark forces of nature; the darkness that follows the blinding light at the center of the canvas. And the darkness of erotic desire, in the drawings that Ruskin hid in a folder intentionally mislabeled "Plants."

That day, with Toby's message lodged in my mind, I went to the Cast Courts and thought about Julian. In hindsight, Toby's story should have been a kind of warning. But instead, it instilled in me an even greater curiosity about Julian that prompted me to accept the offer of the fellowship without pause. Julian intrigued me because he was a figure that lurked in the shadows of the house. I imagined that he harbored within him the same kind of darkness that lies in what I considered, at the time, to be Turner's best works. And for that reason alone, I felt more drawn to him than to Aidan, whom I associated with light—with the bright and airy spaces he designed—and it was a long while before I understood the false appeal of that darkness. Sitting on a bench in the Cast Courts, I looked for a photo of Julian online, one I had already seen during an Internet search. Something in his expressionless face was kin to the stone bodies and faces I saw before me, the meticulously sculpted exterior that covered the bones—or the nothingness—that lay within. I found the photo chilling, but at the same time, it thrilled me, a thrill I had hitherto felt solely in relation to art.

It is the image of the effigies that I recall today in anticipation of seeing Julian again next year. But now, only the chill remains.

After visiting the Cast Courts that day, I wandered through the other rooms at the V&A. I saw a painting that is rooted in my mind, though I have forgotten its title and the name of the painter. All I remember are the shades of umber and the subject: a country house set in the middle of the woods. In the foreground, there was a mysterious circular patch of burgundy, perhaps a small pond. But when I first encountered the painting, I formed in my mind the image of a pool of blood on the floor-boards of a library, seeping into the crevices and slowly staining the fibers of the wood.

Standing in the Loggia dei Lanzi, at the heart of Florence, is the sculpture of a woman being carried off by a soldier who tramples over King Acron, who sought vengeance for the Sabine tribe. The woman's breasts are exposed, her outstretched arm reaching up for divine forces that could not, or would not, save her.

On the other side of the Loggia is a bronze sculpture of the virile Perseus, holding a sword in one hand and, in the other, the head of Medusa. Perseus treads on the Gorgon's decapitated body, which is artfully posed and draped over the top of the plinth so that her breasts and thighs seem to say "touch me," even though she remains just out of the spectator's reach.

What would the Renaissance viewers have thought when they stepped into the Loggia and encountered Giambologna's The Rape of the Sabine Women (1583) and Cellini's Perseus With the Head of Medusa (1545–1554)? Might they have been reminded of the sovereignty and patriarchal power of the Medicis? Would they have seen the sculptures as purely allegorical or metaphorical narratives taken from myth and ancient history? Would they have interpreted the works as lessons for blushing brides, who should understand the perils of losing their feminine virtue? Or would the viewers, admiring the scene of abduction and decapitation, understand that power is built on men's subjugation of women? The spectators might remember that prior to the placement of Giambologna's and Cellini's sculptures in the heart of the city, Donatello's Judith and Holofernes (ca. 1456–57) stood next to the entrance to the Palazzo Vecchio. But the authorities concluded that a sculpture of a woman beheading a man was unsuitable for the civic center of power, and

Donatello's masterpiece was relocated to a less prominent spot in the Loggia.

Two things are for certain. First, the Renaissance spectators would have applauded Giambologna and Cellini for the beauty of their work. Second, the male viewers would have read the sculptures as depictions of glorious conquest, and they would likely have identified with the Roman soldier and with Perseus, who demonstrate the masculine ability to dispossess enemies. Aside from being narratives of conquest, the sculptures were also titillating spectacles of pleasure, throbbing with erotic potential. In the memory of the spectators, the Sabine woman would have stood out for her perfectly sculpted breasts, and Medusa endured as a beautiful, voluptuous corpse lying languidly at Perseus's feet.

Two

October

October 1

In the 1840s, visitors to Turner's studio in Queen Anne Street were astounded by its state of disrepair and neglect. John Hoppner, a fellow Royal Academician, likened the gallery to a filthy stall, with canvases crammed into every nook. Turner had also allowed the rain and soot to fall through the cracks in his studio windows, so that the filth of London was encrusted on his pictures. According to one of his friends, dust and mold had repainted the golden *Dido Building Carthage* into a gloomy scene that resembled the inside of a chimney.

I enjoy this routine of reading and thinking about Turner at the start of each month. It resets my mind.

Herbarium

Album of pressed leaves, flowers, and grasses, *ca.* 1850. Octavo. Caramel morocco. Botanical specimens in excellent condition; each item labeled. Samples have been collected from the author's journeys to places of interest. Author unknown, though presumed to be wealthy, due to the costs of travel in the nineteenth century. Herbarium includes ginkgo leaves from Goethe's tree in Heidelberg Castle; beech leaf from Voltaire's garden; grass from the fields of Waterloo; and flowers from the Forum Romanum.

OCTOBER 2

The sky is gray and flat. Outside, the trees that remain in the park put me in mind of Van Gogh's poplars, with sinewy, twisting arms that stretch toward the barren land.

I spent a good part of the day working on the vegetables. We keep a small vegetable patch in one corner of the old Conservatory. Delicate long stalks bear green leaves, and red fruit climb up the coppiced poles. We share our water ration with these plants in the hope that they will continue to grow. In the garden behind the kitchen, there is also a potato patch. Most of us are vegetarians now, due to the price of meat, which is one of the few good things to have come out of the world's catastrophes.

These vegetables have been easier to maintain than the plants in the glasshouse and gardens. A botanist stayed with us years ago, one of Dad's colleagues from Kew. He took care of the glasshouse, careful to preserve the seeds and log the development of each plant. But a storm fractured the glass roof, and the outside world entered, killing the plants. The glasshouse reverted to sand and debris, much like what it was during the initial phase of renovation when I first arrived at Mornington. After the botanist left, I took over the maintenance of the gardens, using knowledge gleaned from Dad, as we could no longer afford a gardener. A neighbor dropped by every week to help with the lawn-mowing and leaf-gathering until those tasks became unnecessary.

Miranda has been helping me with the vegetables and potatoes. She told me she misses the garden at home, and the sensation of the soil under her hands. She often speaks about the apple trees and the herbs that grew outside her window.

Of course, Miranda said, they were mostly dead by the time we had to leave that house. But it's good to think about them once in a while. I'm sure conditions will improve and we will have a garden again one day.

I admire Miranda's hope that there will be something worth salvaging—a hope that I am not always able to sustain.

Today she sang songs in Spanish as we dug out a few potatoes in preparation for the group meal tomorrow.

OCTOBER 3

From time to time, Aidan and I invite everyone staying with us for a group dinner. Each household has different rations depending on the number of people in it, so when we gather for meals we opt for a potluck, though Aidan and I try to provide extra food, using the funds from the non-profit. Tonight, we shared a loaf of homemade bread; biscuits and cheese; pasta with grilled vegetables; and five bottles of wine that Aidan bought from the village shop. Miranda and I contributed the *gratin dauphinois* that we made together.

There were twelve of us tonight, all adults, including two of the young people staying in the Hall, whom we rarely see outside of their tents. We lit candles and a fire in the Long Gallery, and after filling our plates with food, we each settled into our chosen spots. We exchanged, over the glow of the fire and the plates of shared food, the difficulties we faced and the hopes for the days to come. We complained about government inefficiency, about rising food costs, and about the continuing descent into greater chaos. Aidan loves these conversations and never hesitates to ask others their opinion on a specific policy change or a development in another part of the world. He often takes center stage at these dinners, whereas I prefer to remain on the periphery, listening to others.

OCTOBER 4

Earlier today, I came across a facsimile of von Humboldt's book of botanical illustrations, *Monographia Melastomacearum*. It was one of Dad's favorite books, though he never owned a copy. He once told me that botanical drawings capture the ephemeral lives of plants; to illustrate is to preserve. When I was young, he would often read to me the descriptions that accompany the illustrations. I thus grew up with the language of flowers, full of strange and melodious words that I collected in lieu of the plants themselves: meadowsweet, cinquefoil, self-heal, and feverfew. I combed the gardens for petiolate plants and pinnate leaves. I examined the perianth of a flower and waited for the time of anthesis.

Throughout my childhood, Dad took me to gardens all over the country, sometimes because of his work, other times for pleasure. We toured gardens at country estates, universities, castles, and royal parks, wearing our rain boots and waxed jackets. Glass jars attached to the outside of Dad's rucksack made a jingling sound when he walked. He filled a leather-bound journal with pressed leaves and petals, alongside sketches and notes about rainfall, light, and soil. We also had a kit consisting of a gauge, a thermometer, and my magnifying glass, which was garnished with shells I found on a beach. Dad's hand always held mine a little too tightly, and when I was really young, he made me wear an anklet with bells, so that whenever I walked, the ringing would alert him if I strayed too far.

Those were the days when water collected in pools and drops of rain fell from the leaves and onto our heads as we walked through the gardens. I remember the puddles that blocked the garden paths and the morning petals that were bedewed. Water flowed in streams and irrigated the grass, trees, and flora. Water was lavished on the most insignificant weed, and water splashed on those who walked by fountains or waterfalls. Today, such luxuries are unimaginable for most of us.

OBJECT

Two volumes from a xylotheque, or library of wood samples, *ca.* 1790. Origin unknown. Specimen of oak and pine, in the shape of books, measuring 21.5 x 15 x 12 cm. Spines cut from bark and labeled with the name of the species. Interiors resemble shadow boxes or dioramas, housing botanical specimens: seeds, leaves, flowers, twigs, nuts or cones, all preserved in wax. Volumes damaged by mold.

OCTOBER 5

This week, I have been writing in the guest room that I stayed in when I first came to Mornington. The room has a striking *trompe l'oeil* wallpaper, featuring a garden with green bowers and an open field with trees in the background. Painted garlands frame the window. The space has become uninhabitable due to damage from a storm long ago. The wallpaper is tattered, exposing the bricks underneath; the azure of the painted sky has been marred by streaks of black mold. But sometimes, when a draft blows in through the window, the *trompe l'oeil* seems to come alive, as if the clouds in the painting moved and the branches swayed in the wind.

This room reminds me of the study I'd made back at home, in the house I shared with Dad. I recall those years during graduate school when rain was heavy and I spent my days reading and writing about art, about Turner, in the study set up in the small conservatory. The glass ceiling of the conservatory was leaky, and drops of rain would fall on the manuscript pages so that I had to hang them up to dry on the laundry line. Ink dissolved into the fibers of the damp paper, creating columns of blue that ran down the pages.

Dad laughed every time my writing was rained on, and insisted that I work in the house instead. But the conservatory—with the heat from the sunlight, the sound of the rain, the plants outside—was an integral part of the writing process. Dad had built the conservatory himself, as well as the brick wall that enclosed our little plot of green, to which the conservatory led. On the other side of that wall was a communal garden shared with neighboring houses.

In about two months, it will be the fourteenth anniversary of Dad's death. The image of that house keeps re-emerging in my mind, even though I have seen it only once since he died. It is inaccessible now, submerged in one of the many flooded zones in London.

OCTOBER 7

An unusually sunny day. Aidan and I took a walk in the gardens after lunch. It is our habit to take a walk together, whenever the weather allows, a habit we first established years ago to help me transition back to life at Mornington, after everything that had happened with Julian. We used to walk past the lake in the middle of the parkland, through the Italian, Japanese, and English gardens. There were once red maple trees and a bamboo grove; hedges of bay and laurel punctuated by lavender bushes. We occasionally paused in the neoclassical folly overlooking the lake, or walked through the open fields to climb the small hill at the edge of the estate.

Sometimes, we would sit under the cedar tree and share a bottle of wine. I would read while Aidan worked on a design. He liked to handle a random object—a rock, a pine cone—in one hand as he sketched, turning it this way and that. Once in a while, he showed me his drawings and discussed the projects he was working on. Aidan gestured wildly when describing architecture, stretching his arms or drawing lines in the air. He designed rooms with large panes of clear glass and warm honey-colored wood, structures that blended into the trees and hills in the background. Even the emergency housing for survivors of disasters resembled nests built by an industrious creature using materials collected from the woods.

I don't want anything to intrude into the space, Aidan once said, the way houses like Mornington do, pushing everything aside with such arrogance.

On some of our walks, we ventured beyond the estate or made excursions to the nearby villages. We have spent entire afternoons on a hill or in a field somewhere before coming back here and collapsing into bed. Several times we walked along a brook by which we encountered a row of orange-beaked grey-lag geese that stood perfectly still and glared at us as we walked by. We visited local churches, where Aidan took notes on the architectural details, or climbed up hills from which we could survey an entire valley and narrate the lives we imagined for those who inhabited the distant houses.

One time we drove to the Lake District and, standing atop a summit, seeing the narrow roads like gray ribbons that wound between jagged rocks, I realized for the first time that Julian had retreated into the background, like the sheep and hikers reduced to miniature. I had the feeling that all would be well so long as Aidan walked beside me. The moment atop the summit when I realized I loved him was akin to the moment when the meaning of an artwork suddenly emerges through the cloud of incomprehension. I almost slipped on our way up to the peak, but he was there to prevent my fall.

Gradually, the greenery vanished. The geese no longer appeared by the water, and the river receded until it is now no more than a thin ribbon, squeezed on both sides by the river-banks that widen each year. But we have upheld our tradition of walking, and through the walking, we have grown into our togetherness. The corner we have created for ourselves in this part of the house seems to be the single soft shape in a world that is otherwise full of sharp and jagged edges. With Aidan, everything has changed. From the books in the Library to the paintings on the walls, all the details that had been tainted by Julian's presence have been transformed. I have finally been able to—cautiously, quietly—call Mornington home.

OCTOBER 8

Celia's studio is on the top floor of the northeast pavilion, with a view of what remains of the woodland. When I entered her room this morning, I noticed that she had moved all the furniture, including her bed, to one side of the room, and on the other side, by the window, she'd set up her easel and a table with painting materials and glass jars filled with paintbrushes. I wandered around her studio in the shapeless gray dress that she had prepared for me. Canvases were leaning against the wall. Objects on the windowsills composed still lifes: rocks, a bowl of pine cones, rusted bits of machinery, paperclips bent into varied shapes.

The room was cool and airy. Celia left the windows open last night to air out the odor of the turpentine. When she doesn't have someone coming to sit for her, she keeps the windows closed. The smell is usually unpleasant to others, she said. But when I'm alone, it is a reminder to continue working, every day of my life.

I sat down, took off my shoes. I fidgeted until I found a comfortable position, by which time Celia had already begun drawing. She started with pencil, and I could see on the table the pigments that would blend together into a portrait. The Naples yellow, burnt umber, Indian red, raw sienna, and flake white.

Each sitting would be approximately three hours. Either in the early morning—as it was today—or before dusk, depending on the quality of the light she needed. For this first sitting, Celia said I could bring a book. So I sat with my well-thumbed anthology of Simone Weil's writings, and as my mind delved into her words, and as the sunlight moved across the wall, some version of me materialized on the canvas that I will not be allowed to see until the entire portrait is completed.

After the session was over, we shared tea and biscuits. Celia explained that she draws or paints a subject several times, in separate layers. This was only the first sitting, and she could not tell me yet how many she would need to do before she arrives at the final image. She asked for my patience. It takes time for each layer of paint to dry before the next can be applied, she said; so in between each sitting there will be a period of waiting.

I told her about Turner's process of painting Norham Castle repeatedly, which she had not read about before. The earliest—1798—depiction of the castle was conventional, heavily indebted to other landscape painters. In 1822, he painted the castle again, but this time, the picture departed from tradition. The 1845 version is the one I love best, even though it is unfinished. Despite the fact that nothing is seen clearly and everything is suggested—a few strokes of red stand for the herd of cows, and the history of the ruinous castle is summed up in washes of gray and blue—Turner conveyed all that he had failed to say in the earlier compositions.

The truth of any single thing, Celia said in response, requires time and continual return.

October 8—evening

Am curious as to how I will appear in a portrait. I rarely look in the mirror, and I keep few photos of myself. With age, the fleshy parts of my face have diminished and the bones have protruded. My body has reverted to the awkward and knobby frame I had as an adolescent, though the skin is now stretched taut and marked by everything through which the body has passed.

One of the few photos I have kept is one Aidan took near the start of our relationship, using an analogue camera. The image was out of focus. Part of my body was a smudge, but the face was intact, my eyes like an animal's, alert in the dim light as I stood in the midst of towering piles of books. That picture seems to me an accurate representation of myself at that age, always half-vanishing into books and images.

BOOK
Italo Calvino, *Invisible Cities*. Published by the Arion Press, San Francisco, 1999. Translated by William Weaver. Bound in four-ring metal binding. Twelve drawings by Wayne Thiebaud, of cities and objects, printed on transparent plastic sheets and invisible until the page is turned back onto the preceding page. Edges damaged by water and pests.

OCTOBER 11
Yesterday, a pipe burst in the kitchen. Water flooded into the hallway and Dining Hall. For the whole day, the house was filled with the high-pitched banging of hammer on nails, as Aidan and the others tried to fix the pipes and replace the damaged floorboards. The lost water means we must dip into the reservoir, which I'm reluctant to do. Each diminishing inch of water corresponds to an increase in anxiety. Every time something breaks, I sink into momentary despair. All the mending and fixing seem futile, and regardless of how much time and resources we spend on repairs, the disintegration outpaces us.

OCTOBER 14
The pipes have been fixed. In the morning I set out for a walk in the parkland by myself. Aidan is away for a few days to check on the progress of a construction site. There was pale sunlight and no wind, though I am still unnerved by the silence of a morning without birdsong.

Years ago, we partitioned much of the one thousand acres that previously belonged to the estate. Some of the land was sold to farmers; other parts reverted back into public commons. As I walked across the field, I imagined how the parkland would have once appeared from the vantage point of the house, the Brownian meadows the shade of soft green, framed by the windbreak trees and romantic groves in the distance. Now, the dead and dying trees are skeletal silhouettes against the sky.

I remember the last days of rain—about three years ago. There was a period of increasingly longer droughts, then the last rain was gossamer drizzle that disappeared sometime in the night. The only water that remained was that which had collected in the outdoor fountain and in the buckets placed throughout the garden. We don't expect much variation from the sky nowadays, nothing other than this ashen grey, which covers the earth like a mildewed blanket.

After I passed the ha-has, I checked the small holes inserted into the boundary walls, which allow small animals to move in and out of the estate. I habitually check for signs of life, though I seldom see any. At one time, we saw many hints of animal life in the garden: the mole ridges that extended the whole length of a meadow; the winter shelters made by hedgehogs under the compost heap; the small entrances to subterranean tunnels dug by rabbits. I cannot imagine the kind of changes that are needed in order for abundant life to return to the land.

I walked to the edge of the open field where the grand Lebanese cedar once stood, its umbriferous foliage providing a canopy under which Aidan and I sat many times. Now, in its place, nothing but a scorched stump. I recalled with a tremor how we witnessed the death of the beloved tree, how the fungus turned the green needles of the cedar a pinkish-white before they dropped off, stripping the tree to its bare branches, which also began to sicken. The bark was bruised red and deep purple.

The shoots died and oozed a gum-like fluid, akin to blood from a wound.

Death came for the parkland and gardens long before the rain stopped. Box blight and box-tree caterpillars defoliated the hedging in the formal gardens. Fungal pathogen rotted the roots of the beech trees. The ash woodland—where Aidan spent so much of his childhood—was almost thoroughly destroyed by ash dieback. The fungus hid among fallen leaves in the winter. Then, in the summer to early autumn, their white, fruiting bodies produced countless spores that could travel for many kilometers, eventually landing on the ash leaves, which the fungus ate through before spreading to the rest of the tree. Dark patches, like sores, emerged on the leaves. They withered and blackened, and fell off the branches one by one. Brown lesions developed on the branches and trunks as the trees were being eaten away from within. Over time, the fungus cut off the trees' water transport system and suffocated them to death. The saplings and younger ash trees died quickly; the older trees managed to hang on for awhile longer but succumbed in the end. Most of the dead trees were felled; some trunks were left for the insects.

We took the necessary measures to salvage the ancient woodland. We burned the fallen ash leaves to disrupt the fungal cycle; we planted saplings; we tried to encourage the natural regeneration of native species. But it was all too slow. The droughts sped up the deterioration of the infected trees and gradually killed most of the surviving ones that had been immune to the disease. The death of the trees was followed by the demise of the shade-loving plants that were protected by the foliage. The ferns and mosses, the bluebells and snowdrops that carpeted the forest floor were replaced with a layer of clay punctuated by dead tree trunks.

Today I wandered through the spot where the woodland used to be as if through a cemetery. I always make sure to inspect the remaining trees for signs of disease. A few are still standing, though their papery leaves are sparse and small in size. Thankfully, none of the trees appear to be sick at the moment. I breathed a sigh of relief even as I acknowledged that their death might be delayed but never prevented.

I walked beyond the woodland, past the empty lot where the glasshouse stood before it was torn down, and reached the wall that encloses the neighboring estate, Barrington Grange, which has been converted into a luxury spa. I walked along the wall and climbed the small hill at the far end of the commons. There was a painting that Turner completed in the 1790s—which mysteriously vanished from the Mornington collection sometime during the 1920s—when he was still a young painter and heavily influenced by his predecessors. In the fuzzy reproduction in my Turner book, the painting featured the landscape as seen from this hill, with grand oak trees and a herd of deer in the foreground. In the background, Mornington Hall was encircled by trees. Today, no woodland obscures the view of the house, which looks exposed and vulnerable without the dense woods nearby.

These observations I record cannot possibly approach what Turner would have made of the current devastation, the pathos he would have given to the flinty and dry downs, the bare slopes. The emptiness. Even jotting down these words pains me tremendously. But I must continue to write, to go out there and look, again and again, as a way of paying tribute to all the life that has been lost.

OCTOBER 15

Years ago, on one of the walks I took with Aidan, he related the history of the park at Mornington.

Did you know, he said, that so much of this parkland, this so-called natural landscape, was man-made? The serpentine lake, Aidan explained, is not really a lake. Capability Brown dammed an existing river to create the illusion of a lake. That hill at the edge of the estate was actually a built structure, like a gigantic sandcastle. Most of the eye-catching trees in the park, like the cedar, were planted strategically.

In fact, Aidan told me, many of the trees and flowers were imported from the colonies for the purpose of beautifying the gardens. Any plants that didn't fit the overall aesthetic were removed. The uninterrupted vista was also a fiction—possible because of the ha-has made by laborers over incalculable hours. And the whole estate was built partly on a demolished village.

The costly project, Aidan said, of creating the park and gardens took approximately nine years to complete. It's all so ghastly, if you think about it. I remember reading about Capability Brown and his designs for country houses—there was a passage in which an estate owner was quoted as saying it did not matter that something was artificial, as long as it was beautiful.

When I first learned about all this, Aidan continued, I felt guilty for loving the park and gardens. For having grown up in this house. But I could not resist coming out here. My father, when he was here, liked hosting big parties, and the guests loved the gardens. They'd have picnics on the lawn or sunbathe by the lake. They were everywhere, these strangers. I hid in the old glasshouse. It was humid in there, so no one else liked to stay for long. I was impressed with the glass domes and steel columns, with the way the tropical plants pushed up against the glass walls, like they were trying to break free. Maybe that was where I first began thinking about space and architecture, about how sunlight could enliven a room, or how walls could be transparent.

Aidan later showed me a photograph of the original glass-house, which was in part inspired by the peristyle at the House of Loreius Tiburtinus in Pompeii. In his redesign, Aidan erased all traces of the Roman villa. Where the old interior boasted rows of wooden pergolas clad with vines and a rectilinear pool in the middle lined with plants on either side, the new design replaced the straight lines with winding paths that led to hidden nooks. As the plants grew, they obscured the walkways and built their own arches and columns within the glasshouse.

ATLAS

Part one of John Speed's *England, A Coloured Facsimile of the Maps and Text from the Theatre of the Empire of Great Britaine* (first edition, 1611). Published by Phoenix House, London, 1953. Folio. Foxing and water-stains on endpapers and frontispiece, otherwise in good condition. Nine colored plates of maps; one plate missing. The maps are inaccurate, but remain useful for decorative purposes.

OCTOBER 17

The group of four older travelers left this morning, after a three-month stay. I have posted an official announcement on our website about the upcoming demolition; we will no longer be accepting applications. Everyone who is currently here has already submitted their planned schedule for departure. At times, I can scarcely believe that this house, so painstakingly preserved for the sake of the travelers, will soon be reduced to flat ground upon which another symbol of power might be erected.

Our decision to sell Mornington was finalized earlier this year, on that day in March when Aidan and I walked down to the river beyond the estate.

The last sale didn't get us much, Aidan said as we sat down by the river that is no more than a pebbled rivulet, like a wound cut into the land by a thin blade.

Is there anything else we can sell? I asked.

There are probably various items that are still worth something. Vases, picture frames, some of the chairs. There is the house itself, of course.

We had already had many debates about the potential sale of the house, about the difficulty of giving up the non-profit. But that afternoon, I realized that all our debates had merely postponed the inevitable change neither of us had the courage to confront.

We made the decision that day, by the river. A few days after, Aidan started making arrangements for the sale. We agreed that the proceeds from the sale would go toward his pro bono architectural projects, as well as the house-on-wheels in which we would live, and a future non-profit that we hope to set up one day, after we've settled in a new, undetermined place.

What we could not agree on was whether Julian should be informed—and whether he should be invited back to visit Mornington one last time. The two of us rarely speak of Julian. At one point, Aidan's silence was oppressive, but the silence has become a kind of buffer in which we can remain still, nestled in the world we have constructed, separate from all that happened with Julian. Sometimes we almost forget that Aidan has a sibling, and I think he prefers it that way.

Out of a wish to protect me, Aidan said he did not want Julian to come back. But I felt confident that I would be ready to confront Julian's physical presence. Those days with Julian, I told Aidan, resembled an obscure building in the background of a vast panorama, and I needed to squint my eyes to see it clearly.

This was what I had assumed at the time.

I reminded Aidan that his brother was the only person who had shared his childhood days at Mornington; that they had built a tree house together in the woods, where they would hide and read comic books together.

He thought about the matter for a few days, then decided to call Julian.

You might want to see it one last time, I overheard Aidan saying on the phone. Parts of the house will remain intact after the sale, but it won't be what we knew, when we were kids.

I heard the tension in Aidan's voice. Then he stopped speaking for a while and cleared his throat repeatedly—something he does in moments of anxiety.

When I heard him say my name to Julian, I got up and left the room. I did not want to know how Julian had reacted. I did not want to imagine his voice saying my name back, with trepidation, or disgust perhaps, the way that people utter the name of unclean things. His name, when it surfaced in my mind, once again induced a sense of vertigo. In that instant, I regretted my decision to invite him back. But it was too late. Maybe Aidan had been right in his reluctance to see his brother. Maybe he had been right to assert that some things should not be excavated.

That phone call marked the beginning of Julian's journey back to Mornington, for the first time in over two decades.

PICTURE POSTCARDS
Eight hundred vintage postcards, *ca.* 1890s to 1920s. Touristic images of European cities. Some in black and white; others in color. All postmarked and franked. Fragile—held inside transparent plastic folders. Some are stained; others curled at the corners.

OCTOBER 19
Not long after I started working as archivist and librarian at Mornington, I began to collect ephemera: postcards, found photographs, stereoscopic views, pictorial visiting cards, tickets, pamphlets, trade cards, and stamps. Tangible records of everyday life that were often left out of major collections. I purchased from auctions, trade fairs, and second-hand bookshops.

Occasionally, I would acquire a private collection. Once, an elderly gentleman donated hundreds of vintage bus and tram tickets, all gathered from used books over the course of a lifetime. Another collector sold me a trove of French *cartes de visite*, *circa* 1900.

Of all the ephemera, I value the postcards the most—as though they were my own. They allow for imaginary journeys at a time when travel has become difficult. On many of the cards I have, the streets and monuments of London, Paris, Milan, Rome, and Munich were photographed and reproduced on cards, which were then sent through the mail and collected in albums, where they remained long after the actual buildings were demolished. Sometimes I sit with these pictures and allow my mind to be carried to unknown terrains. For a few minutes, I am elsewhere.

OCTOBER 22

Winter is approaching on rapid footsteps, arriving earlier than last year. In the mornings, the windows fog up as the warm air of the interior collides with the cold outside. Soon, it will no longer be possible to sit under the open oculus in the southeast pavilion and write, as I'm doing today.

I recently re-watched Alain Resnais's *Toute la Mémoire du Monde*, a film that has taken up space in my imagination, and I noticed how the gloomy vault, crammed with dusty crates, resembles the underground storage at Mornington. The edges of the remaining books in our Library have become wavy. The fluctuating temperature and humidity have made it difficult to keep the books and archive in an optimal state. I am constantly engaged in the work of reparation. I think of Ruskin's dedication to rescuing and preserving Turner's sketches: unrolling and flattening all the pages; clearing away decades of dust; laying loose leaves in between sheets of writing paper to protect them

from further damage; enclosing the sketchbooks in sealed pack-
ets; and, finally, glazing and framing the best pictures. I'd like
to think I have been as devoted to this Library as Ruskin was
to Turner's studio. I put ointment on leather binding, glue back
loose pages, and fill in the endless holes made by insects. But
disintegration is always one step ahead. At the end of Resnais's
documentary, there is a mysterious, ghostly figure who stares out
at the camera from behind the bookcase—I see this figure as the
specter of time, reminding me to pick up my pace.

The original Library at Mornington, before the renovation,
had dark wood paneling and mahogany desks. But the Library
I saw in person, when I first came here, had a cathedral-like
interior with white walls and columns that reflected the sunlight.
The flute-like timber columns stretched upward and fanned out
into expansive vaults that formed a wave-like canopy, giving the
Library the appearance of a forest of snow-laden trees. The
floor was lowered to accentuate the sense of height. The interlocking rows of arches articulated distinct spaces, each filled
with large desks and armchairs. Cool air circulated throughout.
There was a reading area that I recognized from one of Turner's
sketches, also re-painted in white, with modern chairs instead of
the leather armchairs Turner would have used. The heavy oak
doors are the sole remnants of the original Library.

In the middle of the forest of white columns rose a cylindri-
cal enclosure housing the book storage system. This glass tower
was temperature-controlled and hermetically sealed, with con-
centric circles of shelves that held the books and archive.

I have never seen anything like this, I said to Aidan during
my first tour of the house all those years ago. Our study back
at home, in London, smells of old books. Dad… my father, he
can't think without the smell, that combination of the glue in the
binding and the mildew. But no, nothing like this.

Aidan told me about the process of designing the new
Library, spearheaded by Julian, who'd insisted on eradicating all

traces of the old space in order to build a new one severed from the past.

My brother, Aidan said during that first tour, did extensive research about library management and archive storage systems. The Spiral, as we call it, extends three levels down, and the shelves spread out into the underground storage space. That was the only way we could keep all the books in the collection without compromising the overall aesthetic. Robotic arms retrieve the books, so no one ever goes into the stacks, unless repairs are needed.

What a strange idea, I said. A library where the books on the shelves can't be browsed or touched.

Years later, Aidan confessed to me how he'd hated the process of designing the Library with his brother; how Julian, who had no architectural training, had tried to dictate everything, ignoring Aidan's professional advice. The house is mine, Julian kept repeating, to which Aidan had no adequate response.

What irritated me even more, Aidan said, was that the finished product was very aesthetically pleasing. I do like the white columns. But it was a lifeless place. I almost prefer the way it is now, with that crack in the wall and the broken robotic arms. I laughed the first time Julian proposed the robotic arms, he said.

Tonight, I wondered if I should tell Aidan about the plants that have been thriving in the fissure. I'd checked on them a few hours ago; more blossoms have emerged. He would have liked the idea of the flowers forcing their way into the Library. But the leaky pipe would bring him nothing but anxiety. And the thought of the Library might lead his mind back to those days of collaborating with Julian. I chose not to tell him.

ALBUMS

Set of three philatelic albums from the Netherlands, undated. Octavo. Paperbound with sea green covers. Incomplete collection of stamps from European countries. Some pages partially torn. Many stamps have fallen out, leaving behind the adhesive tapes used to attach them to the blank pages. Albums were most likely used for a "round robin"—a collection of stamps amassed from a long chain of exchanges between collectors.

OCTOBER 26

While sorting through some personal documents today, I stumbled upon drafts of the essay I wrote for the catalogue entry on Turner's *A View on the Seine*—the writing of which was an important part of the fellowship that brought me to Mornington.

When Aidan gave me a tour of the house on that first day, he showed me *A View on the Seine*, protected behind a glass case in a recessed area in the Library. But for the entire first week of my fellowship, I stayed away from the painting. I had the postcard reproduction taped on the wall in the guest quarters, and every day I would stare at that tiny rectangle; yet not a single idea or coherent sentence emerged in my mind. When I was reminded—via an email from Julian's personal assistant—that Julian expected to read a draft of the essay upon his arrival at Mornington the subsequent week, I finally went to look at the painting.

I stood immobile in front of it for an unknown length of time. Then my vision began to blur. The painted waves and clouds faded away, along with the solid form of the little town by the Seine, until none of it made any sense. I turned away, nauseated.

In the days that followed, I could not write. I ordered books from the catalogue and watched the robotic arms inside the glass tower retrieve the volumes and deposit them inside a metallic drawer, which I could then open to access the books. I spread out all my notes on the desk and pulled up online images showing magnified sections of the canvas. But no words came.

Ruskin had considered *A View on the Seine* one of Turner's finest demonstrations of what color could achieve. Serenity and destruction—these I understood to be a part of the picture. I had vague thoughts about the buildings and the forces of nature depicted, the tableau of waves breaking upon the shore. It took me hours to compose the first sentence, and no sooner was it scribbled down than I was overcome by the impulse to tear the page, appalled by the inadequacy of my own words. I attempted a description of the painting, inserted the quote from Ruskin, and crossed out the sentences straight away. I wrote down a list of adjectives, and realized that none of the words could express the sense of unease I felt while looking at the painting, so I tore the page and began anew. Whatever I wrote, however satisfactory it might have seemed at first, when I read over the words with greater attention, the inelegancies and inconsistencies would jump out like blemishes, forcing me to throw it all out and begin again, only to be confronted with yet another row of banal words. Everything I wrote was subsequently unraveled. The painting called into question not only my ability to convey meaning, but the entire work of writing itself.

This all happened at a time when Mornington Hall was undergoing a series of renovations, which created another obstacle. I often woke up to the clanging of metal and the beeping of trucks as they backed onto the garden path. In the hallways and on the lawn, there were rows of black pipes and heaps of scrap wood. When the crew moved into the house itself, I was jolted awake each day by the drilling and hammering. The vibrations shook the furniture and sent ripples across the surface of my coffee.

I gave up writing for a while and focused on cataloguing Mornington's art collection, which was another part of the fellowship. Eventually, as the deadline loomed, I went back to stand in front of the painting. In one corner of the picture, I noticed a hazy, rough-hewn shape extending above the white waves: the mast of a ship. And next to it, a faintly outlined human limb amidst the frothy foam. So *A View on the Seine* depicted a maritime disaster, even though it is unlike Turner's other representations of disaster. That observation formed my first idea for the essay.

I love this piece, Aidan said to me the next day when we viewed it together.

Me too. It is stunning. But still, it's… I don't know, it's not Turner's best.

No, I suppose it's not as celebrated as some of his other works.

But there's something about it, isn't there? Some quality… maybe it's to do with the light, something I can't quite name. It's killing me, not knowing how to describe this quality. I once attended this Turner conference where the theme was "Incompleteness and Indistinctness." Maybe by calling an artwork "indistinct," we could be freed from the responsibility of having to describe it. Why did your brother purchase this painting, by the way?

I have no idea. A Turner is a worthwhile investment, and there are so few of them in private collections.

Look at that arc there, Aidan continued, pointing to the birds in flight in the bottom left-hand corner of the canvas. Look at how it mirrors the arc of the waves and the clouds.

Aidan's comment gave me the second idea for the essay. I began to write the first paragraph, about the seagulls and the sunken ship. But after that, I stopped, once again unable to move forward.

On the wall where *A View on the Seine* used to be, there is now the reproduction in oil that we commissioned to create the illusion that the painting is still there. We sold the original about four years ago to finance the post-earthquake repairs. By studying the original painting, dusting its frame, protecting it from sunlight and humidity, I came to believe that it was mine, that it belonged to me in a way that far exceeded legal boundaries. But when it was wrapped and transported, when the documents were signed at the auction house, I understood how easy it was for things to slip away, how I might lose, at any moment, through circumstances over which I had no control, something that I loved, including all the things, like the Turner, that I considered a part of myself. The loss was not greater than losing Dad, of course. But loss is unaffected by repetition or experience. Each loss is a fresh cut. And each process of healing subject to its own vagaries and setbacks. I know the reproduction for what it is—a copy—but sometimes, if I dim the lights, I can fool myself into thinking that nothing was ever lost.

MANUSCRIPT
Travel diary of Elizabeth Scott, from May 1 to June 2, 1890, throughout Italy. Duodecimo. Diced leather notebook. Ephemera inserted, along with botanical specimens. An exam paper on the architecture of ancient Rome tucked into the pages. Margins contain edits and errata by Elizabeth; two pages have been ripped out; one page painted over with black ink.

OCTOBER 28
The foundation for the house-on-wheels stands in the open space above the ha-has. Last month, Aidan started working on the mobile house that is to be our home after leaving Mornington. The original plan was to use one of the shipping containers that his studio put aside for their prefab building projects. But Aidan decided to design something from scratch.

He stripped the floorboards from the disused rooms to construct the walls and floors of the mobile unit, and repurposed some of the old furnishings, so that our new home will be composed of bits and pieces of Mornington.

OCTOBER 30

When I stepped into Celia's studio today, she looked at me with great sadness. After reviewing the work that she completed during our first sitting, she has decided to give up on it and start anew.

You're thinking too much when you read, she said. It translates onto the canvas. You seemed anxious.

I was taken aback. I had thought reading Weil would give me a sense of peace.

I'm afraid, Celia said, I'm going to ask you to give yourself over to the experience of sitting. Then we'll see what the result looks like. I'm interested in how people dwell in that silence and stillness. Some people think through a problem. The religious often pray. But try to enter into a kind of reverie. It can be a pleasant experience. You can think about whatever you want. You be in your world and I'll be in mine.

She also said that if she were to talk to me during the sitting, it would distort the painting because too much of her own self would seep through.

Not wanting to disrupt Celia's process, I agreed to sit in silence, despite having no clue how I might get through three hours with nothing to do.

She proceeded to paint over that first portrait of me, which I never got to see.

At first, the experience of being scrutinized was unnerving. I felt locked inside my body. I attempted to sit up straight, to suck in my cheeks, jut my chin out a little more, or widen my eyes. The experience oddly made me feel like an adolescent again, defined by the gaze of others. Celia instructed me to be as still as possible.

That corner of the house was quiet. I imagined I was wrapped in layers of silence—the silence of the park, of the house, and of the studio itself, at the center of which was the listening self. I strained my ears to catch the sound of the paintbrush on the canvas, the noise of squeaking floorboards when someone passed by in the hallway, a distant cough. I avoided looking straight at Celia, so I fixed my eyes on the wall behind her, which had a partial *trompe l'oeil* of a tree. I focused on the tree and visualized it growing. In the end, the work of listening and looking sustained me through the session.

Before I left, Celia reassured me that I mustn't be anxious about her looking at me.

Painting someone, she said, is my way of paying attention. It is not a form of judgment.

She told me that at university she sat as a model, for extra money. I know what it is like to be painted, Celia said. It can be alarming. Some of the portraits the art students did of me turned me into a sort of monster with dislocated body parts. It is never an easy process to find out how someone sees you, no matter how subjective or short-lived that vision might be.

30 OCTOBER—EVENING

The first time Julian looked at me was when we met in the Long Gallery, the day he arrived at Mornington, about two weeks after I started my fellowship. When he called my name, it sounded like a question. He squinted his eyes and lingered on each syllable. I realize now that I have forgotten what his voice sounds like.

I had already seen Julian earlier that day. As he walked along the veranda with a book in hand, he passed by the Conservatory, where I was sitting, and in the brief opening between two palm trees, he turned and glanced at me before proceeding to the other side of the veranda.

It was not until later that day that I spoke to him, when I was dusting the cabinet of glass objects that had been moved into the Long Gallery from the Dining Hall, which was undergoing renovation. I was transfixed by the glass—the flutes, vases, and cups—which resembled the surfaces of icy lakes, with flecks of reflected light.

Be careful not to break anything, a voice said from behind me.

I turned to see the face that I had already learned through photographs. That face which I found at once unsettling and electrifying, with its steady gaze and sharp angles, drawing me into its depths.

I wasn't going to touch anything, I said.

You can touch them, just don't break them. He reached into the cabinet and took out a glass flute.

It's quite all right, he said. I own all this, he gestured to the cabinet and the walls.

Julian began to play with the flute. I remember the way his fingers curved over the thin handle of the flute, and the way he tilted his head to one side, not really looking at the thing directly. I remember that the skin on the back of his hands appeared bruised, with protruding lines of blue veins. I remember the extraordinary green of his eyes, like crushed malachite.

Julian touched my hand and elbow lightly as he handed me the flute and asked me why I was interested in the glass objects.

They're beautiful, I said. There's a sturdiness to them, even though they're fragile.

He grinned as he leaned against an empty pedestal from which a marble bust had been removed. Let me ask you, Penelope, he said. Wouldn't you rather have something that could not be broken, that could be rebuilt, even if it assumes another form?

That is a very odd question, I stammered as I placed the flute back. I'm not sure I know what you mean.

He smiled as though he had won an argument. Do you think art endures? he asked.

I flushed and struggled to find the right words, as I could not tell whether he was using a mocking tone. I don't know, I said. Individual artworks, no. They require a lot of conservation. But Art, with a capital A, I have no idea. What an odd question, I murmured.

He shrugged and tapped the top of the pedestal. I like asking strange questions, he said. They put things in perspective.

He turned away suddenly, and for whatever reason, I followed him to the other end of the Long Gallery, where his briefcase was placed next to a statue. He took out his laptop and sat down on the chaise lounge, gesturing for me to sit down next to him.

I grew up in this house, he said. Houses like this are very mortal.

Julian then showed me something on the computer that I cannot recall. Maybe it was an image; maybe it was words or symbols. This will remain, he said. Nothing lasts forever, as they say. But I think this will still be here when we're all gone.

I glanced at the computer and could not think of what to say. All I remember are his eyes and profile, illuminated by the screen. Sometimes, when I close my eyes, I can still see that face—the slight grin at the corner of the mouth, and the look of complete self-assurance as he turned to smile at me, like one who was smiling for the camera.

Arms reach into the air. Mouths agape. The women twist their bodies, attempting to flee. Abandoned infants lie in the foreground, alongside pleading old men and women. The Abduction of the Sabine Women *(1633–4) is the first of Nicolas Poussin's two interpretations of this myth about the founding of Rome, which was painted by numerous artists, among them Peter Paul Rubens, Jacques-Louis David, and Pablo Picasso. In Poussin's version, the colors are vibrant. The pale flesh of the women and the horse are set against Poussin's intense blue. The Romans are muscular and virile, embodying a specific definition of the heroic. The godlike Romulus, standing above the crowd, presides over the chaotic dance of violence and desire. In the foreground is a half-naked Roman soldier who holds a sword, the tip of which gestures toward the focal point of the painting. In that central spot, framed by the monumental buildings and by the outstretched arm of another victim, is a woman in a sapphire-colored robe, who walks away willingly with one of the Romans. While the other figures seem frozen in their suffering, she alone is moving. Toward union. Toward the abductor who would become her husband.*

Assault and marital rite could overlap. In Ars Amatoria *(2 BCE–AD 2), Ovid portrays a woman's struggle during an attack as part of an elaborate ritual of seduction: "Perhaps she will struggle at first and cry, 'You villain!' Yet she will wish to be beaten in the struggle... She whom a sudden assault has taken by storm is pleased... But she who, when she might have been compelled, departs untouched... will yet be sad." In Rubens's* The Rape of the Daughters of Leucippus *(ca. 1618), viewers are invited to* see Castor and Pollux not as predators, but as lovers; the painting depicts erotic union in spite of the word "rape" in the title.

Raptus, *"to seize," also signifies "rapture" or "transport," so that the Sabine women, by being seized, are also transported into a state of sacred union with the abductors. Thus the woman at the center of Poussin's painting leaves the scene of suffering behind and turns to gaze longingly at the Roman soldier, who wraps his arm around her. As the Roman historian Livy suggests, the Sabine women forgot their resentment and pain once they were rewarded with marriage and motherhood. The Poussin might also recall Antonio da Correggio's* Jupiter and Io *(ca. 1530), in which the nymph embraces the gray cloud that represents the predatory god. Like the Sabine woman, Io's back is turned to the viewer, though her face is visible, her expression one of dreamy sensuality and rapture.*

THREE

APRIL 7, EARLY AFTERNOON

Julian arrives at the train station half an hour before the scheduled departure time. The heat is oppressive, even by the standards of early April in Rome. As he waits on the platform for the 12:30 p.m. train bound for Milan, he wonders why he did not delay the trip further or take the slower six-hour train instead. He has already chosen to take the train back to London, as opposed to flying in directly, prolonging the journey as much as he could. From New York he had taken a twenty-hour flight, with stopovers in Frankfurt and Brussels, before arriving in Rome at 5 p.m. on the previous day. The journey still seems too short.

He takes out his phone and goes through all the photos he took during his walk in central Rome. Like many other cities, the touristic heart of Rome is protected under a series of climate-controlled geodesic domes that provide a harbor against the volatile environment outside. At 7 a.m., he'd left his hotel and wandered around the empty space where the Colosseum formerly stood, before it was removed, stone by stone, and reassembled on other lands. A large-scale holographic projection of the amphitheater remains. Julian had watched as the image flickered, reminding spectators of its unreality.

The Forum was nothing but fragments dispersed across an open space surrounded by food and souvenir vendors. As he walked among the scattered stones and broken colonnades, Julian tried to reconstruct the glory of imperial Rome at the height of its power, before the temples, triumphal arches, and circuses were altered by the passage of time. That grandeur, free from fragmentation, would have been worth seeing.

From the Forum, he walked to the Pantheon, which was intact, though he could not understand the function of the oculus, a hole in the otherwise complete dome. As Julian now studies the photos he took of the temple, he thinks of Mornington Hall. He opens an aerial image of the house he downloaded long ago, before the dilapidation became visible. He has kept an eye on Mornington from afar. Julian knows about the artist residencies and, later, the shelter for refugees, which was a waste of resources in his opinion. But it has been two decades since he last visited the house in person, and the prospect of seeing it again in a few days unnerves him.

"You might want to see it one last time, before it's demolished": that was how Aidan had phrased it on the phone one year ago. "Parts of the house will remain intact after the sale, but it won't be what we knew, when we were kids."

"You mean the buyers are not planning to refurbish it?" Julian replied after a brief pause. He could not remember the last time he spoke to his brother, and the shock of hearing Aidan's voice through the phone had unmoored him temporarily.

"No. They're keeping some parts, like the Library, which will be removed in whole and re-installed elsewhere. But they're mostly interested in the land."

"I see."

"It's up to you. If you want to come back for a visit," Aidan said in a quiet voice.

"You want me to go back?" Julian asked.

An interval of heavy silence followed. Aidan waited then replied at a louder volume, "It's not about what I want. It's just an idea. Don't you want to see the place where we grew up, one last time? The woodland, or what remains of it?"

"Don't be sentimental."

Aidan cleared his throat multiple times and sighed. "Anyways, the place was once yours."

"I remember. There's no need to get upset."

"I'm not upset. Can you stop making assumptions? I've put the request out there. You can take it or leave it. In any case, I'm not doing this for you."

"Ah, I see. At last, something truthful. You're doing it for her then?"

Aidan cleared his throat again. "I don't know what you want me to say."

"If I go back, I do not want to see her," Julian said as he listened to the sound of furniture being moved on the other end of the line.

"That's an absurd thing to say. Penelope lives here. And she has done more for this place than you ever have."

"This is entirely your fault, you know?" Julian said in an unhurried tone. "You've bankrupted the estate with your ridiculous schemes. We wouldn't be here if you hadn't messed it all up."

Through the phone, Julian heard the high-pitched sound of something scraping against the floor. Then Aidan's voice, trembling yet clear: "Do whatever you like, which is what you always do anyways."

"Right," Julian said. "I have to go now." He ended the call without waiting for a response from the other end.

He and Aidan were never good at talking. As children, their time together was occupied with playing, racing each other, and building dens. But the silence over the event that happened with Penelope ballooned between them until it created an unbridgeable chasm of resentment. Since Julian's move to New York, they have seldom spoken, and then solely in relation to the house or legal matters. Julian knows his brother despises him, but he cannot decide whether he cares. At times, he forgets that he has a younger brother. He is glad that they look nothing alike, so no one would really mistake them for siblings in the first place.

He intends to deal with the loss of the house the way he has dealt with all other losses. After his father's sudden death twenty-five years ago, Julian responded by turning to work. He refused to attend the funeral, even after he inherited the estate in its entirety. He did not see the point of rituals of mourning, especially since he felt little more than indifference to his father. To Julian—and he was sure to Aidan as well—their father was banal. He'd spoken of properties and investments, everything that demanded vigilant concentration but no imagination. For most of their childhood, he had lived either in his London home or abroad, leaving Julian and Aidan with their mother—and after her death, the staff who took care of them. When he did appear on holidays, his interactions with the children consisted of commands: "Stand up straight"; "Don't run in the house"; "Do better." He hosted lavish parties, and the crowds of bodies formed, in Julian's eyes, a wall his father had erected to separate himself from his family.

The train arrives belatedly at 12:35, and Julian puts away his phone and the picture of Mornington Hall. He caught a glimpse of himself in the reflection of the windows as the train slows into the Termini station. He feels a vague sense of aversion so he looks down to examine the scuffmarks that have damaged his leather shoes.

The first-class carriage is empty except for one other passenger. Julian settles into his seat. Trains played an important role in his childhood. The few times that his father took him and Aidan on holiday, they found themselves on overnight trains. The nocturnal scenes always entranced him. First there was the darkness of the outside world, and the feeling of rushing head-on into the unknown. Then there were the towns and villages, like glow-in-the-dark toys. There were also the tunnels and the moonlit fields. Later in life, Julian has often taken long train journeys by himself. He is exhilarated by the rapid movement across vast terrains, and the way the views glide past him, without leaving him time to absorb all the details.

The train passes through the outer districts of Rome, with their heavily graffitied buildings that Julian has always deemed distasteful. The countryside soon emerges. Outside the window, there are scant traces of spring, only the bare branches of dying trees and the fractured ground speckled with dry shrubbery. He has little interest in the open landscape in daylight. He was never fond of the rolling hills or dense woodland that surrounded him in his childhood at Mornington Hall, and the loss of these did not wound him as it had wounded Aidan. Julian admires landscape paintings—the way the colors of nature are softened, as in a Constable or a Monet, where the browns and greens of the earth, the yellow of the sun, and the gentle blue of the sky are blended together into a harmonious whole, so unlike the blandness he sees outside the train window.

He draws the curtain closed and tries to read Kafka's diaries, a book he has been dipping into for years, though he has never managed to finish it. After two paragraphs, he is interrupted by an announcement about the dining car. Someone's phone rings. The disheveled man is the only other passenger in the first-class carriage, though judging from his attire, Julian wonders whether he didn't steal the first-class ticket. He turns around and glares at the man, though the latter does not react in the slightest. The ringing finally ceases, and Julian turns back to his book.

But Kafka fails to engage him, so he takes out the notebook that he prepared for the trip—leather-bound in camel morocco, with marbled endpapers and a mottled fore-edge. He also packed a specially selected fountain pen, with green resin shell and solid gold nib. The notebook remains blank, and he has not yet thought of an appropriate title. Perhaps "Train Journey" would do.

He puts down the writing instruments, and reluctantly looks out the window. There is a hillside covered with leafless vines, and a rundown farm standing by a road that twists behind a grove of trees and reappears beside a semi-derelict church. Buildings lead Julian back to the concept of greatness, which he discussed extensively with his classmates at Cambridge, at a time when the world was very different. As an undergraduate, he had collected stories about the accomplishments of others, stories about how so-and-so received a prestigious award, how someone was offered an internship at an international conglomerate, how another invented something and joined the ranks of the world's billionaires. He noted down the facts in a notebook that he still carries with him, and these stories fueled him through the days and nights when he locked himself away in his room overlooking the medieval courtyard, neglecting sleep and food, admitting no guests, and labored over his business plans. Julian has always prided himself on the willpower to attain his goals. It is this quality that he in turn admires in others.

As the train speeds past yet another crumbling building, a villa, he thinks about those Cambridge days. He takes out his tablet and visits the homepage of the company he founded shortly after graduating; he sold the company for a life-changing sum that allows him to spend most of his time traveling. One of his favorite innovations for the company was the Ex Libris app, which filled a gap in culture at a time when serious reading was becoming less appealing. He once came across the famous Victor Hugo quote on how the book killed architecture—but he knew Hugo's prediction to be premature, for something much more powerful had killed both architecture and the book.

He opens a separate file and examines the logo he designed for the app. It was a sketch of an open book with the page on the right-hand side fading into a wing. Technology enables flight—that was what he tried to convey. During adolescence, Julian experimented with book art; he bought cheap paperbacks in bulk and transformed the books into unexpected forms. *The Great Gatsby* became a pile of paper leaves; *Tess of the D'Urbervilles* was turned into papier-mâché sticks; and *King Lear* was reduced to shreds attached to a branch. He worked on his book art late at night, cutting and reassembling the pages until an appealing shape emerged. There was a copy of *Frankenstein* he was fond of, into which he glued variegated feathers. That was the inspiration for the app's logo. Later, when he saw Anselm Kiefer's sculpture of the book with wings, he felt a little embarrassed by his own design. By that point, the acid from the glue had eaten through the pages of the *Frankenstein*, so Julian discarded the book.

The train reaches a mountainous region and passes through several long tunnels. He puts away the tablet and takes a nap, soothed by the droning of the engine. When he awakens, he finds that the train has stopped at Florence. The man with the ringing phone has left. A dense crowd waits on the platform outside. But the first-class carriage remains empty. The Duomo, Julian recalls, has been partially gnawed away by weathering and insufficient funds. A holographic projection fills in the missing parts and gives the illusion of a complete building. That combination of the real and the virtual is the sort of thing that Aidan would mock, Julian thinks.

As the train moves forward again, he starts listening to Mahler's Symphony No. 2, the "Resurrection Symphony." It is a piece of music he has listened to again and again. A program he once read at a concert explained that the first movement represents a funeral and asks whether there is life after death; the second movement offers a remembrance of the life of the deceased; the third movement illustrates despair; the fourth calls for a release from a life of suffering; and the fifth, final movement of the symphony presents a triumphant choral close that signals transcendence. Julian enjoys the music, even though he does not believe in rebirth or life after death. The concept is wishful thinking or an excuse for cowardice. If life were lived properly, he concludes, there would be no need for a second chance.

When the first notes of the symphony start up, the train passes by an open lot filled with defunct train cars. What a colossal waste of machinery, Julian observes. Trains mediated his first encounter with Turner. A school visit to the National Gallery introduced him to *Rain, Steam, and Speed: The Great Western Railway*, his favorite Turner. He likes the idea of the locomotive, the dark, gleaming thing emerging from the smoke and charging onward to a new world. The teacher had pointed out the hare, barely visible near the bottom of the canvas, running on the train track and trying to escape certain death. The other students felt sorry for the hare, but Julian found the scene amusing.

The teacher also mentioned that the artist had witnessed the effects of volcanic eruptions, such as the 1815 Tambora explosion on the Sunda Islands, which sent clouds of volcanic ash into the atmosphere. The aerosol particles eventually drifted to London and scattered the sunlight, creating lurid sunsets and enshrouding the city in a veil of fog. Perhaps Turner had merely recorded the remembered effect of the volcanic eruption. Or perhaps the haze in the painting was generated by the smoke-producing engines that heralded the future. Julian tried to purchase *Rain, Steam, and Speed* when it finally went on sale, but was outbid by another buyer, an incident that still fills him with regret.

He pauses the symphony and finds an image of the painting on his tablet. He does not like to dwell on Turner much anymore, especially not since *A View on the Seine* was sold. Thinking about Turner meant thinking about Penelope. Meeting her had changed his relationship with Turner, and with all the artworks in the galleries. Julian traces his fingers over the black smoke and brilliant yellow of *Rain, Steam and Speed*. When he first met Penelope over twenty years ago, he had just returned from a trip to Central America. He remembers how he had followed a guide through the dense jungle and emerged to find a clearing filled with ancient ruins. For some inexplicable reason, he later associated Penelope with that view: greenery and dark groves and sunlight in winter.

A slight change in the speed of the train rouses him, and he gets up to stretch in order to stop thinking about her. As the train enters the outskirts of Bologna, Julian is overcome by the need to walk, to leave this space suffused with thoughts of Penelope.

Having nowhere else to go, he decides to walk through the second- and third-class carriages, separated from the first-class carriage by a passcode-protected door.

Humans, sitting, squatting, or standing, occupy every inch of the carriages. In some places, children are almost piled on top of one another. Garbage fills the crevices, and heat has created a veil of steam and human stench that permeates the space. Julian squeezes his way down the aisle, already regretting his decision to leave his seat, yet compelled to keep moving. When the train stops at Bologna, he presses himself against the wall in the gangway to let the crowd pass. After the train starts moving again, he notices a gaunt woman with wrinkled breasts breast-feeding a sickly child. A few construction workers start smoking in the gangway. Upon smelling the cigarettes, Julian steps back and bumps into a small boy sitting in the corner, wearing a black garbage bag as a jacket. The boy appears overjoyed to see him, as if he recognizes him. He speaks, but Julian does not understand the language, which is not Italian. Then Julian realizes that the child is admiring his dove-gray linen jacket with its leather buttons and flawless stitching. When the child reaches out to touch the jacket, Julian pushes his hand away and turns back toward the first-class carriage, picking up speed as he proceeds down the aisle and glancing behind him to check whether the boy has followed him.

In front of the door that leads to his carriage, Julian sees a young woman lying on her side, clutching her stomach in pain. Something in her composure compels him to throw some coins at her. A few individuals begin to crowd around him. Julian frantically enters the passcode for the door and steps through the threshold. He brushes his clothes and sanitizes his hands, making sure the spectators on the other side of the besmeared glass door witness him doing so. He takes a minute to breathe in the cool, filtered air of the carriage before returning to his seat.

A fellow traveler, who must have boarded the train at Bologna, is seated across the aisle from him. The elderly man has an open briefcase filled with books and loose sheets of paper that he flips through with great care, bursting into laughter at intervals.

"De Quincey is the most extraordinary man," the old man says, leaning over and trying to make conversation. "You know, I spent three months collecting these notes. Three months. I write everything longhand. It's a wonderful experience, isn't it, the feeling of pen on paper." The man pats his stack of papers.

"Indeed," Julian says, without looking at the man directly.

"And did you know"—the man leans even closer in Julian's direction—"that there is an unpublished, virtually unknown letter written by the poet Shelley, addressed to a publisher, just sitting under layers of dust in an archive in Warsaw?"

"Is that so? How interesting," Julian replies, while attempting to return to the Kafka.

"Yes, isn't it? Archival work unearths the most extraordinary things. Simply extraordinary." The man slides his papers back into the leather briefcase. "You're English? I hear an accent."

Julian hesitates. "Yes."

The old man seems delighted. "Where from? London?"

"Yes."

"Oh, I love London. I'm from Los Angeles myself. What is it that you do, if I may ask?"

Julian hesitates again, still avoiding eye contact. "I'm an art historian."

"Oh, how wonderful! There are so few of us scholarly types left, aren't there? I'm retired myself, but the work never really ends." He laughs. "It is wonderful to meet another scholar. Not many people pursue such a life nowadays." The man pauses for a few seconds in thought. "Do you do any work on Titian? I've just seen some of his paintings."

Julian shuffles in his seat. "No, I'm afraid I don't have much interest in that era."

A moment of awkwardness ensues, but the man is determined to continue talking. "So, what is the purpose of your trip?" he asks. "Heading back home?"

"Yes. My father has died. I'm attending the funeral."

"Oh, I am so sorry. So terribly sorry. My condolences." The man leans back into his own seat.

"Don't be," Julian says and looks the man in the eyes. "These things happen."

The scholar clears his throat and smiles before going back to his papers. At some point, the old man falls asleep and snores, the booming sound audible even against the background noise of the train.

At a small station right before Milan, the scholar returns his papers to the briefcase, smiles at Julian, and disembarks the train. From where Julian sits, he can observe the old man standing on the platform, busily entering a number into his mobile phone, with his briefcase on a bench next to him. As he fumbles with the keys, a teenager sneaks up to the bench and silently takes hold of the briefcase. The elderly scholar focuses wholeheartedly on keying in the number and waiting for a reply. By the time someone picks up on the other line, the briefcase and the young man are long gone. All this, Julian witnesses. When the scholar finally notices that the briefcase containing months of work is missing, he lets out a cry of such anguish that it makes Julian feel he ought to have opened the narrow window and warned him. But the feeling is fleeting. As the train pulls away from the platform, he turns back and sees the old man in a tearful mess, surrounded by concerned bystanders.

That someone could be distraught over a pile of papers fascinates Julian. He likes the idea of a buried letter, unearthed after days of digging through the archive. He and Penelope had undertaken their own project of excavation, during those days they spent in his old apartment in London. They flipped through second-hand books, hunting for ephemera. They combed the pages to see who would find a larger selection of old train tickets, letters, postcards or pressed flowers. Penelope was better at that game. He still has in his wallet an old train ticket from the 1960s that they found in a bookshop on Charing Cross Road. He takes out the ticket and sniffs it; the paper gives off a scent that has become more distinctive over time. He does not know why he kept the ticket and why he is thinking of Penelope yet again as the train moves on toward Milan.

The bull has a placid expression on its face. Its bright, watery eyes gaze out at the viewer. Europa grips the bull's horn with her left hand, while her right arm is outstretched, casting a shadow on her face. She waves a red silk veil in an effort to call out for rescue, as her companions in the background look on helplessly. Her right breast is bared, her fleshy thighs opened, and the sumptuous folds of thin drapery converge at her half-concealed genitals. One of the cherubs, Zeus's minions, leers unashamedly between Europa's legs. All the sensuous textures of the radiant painting—Europa's rolling flesh, the soft, clinging fabric, the frothy sea foam—suggest pleasure, or the expectation of pleasure. Europa is supposed to be terrified. But in Titian's pictorial reimagining, she appears to be in a state of ecstasy. It is almost possible to believe that her story ended happily (as an art historian has claimed).

Titian's The Rape of Europa *(1559–1562) was one of six works comprising the* poesie, *visual poems on the theme of erotic love, each showcasing a different female nude from Ovid's* Metamorphoses. *The series was painted for King Philip II of Spain, who imagined himself to be a descendant of Zeus, holding dominion over a growing empire. The desire for imperial expansion, like the desire to conquer women, must have burned like a blaze that consumed the mind.*

A similar scene of eroticism appears in Titian's 1571 Tarquin and Lucretia, *a story which he painted three times. In the 1571 version, Lucretia is nude, lying prone on a bed, with the white sheets bundled at her pubic region, thus drawing the viewer's eye there. Tarquin raises the phallic knife over her head and thrusts his knee between her splayed thighs. Lucretia, though vulnerable, is also voluptuous and beautiful. One eminent art historian claims to see a faint smile on Lucretia's face, as if she were unable to resist her own lust.*

In these paintings, where does the viewer stand? Is he like the voyeur in Titian's Tarquin and Lucretia, *peeking from behind the curtain, and standing right next to Tarquin so as to watch this display of desire and pleasure from his perspective? Is the voyeur unable, or unwilling, to intervene, caught up in the work of looking that can also be an act of violation? Does the viewer spot the barely perceptible tear glistening on Lucretia's cheek? Do we recognize the beguiling look in the eyes of Europa's bull, in the act of transporting his prey, as the look of mutual acknowledgement, of complicity?*

Four

November

November 1

Despite how poorly Turner treated his works, he had a collector's mania. He compulsively bought back pieces he had previously sold, and sometimes refused to sell the ones that were dear to him. Of his paintings, he is said to have remarked, "What is the use of them, but together?" Accordingly, in the 1848 codicil to his will, he left his collection to the nation in the form of a "Turner Gallery."

His friend, the architect Sir John Soane, had a similar impulse. In his house at Nos. 12–14 Lincoln's Inn Fields, Soane collected hundreds of architectural and decorative stone fragments, alongside over sixty thousand drawings. From antique relics to Gothic sculptures, the house culminated in the sarcophagus of Pharaoh Seti I, the kernel at the center of the collection. Prior to his death in 1837, Soane bequeathed the house-museum to the nation by an Act of Parliament.

Although Turner, like Soane, wished to preserve his legacy for posterity, he did not treat his collection with the same care. The painter accumulated his own works only to let them rot in his studio, to be pasted on walls, rolled up in filthy corners, or used to patch holes in broken windows. Why collect if the collection is allowed to disintegrate?

ALBUM

Entitled "Homes of Famous Men," *ca.* 1900. Consisting of twenty-four individual cards, each with an image and description. Octavo album, covered with heavy cream-colored paper; water-stained. Collection includes Byron at Newstead, Dickens at Gad's Hill Place, and Turner at 119 Cheyne Walk in Chelsea (Mrs. Booth's house). Collection incomplete. Contemporary ink inscription: "O. D. W., seven-years-old."

NOVEMBER 2

A family of five has joined us. We rarely have children here, at least not for an extended period of time, because Mornington is too far away from schools. The parents of the three kids— aged five, six, and eight—told me the family has lost their home after the last round of evictions, part of the infuriating policy to segregate those who have the right to stay from those who have been denied that right due to complex reasons obfuscated by the language of bureaucracy. The family will stay here for approximately a month, as they await their visas.

NOVEMBER 3

Fell asleep this afternoon in the Library's underground storage space, exhausted from work. In the liminal state between waking and sleeping, I thought I saw a figure weaving between the stacks: a figure with Julian's gait and slightly hunched back, his way of pausing suddenly in thought. When I woke up fully, I realized there was nothing there at all. Felt a sudden chill. What frightens me is not the possibility of his physical presence here, but the possibility of his re-entering my subconscious, from which I had purged his image so long ago.

NOVEMBER 4

A new traveler arrived today; his application was the last that I processed before posting the announcement about the closure. In his application letter, Alex mentioned being fired from his job as a security guard after getting into a fight with colleagues who had attacked him verbally. He had lost most of his savings paying for his mother's medical treatment, but the treatment was ineffective, and she died anyway.

When I showed Alex to his room, I invited him to tea and asked if he would like a tour of the rest of the house. He promptly said no and shut the door without waiting for my reply. He is not the first traveler to act with such coldness, but I understand the need to be left alone. And I must admit a certain sense of relief that he turned down my offer, as I did not really want to sit down with him over tea, even though I felt obliged to invite him, as I do every new traveler. There was something about him—and this is a sense of unease I've felt in the past with certain men—something menacing. The bland, matter-of-fact way in which he spoke of his mother's death, without any hint of sadness, unnerved me. But his eyes were actually quite expressionless, so perhaps I'm imagining the menace. I must refrain from judgment.

NOVEMBER 5

The three children who are staying with us are not very interested in the few children's books we have. Today, when their parents went to the nearest city to process their applications at the government agency, I asked the children to help me dust the books in the Library. Afterward, I watched over them as they wandered through the gardens, filling cardboard boxes with pieces of wood, twigs, and rocks. They brought these found objects back into the house and constructed a makeshift fortress in one corner, using the chairs and old bedsheets I had given them. Into this haven they carried their relics.

These children, like many others in the world, live a childhood untethered from the material comforts that once bespoke a wholesome life. Their bodies learn of cold and hunger before they learn of pleasure. From a young age, they become experts in longing, and for that, I admire them.

NOVEMBER 6

Today was our anniversary. Aidan and I celebrated by having a candlelit dinner in the Library, as is our tradition. I bought a bottle of wine and a cake from the village shop. He gave me an exquisite object: a paperweight with a real cornflower preserved in clear resin. I have decided to store it inside an old jewelry case that was a present from Dad, a black Japanese lacquer box with sakura blossoms painted on top. Inside, there is a velvet lining, indented in places where jewels once sat. The paperweight fits imperfectly into one of the hollows.

SCRAPBOOK

Album with pressed seaweed and seaweed collages, date unknown. Octavo. Speckled brown morocco with gilt borders and marbled fore-edges. Dedicated to Alice M., with love from her sisters. Approximately sixty collages, made using seaweed, photographs, and postcards. In extremely fragile condition; many seaweed specimens affected by damp and pests.

NOVEMBER 8

Have not been sleeping well lately. But still had to do the supply run today, which we have not done for a few months. Aidan and I left for London in the morning and arrived before noon.

The temperature was unusually warm, despite the cement gray of the sky.

The drive to the city yields many sights that both disturb and fascinate. In the outer boroughs, there are former high streets with shops overrun by wild weeds. Where we once saw billboards advertising overseas vacations or real estate developments, we now see announcements about the hazards of contaminated water. Many alleyways are clogged with broken furniture, abandoned cars, and fractured pieces of cement.

Innumerable structures closer to the city center were dismantled in the early days of unrest, after the flames, left unchecked because of cuts to fire services, turned whole blocks to cinder. For a while, the charred ruins were the city's greatest spectacle. Photographers, artists and filmmakers made much use of them. Activists and politicians repurposed the rubble as symbols of the plight of the oppressed, and disseminated images of the wreckage in their fight for political change. But as the physical environment became more inhospitable, as the water level and the temperature rose and the possibility of rebuilding became more remote, both the aesthetic appeal and the symbolic usefulness of the ruins receded.

Being in London reminds me that people once filled the streets, banners in hand, crying for change. There was a time when brightly lit screens flickered across the faces of young and old, the same screens held up to artworks and scenery, or positioned before carefully poised bodies. A time when freedom meant having the right possessions, eating the right foods, and being far away from the crowds gathered at closed borders. That was a time when "home" seemed easy, filled with comforting narratives; a time when the world was a beautiful blue-green orb that appeared unchanging. It was a time of both comfort and unease, of decadence and the awareness of imminent loss.

It is reassuring to be back in our room, in bed, with Aidan reading next to me. The exhaustion from the day will hopefully send me into a deep sleep tonight.

NOVEMBER 9

Startled by the news this morning. More bodies in seas. Whenever I learn of such tragedies, I am confronted by the enormity of the task before us and the insufficiency of all that we have done.

I keep thinking about the trip I took with Aidan all those years ago, to the refugee camp near the Mediterranean, where his firm had built emergency shelters. He recounted his first visit to a similar camp, with the senior architect who trained him. Seeing the groups of people stranded behind a fence, Aidan was reminded of something he'd seen when he was young. There was a barn that belonged to one of the farms on the Mornington estate, and birds had bored a hole in one of the outer walls of the barn in order to build a nest. Aidan, who was about ten, heard the twittering of the nestlings and he went back daily to watch the adult birds fly out and fly back in with worms to feed their young. But one day, the farmer covered the hole with a wire mesh, leaving the nestlings to starve to death; the adult birds frantically tried to remove the barrier, to no avail.

For a long while afterward, Aidan had nightmares about that blocked nest. Witnessing people forcibly removed from their homes, or families divided by arbitrary barriers, he thought of the birds he failed to save.

The turning point in his career was when his team's award-winning design, originally intended to regenerate a run-down housing project, instead developed into upmarket properties that forced out the low-income residents.

I contributed to that, Aidan told me that evening in our tent on the periphery of the camp. Some of the features that made the place attractive to investors were my ideas.

He subsequently left that firm and founded his current studio with a colleague who shared his sense of dismay about the direction the profession had taken.

Aidan's belief in something outside the self was infectious. It was partly his radical optimism that turned me away from the shadow cast by Julian's presence. Aidan never became disillusioned, in spite of criticism from his peers, in spite of the financial precarity his studio faced. He held on to the idea that even in the midst of the inferno, there are people and things that endure, that resist the fires and pestilence.

NOVEMBER 10

Wintry dryness and frost. There are cracks on our hands and faces, like fissures on bedrock. Outside, the bare trees, dried and brittle, appear weightless.

One wall on the veranda, on the exterior of the Long Gallery, has begun to rot again—this time, from termites, those relentless, indestructible armies that survive heat and cold alike. We have decided to use the emergency fund for the extermination.

A part of me pities the insects, as they will be slaughtered in great numbers. But they sicken me and hasten the death of the house. I shudder at the thought of the insects burrowing away, eating the building from inside out. When I close my eyes, I can almost feel them crawling on me. It is impossible to work until they are gone.

NOVEMBER 11

Slept without dreams after taking a sleeping pill. Still had difficulty focusing all day. I must stay away from that section of the wall where the termites can be seen.

The group of young travelers who were staying in the Hall have left. I hardly spoke to them over the course of three months. Alex has asked to move into the Hall, even though he was assigned a bedroom in the pavilion. He likes the open space, he said. He set up a tent in a corner, behind a marble column. If it were anyone else, I'd worry they'd be lonely there, but Alex does not strike me as someone who's easily affected by isolation. This evening I paused by the entrance to the Hall and peered in, and I heard—nothing. There was complete silence, though I could see his silhouette on the side of the tent. That silence was unnerving. Was he just sitting there, doing absolutely nothing? Maybe he was meditating? I still do not understand his request to be moved into the Hall. He could have set up the tent in one corner of the bedroom. Inside the Hall, any movement might generate sounds that would reverberate through the marble space. Maybe that is the challenge that he has set himself, to remain as still and quiet as possible in order to avoid the echo.

NOVEMBER 12

Today was my third session of sitting for Celia. She said the portrait is progressing nicely, though I am still not allowed to see it.

It is surprising how quickly the mind wanders in stillness. Sitting and being observed has the curious effect of pushing me into memory. The present—the sounds in the house, the *trompe l'oeil* on the wallpaper—receded. Unable to read or speak, I fell headlong into the past, dredging up details that I had assumed were forgotten.

I thought of the Library and the remaining tasks that I have to tackle. I thought of what the Library looked like in Turner's days. I thought of how Julian rejected the first version of the essay I wrote on *A View on the Seine*. What I had considered completed work was, for him, still an undeveloped draft. So I deleted everything I had written and started again.

Almost as soon as he arrived at Mornington, Julian began working on the collection. His goal was to turn the Library into "a meeting place of minds." He showed me his folder of quotes about libraries, with accompanying illustrations. "Inspiration is the lifeblood of any important institution." He was fond of sayings like that, though I was never certain whether these were quotes from the Internet or lines he had written himself.

At the time, he was also writing a speech that he had been invited to give at a conference, on the relationship between the digital world and the world of books. We sometimes sat together in the Library, me with the essay on Turner, Julian with his speech. He would pace from one end of the Library to the other as he muttered to himself, periodically pausing to write on the piece of paper that he kept neatly folded in his pocket.

Sometimes he would retrieve an antiquarian volume from the archives and examine it, scrutinizing its cover and flipping through the fragile pages. He was attracted to books with elaborate bindings or intricate woodcuts and etchings, though he did not comment on the images, except to say that it would benefit the collection to have more rare books.

About halfway into the three-month fellowship, Aidan left for an extended work trip, and during that time, I spent most evenings with Julian, sometimes in the Library, other times, over a meal. I offered morsels of memory—about childhood visits to gardens, my travels abroad, or my discovery of Turner. I extended a hand to Julian, as it were, inviting him to take it, and in return, offer fragments of his own past from which I might construct a fuller picture of him. Except he never took my hand. In response to my memories, he spoke of the Library, of his ongoing projects and his investments, as though they were the only things he had ever collected in life.

When asked about his childhood, Julian spoke of Aidan's experiences instead: "Aidan liked racing in the garden. He usually won"; "the house was great for hide-and-seek. That was Aidan's favorite game for a while"; "Aidan liked the tree house in the woods, and we would go there and pretend to be Robinson Crusoe. It was our secret hiding place."

On warmer evenings, we would sit outside on the veranda and read together. Julian would ask me questions about art. He absorbed everything in an almost childlike manner, taking notes and asking one question after another—about colors, about Turner's life, about my opinion on particular artworks. In those conversations, I saw a curiosity and thirst for knowledge that I recognized in myself at a time when I had assumed the accumulation of facts and ideas to be the key to the world's mysteries. In hindsight, I wonder if that erroneous assumption we shared—about knowledge—created a false sense of affinity between us.

One time Julian asked me whether Turner painted scenes of violence. I pulled up on my phone an image of *The Field of Waterloo*, with the moonlit battlefield, to which he displayed very little reaction. Then I showed him *War. The Exile and the Rock Limpet*, portraying Napoleon in exile, standing against a sunset that the painter had called "a sea of blood." Julian nodded but did not say anything, waiting for me to find something else. I thought of the poignant *Slave Ship*, with the bodies of the abandoned slaves entangled in the violent waves. He leaned in to take a closer look at the painting displayed on the screen, and nodded. I told him about the unfinished poem that Turner appended to *Slave Ship*, which ended with the lines "Hope, Hope, fallacious Hope! / Where is thy market now?" Julian seemed unimpressed with that bit of information and asked me if there was anything else.

I then remembered *The Fall of Anarchy* and found an image of the unfinished painting. The skeletal, phantasmagorical figure of Death, like a mangled cadaver, is draped over the back of a horse, as it disappears into the orange and blood-red mist. I went on to explain how people have interpreted this piece in divergent ways—as Turner's expression of grief over the death of his father, as a meditation on the cholera epidemic of 1832, or as a response to Shelley's "The Mask of Anarchy"—but Julian did not hear any of that. He opened the same image on his phone and, holding the phone in the palms of his hands, stroked the screen as if he were petting an animal. As he walked away, he turned back and said to me, It's nightmarish, isn't it? It's exactly what I was looking for.

At the end of the session, Celia smiled and said that I'm finally dwelling in stillness. I did not tell her what I was thinking about, but she somehow sensed that I'd been pulled into the past.

Many people, she said, tend to sink into their memories when they sit. And there's always an instant, when something delights or pains them, and the sitter comes fully into him or herself. I want to record that moment. I feel like I'm capturing a backward glance—whether unflinching or hesitant—even though the subject is facing me, looking forward.

NOVEMBER 13

Slept badly. A dream about termites. I was watching them through a camera lens, moving and digging, and laying their horrifying eggs. They were eating their way through a house, hollowing it out from within. They drilled and drilled until they dug a labyrinth of tunnels in the walls and under the floorboards, an unmappable network of subterranean channels and cavities. Then the whole edifice caved in. When I woke up, sweating and with my heart pounding, I imagined I could feel the insects crawling on me. Impatient for the exterminators to get here and eradicate the colony.

NOVEMBER 14

Felt unwell all of yesterday and this morning. Sense of queasiness after reconstructing those scenes with Julian. I realize that I am afraid of the physical strain of remembering, afraid also of the enormous abyss that might open beneath me, sucking in everything and everyone in the present. At least last night's sleep was free from termites. Had to force myself to get out of bed, to take clothing and food donations to the village. Spent most of the day helping the volunteers sort through the items.

In the evening, Celia and I helped Miranda with her sewing, which was calming. My sewing skills are no match for Miranda's, but I can make simple stitches, albeit slowly. Miranda is working on a quilt, using scraps of fabric she has collected throughout her life. She told us today she learned how to sew when she was very young, as it was one of the few skills her mother was able to pass on to her. As an adolescent, Miranda also worked in a clothing factory. She showed us a scar on her arm, left by a malfunctioning machine.

NOVEMBER 15

The exterminators have finally arrived to do their work. We vacated the house for the day to avoid the noxious fumes. Aidan and I set up desks in the folly by the lake. But I spent the day pacing back and forth, looking in the direction of the house, unable to concentrate on anything.

NOVEMBER 17

The extermination is complete. The termites have been eliminated, and the damaged wall will be rebuilt. We celebrated by hosting another group dinner, for which Miranda made lasagna, and David, the father of the three children, made chocolate cake. After dinner, we took out an old video game console for the children. Alex turned down the invitation to join us for dinner; he preferred to bring the food back to his tent.

Throughout the evening, my mind was elsewhere. I kept picturing the heap of dead termites piled up and burnt. I could not determine whether I felt pity or relief. For some reason, I am adamant they will reappear, one way or another, despite the assurance the exterminators gave us that the colony is gone. My eyes have become sensitive to the most minute movements—a sheet of paper fluttering in the draft, a rolling dust ball—fearful that the movement signals the return of the insects.

BOOK
Jane Austen, *Mansfield Park*. First Bentley edition, 1833, published by Richard Bentley, London; third edition overall. Octavo. Half-bound morocco, with marbled decorative board. Illustrations by Ferdinand Pickering. Extensive worming throughout, obscuring portions of the text.

NOVEMBER 18
Went for a solitary walk today to clear my head. I took a different route than my usual one, down the rough, narrow track that leads toward the river, past the spot where the boundary trees—the sycamore, beech, and oak—once stood, and past the old hawthorn, which is nearing the end of its life.

I passed an old granary that belongs to one of the neighboring farms. The roof has collapsed. Abandoned farm machinery, rusted metal parts, and fallen tiles lay around the dilapidated building. There were lesion-like holes on the sides of the structure where the wood has rotted away. A little further down the path, I stumbled upon a mildewing hay rick and a stack of beech leaves turning to compost. No humans have been there for a while, but I know that someone owns the farm, which has changed hands so many times that we can no longer keep track of the owners.

The footpath I originally planned to take led to a barbed-wire enclosure. I had to take another route and passed through the fields that belong to another farm that was formerly a part of the Mornington estate. The fields were empty. There were once cows in those fields, and horses too. I remember standing by the fence and watching the cows rambling across the pasture. They paid no attention to the world around them and focused their energy on the act of eating. Yet they lived among forgotten things, and they themselves were half-ruins, destined for a place that I could not bear to think of.

For a long time, the suffering of animals was indistinguishable from my own. Any news about factory farms, endangerment in the wild, or death from anthropogenic disasters was unbearable. It became impossible to go outside, to behold the atrocity of the force that turns all living beings into mere things. Aidan told me I needed to protect myself, to prevent my mind from becoming too porous. Yet my heart would shatter and my sleep tormented by nightmares for days after coming across a dead animal in the woods.

We started adopting rabbits, after conditions became too inhospitable for them in the wild. Our first two were rescued from the ash woodland after we found them abandoned as kits, their mother possibly killed. They were the sweetest creatures. When we first brought them home, they were terrified of everything, suspicious of our every movement. But they overcame those fears. Despite being among the most vulnerable animals in the world, with so few defenses, the rabbits nevertheless managed to find repose and joy. Their days were filled with eager munching and dazedness and contentment. When they were truly excited, they would do a little jump and twist in the air. Watching them provided an antidote to all the horrible changes we were witnessing in the world.

PICTURE POSTCARD

Postmarked 1904. Black-and-white photo of the Egmont Castle, in the Belgian city of Zottegem. The original building dates back to the twelfth century; it has undergone numerous cycles of disrepair, partial demolition, expansion, and restoration. Since the 1980s, a public library has been housed on the site. Undivided back—address written on verso. Message, in microscript, written in the margins of the recto side. Fine condition. First vintage postcard in the Mornington Ephemera Collection.

NOVEMBER 19

The first time I saw this postcard in a bookshop, tucked into a tattered copy of Rilke's novel, I was stopped in my tracks. It is not beautiful, but it wasn't beauty I was interested in. Rather, I was stunned by the improbable survival of something so fragile. That delicate piece of paper, despite the fraying edges and spots of mold, still displayed a picture and conveyed a message. At the time, the postcard spoke to me of permanence, a word that I naïvely attached to a fantastical life of companionship with Julian that I envisioned, without any clear understanding that such a life would have been impossible.

I discovered the postcard on one of the "collecting trips" I took with Julian in London, toward the end of my fellowship. He requested my help with the purchasing of items for the Library and the art collection. I stayed with him in his apartment in the city, a place with blindingly white walls and white furnishings, interrupted by the pale brown shade of birch. Julian said he found dark-colored furnishings suffocating. Even the painting hanging in the living room was black, white, and gray. It was one of Francis Bacon's crucifixion pieces, with a spectral figure—either a ghost or the skeletal remains of a flayed carcass—hanging from hooks. It frightened me, and whenever I was in the room, I kept my back turned toward it.

Julian's space, with its aura of cleanliness, suited him, since he too appeared impeccable—in his expensive, freshly pressed clothes, his hair styled with gel, and, at his wrist, the carefully selected watch that was coordinated with his outfit. But all his belongings were concealed in cabinets and drawers. The surfaces or countertops were completely clear. I once snooped in his bathroom to find nothing but a travel pouch with a toothbrush, toothpaste, a shaver, a comb, deodorant, and a bottle of aspirin. He seemed ready to flee at any moment.

For approximately a week, Julian and I frequented galleries, auction houses, and bookshops every day. We made notes on the artworks or antiquarian books that might be suitable for the collection. He consulted my opinion on each piece, and I shared any knowledge I might have had. He then either made a purchase on the spot or took a few days to consider the investment.

We visited a few exhibitions for fun. At one gallery, there was an installation that consisted of found images—photographs, postcards, letters, advertisements, newspapers—all displayed in vitrines, resembling archaeological collections in a museum. There were no obvious themes in those archives of heterogeneous images. I was captivated by the apparent randomness. I recommended purchasing a few of the vitrines, but Julian disagreed, for he disliked artworks without an obvious meaning.

In second-hand bookshops, we hunted for the same kind of ephemera that were used in the vitrines. That was when I came across the postcard of Egmont Castle. In the photograph, the castle sat in the middle of wintry woodland. All the curtains were drawn on the upper level; two windows on the lower levels were open, resembling dark voids. I was arrested by the way in which the message, written in French, surrounded the image of the castle, encasing it like a cocoon; the building, in turn, formed a kernel inside the written text. I tucked the postcard back between the pages and paid for the book.

Later, in a café, I showed Julian the postcard. He turned the card over and over in his hand.

Fascinating, he said, how a piece of paper has survived for over a hundred years. Are there many more of these we could find? Ones from the early twentieth century, or even the nineteenth century? Why don't you start a collection for the Library?

From that point on, Julian acquired the habit of flipping through second-hand books to search for ephemera. He contributed to our burgeoning collection a few vintage tram and train tickets, distinctive for their muted tones of pink, green, and mustard.

NOVEMBER 21

Sleep was thin. My dreams populated by legions of termites that dig and dig. The sense of disgust I feel is barely expressible; the words at my disposal are like blunted tools. Yesterday I saw a line of crawling insects and panicked. Turned out they were ants, and the line led back to the garden, so at least the colony lives outside and not in the house.

I shivered throughout most of yesterday. Even after I put on an extra layer and started a fire, I continued to shiver. Eventually fell asleep on the armchair, having done absolutely nothing, made no change whatsoever.

NOVEMBER 22

Walked past the Hall and once again saw Alex's motionless silhouette on the side of the tent. Statue-like. He has met the challenge of eradicating all echoes from the marble space. Is this perhaps his way of mourning? The stillness as a kind of tribute to his mother?

November 23

Cannot believe it is snowing! The world seems improved by the snow. All of us—except Alex—spent the afternoon in the gardens, playing in the snow and admiring the whitened hedges. There is such beauty in the first soft layer, the glistening line of white that brings everything into sharp relief. Snow dusted the footpaths that led to the gardens, dusted the bare branches and shrubs, and outlined the house, rendering its abrasions less visible in the snow-light. After snow, we can hope for rain in the spring. The cold also means there is less chance of the termites returning anytime soon. For the moment, they have stopped burrowing in my mind.

November 24

During the sitting today, I made a conscious effort to keep my mind in the present. I recited to myself, as a mantra, a line from Louise Bourgeois that I have always loved, about memory being moth-eaten, full of holes. The more I recited, the more I resisted the images from the past that sought to latch on to me.

I noticed, during the sitting, a lovely painting leaning against the wall. It depicts a sleeping child, who has one hand clutching a teddy bear and one thumb in his mouth. After our session, I asked Celia about the portrait. My son, Jamie, she said, when he was about three. I could only paint him when he was sleeping. It was the only time he could be still. Otherwise, he was full of energy, everywhere all at once.

I asked her if it was difficult balancing motherhood and a creative life.

It was so hard to guard that space, she said, the space of silence and solitude I needed for art. Sometimes, a thousand things threatened to invade. Motherhood, and being a single mother, was a constant battle with guilt. I felt guilty when I was in the studio and not with Jamie. But I felt equally guilty when

I was with him and not painting. I was torn between two kinds of love.

Her ex-husband, Celia went on to tell me, was also an artist, who struggled throughout his entire career to find a gallery for his sculptures. He did not take Celia's success well. When the baby was born, he retreated even further into his studio, producing pieces that were like caricatures of famous sculptures.

He was completely uncompromised by parenthood, Celia said. In fact, he was not compromised by anything. So I left him to his sculptures. Then it was just Jamie and me. And the art.

She told me that at her worst, she felt possessive of Jamie, even though she saw it as a form of protectiveness.

The picture I always had in my head, she said, was a portrait by Paula Modersohn-Becker, of a mother holding an infant close to her, her naked body a kind of shelter from all the pain that flesh is heir to.

But at a certain point, Celia continued, I had to let Jamie go. When he first moved away for university, I wept for an entire day. Now I'm used to seeing him once in a while. He lives in London with his partner and kids. But that first separation was unbearable. It was a difficult lesson for me, to learn that a child was not mine to keep.

After the painting session, on my way back to the Library, I thought of my own mother. I wonder where she has lived, what kind of work she has done, and what populates her life that remains hidden from the Internet. The only reference I have of her is a blurry photograph tucked into one of Dad's books. I doubt he even remembered it was there. In the picture, my mother was wearing a floral top and a long white skirt, with white sneakers. She looked no more than twenty years old. She sat on the edge of a boat with a companion, her body leaning forward awkwardly, her hands on her knees, whereas her companion was much more relaxed, sitting upright with one arm around my mother's shoulders. The boat appeared to be stranded in the middle of a marsh. The girls' feet were perched precariously on the side of the boat, the only dry surface in the photo. The mast of the boat rose up behind them. On the back of the photo, someone had written "Evelyn and Winifred at the beach." I had no idea who Evelyn was. Was she someone who continued to be in my mother's life after she abandoned my father and me? Would she have agreed with my mother's decision to leave? Was my mother able to throw me away because she regarded me as a possession, something easily acquired and therefore easily discarded?

NOVEMBER 24—EVENING

I suppose I too have been possessive of things and people. I've felt possessive of art, of Turner's works. When I first saw his signature in the manuscript room at the Tate—next to a tiny drawing of a mallard with which he often signed his letters— I touched the ink and pen marks with my bare fingers. This was against the rules of archival research, but in that contact between my skin and the paper that Turner had touched, I felt I possessed him in a way that no one else could.

I recall how, as a child, I was possessive of the miscellany that Dad and I collected on our visits to the gardens—the pressed leaves and flowers, the acorns and pine cones. I also laid claim to the artifacts in museums, such as the miniature model of the Crystal Palace in the V&A, and I had—according to Dad—gotten angry at a group of tourists for photographing it. I would study the model for hours and imagine what people in the Victorian era would have remarked when they attended the Great Exhibition. Sometimes, I would put on the costumes that were available in the children's corner and enact imaginary stories. This was how I passed the time when Dad visited exhibitions with a girlfriend he had when I was around seven. Giselle was a geologist who was much taller than Dad and with whom he had conversations I could never understand. I do not remember ever seeing Dad with another woman.

I have not thought about Giselle in a long time. I wonder where she is now, if she is still alive, and how she has fared in the world. I remember she made delicious stew, and she came over often to cook with Dad. Sometimes she baked banana loaf and told me about her childhood in a faraway place where there were banana trees and forests filled with fairy-tale creatures. These I assumed to be stories she made up for my benefit, but I loved hearing them nonetheless. I also loved listening to her talk about rocks. She showed me the box of geological samples that she used for her lectures—feldspar with shiny specks embedded in the dark stone; pyrite with its golden sheen; onyx and agate with swirls of white, brown, and caramel bands. She called the box her lapidarium, a word that I found strange and beautiful.

I gradually became possessive of Giselle. Although I never felt the impulse to call her Mum, I cannot deny that she was a sort of mother figure. She took me to the shops for new clothes; selected my readings for the holidays; checked my homework; and mended my clothes when they were torn. For a time, I aspired to be like Giselle. I began to dress like her, wearing a lot of green, which she was fond of. I had also hoped that she would give me a sibling who would resemble the both of us.

I remember that day when I came home from school and found Giselle in tears. I tried to comfort her, without knowing why she was crying, but she ended up comforting me instead. Everything will be okay, she said. Always be kind to yourself. At the time I was not sure whether she meant that for me or for herself. That day, Giselle packed up all the things she left at our house—a set of clothes, two mugs, and a few books. She left me the collection of rocks and minerals, and these I have kept to this day.

Dad never clarified what happened between them and I never asked. He continued his work and daily routine as if nothing much had changed, as if the preceding four years had not occurred, as if Friday nights had not been filled with Giselle's cooking, and Sundays with trips to the market. His silence angered me. I believed I alone understood Giselle, that I alone knew what it meant to love her, and no one else could possibly share with her the bond I had established with her over hot cocoa and glittering pieces of rock.

Giselle taught me about weathering and geologic time. Of all her lessons, this was the most important. Stone endures, in a way that is difficult for humans to comprehend. Yet even stone can be chipped away, by wind and rain, or cut by streams of water. I think of Giselle often these days when I recognize stone weathering here at Mornington, spreading like a disease to all parts of the house. When repairs became too expensive and erosion overtook conservation, surfaces with seemingly perfect solidity slowly became perforated. I remember the photos Giselle showed me of rocks sculpted into bizarre shapes by the waves, with honeycombs forming in the rock bed and deep trenches furrowing the stones. Nature is a brilliant sculptor, she once told me.

NOVEMBER 25
The next person whom I wanted to possess was probably Michael, my first boyfriend. We took long walks around the university campus and strolled along the Thames, under the blue fairy lights. On all those walks, I held onto his hand a little more tightly than he held mine. At one point, I jokingly used a Sharpie and wrote my initials on the side of his arm, where a tattoo might be. When the ink faded, I wrote it again.

Michael was an art student at the Slade and specialized in mixed-media installations. I fell in love watching him set up the installations, his face beaming each time the lights lit up as planned. Perhaps it was the art I loved, and not Michael, or maybe not even his projects, but the way in which he made them, with such conviction. I sometimes stayed with him in the studio till late at night, taping wires, adjusting the alignment, or reconfiguring the layout. I felt it was a collaborative effort. But at the graduation show, my name was not included on the list of acknowledgements.

Michael once asked me what kind of installation I would make if I had the opportunity. It took me days to ponder this hypothetical project, and the image that surfaced was that of ash piled into assorted shapes or spread across the gallery floor. Michael laughed for ages.

For our first anniversary, he gave me a pendant with a hand-written note in it, folded into a tiny square, but I could not decipher his cursive script. I wore the pendant every day, even when parts of the chain became rusted from overuse.

At some point, the conversations about art turned into misunderstandings and accusations. I didn't feel hatred. Rather, I felt my sense of self being eroded until I did not even have possession of my own mind.

BOOK
John Berger, *Once in Europa*, 1987. First American edition, published by Pantheon, New York. Signed by author. Book two of Berger's *Into Their Labours* trilogy. Severe water damage. Worming at back affecting sections of the text. On the front pastedown, a pencil drawing of a rabbit.

NOVEMBER 26
An acquaintance at college—whose name I can no longer remember—told me how he'd remained faithful to A. E.

Housman's *A Shropshire Lad*, that fantasy of green and pleasant lands, despite having read many other collections of poetry. "Faithful" was the word he used. He kept a copy of the book in every room of his house, in every bag he carried, in the pocket of every coat. He lived in fear of losing the book. Each night before sleep, he would read a poem from the collection, and he would be convinced that all was well. Being with Michael had felt a little like that, the longing to possess entangled with the fear of loss. But even after two years together, it became evident that I had never owned any part of him, that the frantic attempt to insert myself into his life had ended with my complete erasure from it anyway.

In the weeks I spent with Julian in London, I gathered facts about him the way collectors amass artifacts in a cabinet of curiosities, hoping that through the collecting, I could possess him in a way that I never could Michael. I recorded notes on my phone throughout the day, which I have since deleted: the part of his hair that was a lighter shade; a passing reference he made to a movie; his love of skiing. I also documented the incidences of fleeting touch. His arm occasionally brushed mine as we walked down the streets, or when we sat shoulder to shoulder on park benches. One time, when we were moving items into his living room, we touched briefly, his hands held over mine as he took a box from me.

In retrospect, in spite of all the time I spent with Julian that year, in spite of the quotidian details I accumulated, I was ignorant of who he really was. At times I looked at him and thought of Turner's *Interior of a Great House: The Drawing Room, East Cowes Castle*. There are indistinct objects strewn in the foreground of the painting, and in the back, a shadowy figure in the doorway, whose features cannot be discerned. Far from deterring me, that mysteriousness spurred me on. If someone had asked me why I was compelled to get closer to Julian, I would not have been able to say. Something about his voice at night, the shape of his hands, and the line of his neck.

November 27
Have not seen Alex for a few days. He goes out during most of the day, and in the evening, he eats after everyone else has vacated the kitchen. He takes his food back to his tent, where he eats without much noise, the sound of his plastic cutlery dulled against the paper plates. I wonder how I, too, might achieve such stillness, such silence, free from the clamor of memories.

November 27—late night
Feel as if I did not sleep at all, despite the hours that have elapsed. Vivid, half-remembered dreams mean I did sleep, yet I have been running through fields, chasing unknown monsters or being chased, scurrying along with a thousand weak legs that keep collapsing under me. I woke up to the shattering realization that he is coming back to Mornington. Of course, I have known this fact for some time, but the reality of it has not struck me until now.

I read this somewhere—but I have forgotten the source or the author—and the image has stayed with me: a creature is tied around the neck with a rope, then dragged by an invisible force through the ceilings and floors of a house, the limp body yanked and banged against walls and furniture, bloodied and broken. That sums up how I feel.

November 29
Snow blanketing the land, blocking entrances and burying footpaths. We collect snow in buckets and add the water to the reservoir.

Could not write all of yesterday and today. The deeper I fall into the past, the more I seem to feel insects crawling across me. I keep reminding myself of Simone Weil's words, on the problem of attention, on where one directs it, and how one attends to what is important. The first encounter with her writing, in the early days of our non-profit project, was akin to finding a light in a dark forest, guiding me away from the self and toward other. Her words forced their way into the innermost part of me. But now it's as though I never read anything at all.

Nineteen weeks until he returns.

BOOK

Eden Warwick (*nom de plume* of George Jabet), *The Poets' Pleasaunce, or, garden of all sorts of pleasant flowers*. Published by Longman & Co, London, 1847. First edition. Octavo. Maroon, gilt-stamped morocco; beveled covers. Illustrations by Noel Humphreys. Fore-edge painting—of an erotic scene in the middle of a grove—partially obscured due to water damage. Heavy foxing throughout.

NOVEMBER 30

I once read somewhere that being desired is the closest a mortal can feel to being immortal. Desire is an amorphous thing. Michael's desire felt insubstantial, and sex was something he slotted into his busy schedule like a task to be ticked off the list. With him, and later with Julian, desire was inextricably connected with possession—the desire to possess and the desire to be taken. But with Aidan, desire meant being offered shelter from the outside world in which the body is vulnerable. The intimacy that I shared with Aidan, which began in fits and starts, fraught with my recollection of pain, gradually developed into a space in which we could both recuperate at the end of a day. But it is astonishing how long it has taken me to find this harbor.

My first real glimpse of human desire was on one of the botanical trips I took with Dad, when I was around fourteen. We traveled to Cambridge to visit the Botanic Garden of the university. In the late afternoon, Dad went out for drinks with friends and instructed me to stay in the hotel. But as soon as he left the room, I disobeyed and snuck out to wander around the town. I ended up in the Fellows' Garden of Clare College, which had an inner garden with a pond of floating lilies, accessible by two small openings in the tall hedges that surrounded it.

I lay down on the riverbank. Students were relaxing on the opposite bank; punts glided by on the water. It was early evening in spring, and the garden was empty. Above, the first stars were becoming visible.

When I heard the clinking of the chains that barricaded the opening of the garden, I turned to see two people, probably undergraduates, jumping over the chain, laughing as they ran into the inner garden. Curious, I followed them. From the opening in the hedge, I peeked in and saw them sitting on a bench by the pond. They were just kissing at first, their bodies twisting toward one another. Then they looked around and, seeing no one else in the garden, they rolled onto the grass and held each other more tightly, one pressing down on the other, their bodies undulating to a shared rhythm. The sounds they made were scarcely audible.

My second image of desire was one of Turner's erotic drawings, which scholars speculate might not even be his work. In the sepia-colored drawing, a satyr-like male figure kneels next to a woman or nymph, who grips his shoulder and head in the throes of passion. His hand appears to be inserted into her. Their faces are not shown. On the same page is a smaller sketch showing disembodied limbs that converge at the point of penetration. I wondered if the drawings were rooted in memory or fantasy.

There were many images that I later encountered in the works of Turner and other artists. Some were similar to academic studies of nudes. Others were rough, almost abstract, with one body part made indistinguishable from the next, evoking the dynamism of figures in movement. There were nudes entangled in wrinkled bedsheets; soft flesh draped over flesh; perspiring bodies in repose after the moments of ecstasy; women's legs opened wide and suspended in the air, in anticipation. Those depictions neither titillated nor repulsed me. In a few drawings, the female pudendum was represented by a swath of red. In others, female and male genitalia were disembodied, floating in the middle of the page. Then there was the sex portrayed by Francis Bacon, the bodies contorted into one mass of flesh, melting into pools of red that put me in mind of what hangs in butchers' windows.

During those days in London with Julian, the image to which my mind returned was that of the nymph held and penetrated by the satyr.

A man and a woman. A dimly lit bedroom. Three pictures on the walls, and a mirror over the fireplace. A single bed, where the woman sleeps. This is the setting of Edgar Degas's 1868–9 painting, one of the most important representations of an interior in the late nineteenth century. The viewer is invited to step into the bedroom, and immediately, there is a sense of unease. What is the relationship between the man and the woman? What explains this moment of stasis and tension between the two figures? Is it the scene of a lover's quarrel, inspired by a Zola novel? Or perhaps a confrontation between a prostitute and a client? Degas did not name the piece, but should it have been given the neutral title Intérieur? *Or should it be called* Le Viol *("The Rape")?*

In the lesser-known The Misfortunes of the City of Orléans *(1865), Degas painted an unequivocal scene of violence and femicide: three men in medieval costume, on horseback; a naked woman trampled under the hooves of a horse; another victim carried off by a rider. In one corner of the painting, a pile of naked female corpses. In the background, four more women are attempting to flee while a horseman raises a bow and arrow to shoot in their direction. This painting has been interpreted as an episode in the Hundred Years' War.*

Intérieur, *or* Le Viol, *does not offer such unambiguous signs of aggression. The woman in the picture turns away from the man, her body bent over, seemingly in pain. Her white garment is slipping off her shoulders; her corset and other items of clothing have been thrown on the floor. Behind her, a trail of blood is discernible on the white bedspread. Three areas are highlighted in a painting that is otherwise full of heavy shadows: the woman's half-undone dress, the white floral-patterned lampshade, and, on the table in the middle of the room, the sewing box, an object associated with the domestic, opened and exposed. The man stands against the door, his hands in his pockets, and his eyes fixed on the woman. His body casts a large shadow on the wall behind him, creating the illusion of a* doppelgänger, *a shadowy, predatory self. His entire figure is painted with dark tones, except for the area directly below his waist, which is illumined by the lamp.*

This is one reading of the scene: the man has invaded this cozy domestic space, violated the woman, and in the aftermath, as she attempts to recover from the pain and humiliation, he stays to contemplate the act, perhaps in a moment of conquest or pleasure. He has become the spectator of his own work.

FIVE

DECEMBER

DECEMBER 1

In 1807, Turner purchased a small parcel of land at Twickenham, where he built a villa-like structure to his own designs. The process spanned three to four years, and the ideas—in the form of topographical drawings—were distributed across eight notebooks. The painter designed in fits and starts, jotting down ideas in a disorderly fashion. In the sketchbooks, one page might show a drawing that diverges from those on the preceding pages. Eventually, the multitudinous ideas came together in the final scheme of the villa—a simple two-story house flanked by wings on either side.

Today, as I flipped through the facsimiles of Turner's sketches for Sandycombe Lodge, I felt my life resembled his designs, scattered and confused. If only things would come together into a cohesive whole as they did for him.

DECEMBER 2

I have been dropping by the entrance to the Hall almost every day to check on Alex; and every day, that same silence. In contrast, the Hall was filled with the noise of chatter and music when the group of young people stayed there. Alex's silence haunts me. How does he achieve such stillness? Is he not plagued by thoughts and memories as he sits still? Does he not feel the temptation of any form of entertainment?

I confessed to Aidan about my repeated visits to Alex. He said that I should not be nosy. Everyone has their own way of dwelling in time, he said, of dealing with whatever they are going through. He was perplexed by what he called my obsession with Alex. I told him it's simply curiosity. I've also asked Celia and Miranda what they think of Alex, but since they encounter him infrequently, they have not been able to form an opinion.

Perhaps Aidan is right. Perhaps there is nothing at all suspicious about Alex's stillness and silence. Perhaps this is how he copes with all that he has lost. It certainly seems more effective than my method of dealing with the past, which has led to constant tossing and turning in bed and aimless drifting of thoughts, followed by a few brief hours of shallow sleep. I must refrain from going to the Hall again, at least for a few days.

DECEMBER 3

Migraine upon waking. Incapable of sustained focus on anything important. Still seeing termites behind closed eyes, despite knowing that they have been eradicated. Decided to take out the postcard reproduction of *A View on the Seine*, and recalled the discussion I had with Julian, on the train journey back to Mornington, after our week of collecting items in the city. Our conversation touched on the painting, and I asked him why he had purchased it.

I saw it at an auction, he said, and it just struck me. That contrast of light and dark, the lighthouse and the church in the middle. I also liked how there's very little commentary on it.

No, I said, not even Ruskin wrote much about it.

Julian pulled up an image of the painting on his tablet, and said that the scarcity of commentary made the painting a little mysterious and all the more desirable.

I went on to say something about Turner; I have forgotten the details. I was looking at *A View on the Seine*, and not at Julian, when he leaned in and kissed me, his face temporarily blocking my view.

I remember that as he moved away after the kiss, I glanced outside the window and noticed how the speed of the moving train softened the outlines of the houses and hedges, so that every image dissolved as soon as it came into focus.

PICTURE POSTCARDS
Series of ten *Gruss aus* ("Greetings from") cards, late 1890s, depicting Munich, Berlin, and Leipzig. Undivided backs; short messages on recto. Edges worn; colors faded. Unlike other touristic postcards that presented panoramic views, the *Gruss aus* cards portrayed the city as a collection of three or four iconic sites. Frequently, buildings from different eras and locations were illustrated alongside one another; the cards therefore elided the difference between past and present.

DECEMBER 5
Today I brought Celia a postcard from the archives. It shows a woman in an Edwardian outfit, standing in front of an easel, in the middle of the grottoes at Vals-les-Bains. In one hand, she is holding a paintbrush; in the other, a cup, presumably filled with the healing spring water from the caves. That commingling of art and nature reminded me of Celia.

But the woman on the postcard is also me, her figure framed by the massive rocks that seem to bear down on her. I have been exhausted as of late, and I no longer have the strength to fight the gravitational pull of memory. My constant return to the past, to those days with Julian, borders on madness, a kind of frenzied grasping after slippery things that concern no one except myself. I feel as if I might die of the past.

As I sat for Celia this morning, I thought about that kiss on the train and its aftermath. When Julian and I returned to Mornington, I immediately began rewriting the essay on Turner. I worked for hours without stopping. The old doubts about language fell away and something unfamiliar emerged. It was the antithesis of the academic discourse to which I was accustomed, and utterly unlike a conventional catalogue essay. It was strange and amorphous, a conglomeration of all that I had seen and felt. *A View on the Seine* was there, and the desire of touch, and the image distorted by the speed of the train. To this day, I have not been able to write anything else that approaches that effect.

In the week that followed, as the essay was being finalized, the house also reached the halfway point of its renovations, with refurbished rooms and a redesigned glasshouse. Paintings came back from restorers; the collection in the Library grew.

But my fellowship was coming to an end, and with another rejection letter for an academic post, I faced a new period of indeterminate waiting. It was then, a week after our return from London, that Julian offered me the position of librarian and archivist, despite the fact that I had no formal qualifications and would have to complete a degree remotely, alongside my work at Mornington.

I just want someone to keep adding to the collection, he said, though he did not specify what he would like me to add. Someone who has an eye for intriguing pieces, as I know you do.

On the day I signed the contract, Julian kissed me for the second time.

After the session ended, Celia and I sat down with tea and biscuits. We talked about Berthe Morisot and Paula Modersohn-Becker, two of Celia's favorite artists, and about Francesca Woodman's self-portraits in which the blurred female form fades into walls and floors. The conversation was a welcome break.

Tomorrow, Celia will be leaving to spend a few weeks with her son in London. She's planning to return after the holidays, and we will resume the sessions in January. I'll miss her company.

December 5—evening

In spite of the cold, I have come to the abandoned room in the southeast pavilion, for the quiet and the solitude. I have set up a desk with a lamp and heater. Snow drifts in through the hole in the roof.

I am torn between the past and the work I want to do here in the present, with the archive, the house, and the world outside. The nearest I have come to Celia's sense of being divided between her son and her art is the conflict between my obligation to others and this sinking into memories. The John Berger book I brought with me today, with its lessons on ethics, puts me to shame. But I nevertheless force myself to skim some passages, if only to remind myself of what is at stake. It is as though I were very small, surrounded on all sides by towering things that might squash me at any moment, yet I have no choice but to scuttle along, keeping to the walls, evading death. Tomorrow I will return to the archive and continue my work.

December 6

Self-discipline means:

Not being distracted.

Not upsetting balance.

Not dwelling.

Not giving in.

BOOK

The Microcosm of London. 1904 facsimile of the original 1808 edition published for Ackermann's *Repository of Arts.* A pictorial survey of Regency London, with illustrations by Pugin and Rowlandson. Three volumes quarto. Diced camel calf binding, scuffed. Marbled endpaper, water-stained. 104 hand-colored plates—though four plates have been cut from first volume. Severe foxing in all volumes.

DECEMBER 7

This morning, I was shocked to find Alex waiting for me outside the Library door. I froze when I saw him, and my face must have expressed fear, which I hope he did not notice. His voice was surprisingly gentle. He asked if he could borrow books, not antiquarian volumes but regular paperbacks for reading. So he does need some entertainment after all. He seemed, not exactly agitated, just impatient, in a great hurry, though I can't imagine what he has to get back to, except his sitting-still in the tent. I led him to the shelf where I keep the books from my personal collection. He picked up a book without reading the back cover, and said it would do. He placed the book in his pocket and set off for the garden. I did not have a chance to start a conversation. I wanted to ask him why he chose *Austerlitz* and whether he knew anything about the author. But really, I would have liked to ask him why he sits in the tent in silence and stillness.

DECEMBER 8

The family who has been staying with us is moving on. They have obtained their permit and will relocate to Dublin, where the father will continue his work as a chef. We will have a small farewell dinner tonight. There will be eight travelers left, who will stay with us through the winter, and possibly until the demolition, at which point, they, like us, will leave Mornington.

DECEMBER 9

Incapable of concentrating. My resolve to avoid distractions has remained a passing resolve. The progress on the archive has slowed. I feel the strange urge to check on Alex again, to see if he is still sitting there, if he is in fact reading the book. Why have I developed this obsession with him? Why am I incapable of imagining an inner life for Alex that is free of suspicious thoughts and dark fantasies? I really cannot say.

Aidan has been making progress on our mobile home, which now sits in the stables so that it can be protected from the snow. He has hired Carlos and a few local contractors to help with the carpentry. The outer shell is almost complete. The house is a minimalist gem, an asymmetrical box with large windows and sliding doors. From afar, it resembles a boulder. The corrugated fiberglass and steel façade is decorated with slats of plywood that have been weatherproofed with pine tar. Because of Aidan, I have developed a real appreciation for this kind of architecture. It is the antithesis of Mornington.

DECEMBER 10

Took extra sleeping pills last night in order to wake up early for the supply run in the city. The market was busy this morning, filled with stalls that hold their own archive of mostly defunct detritus of the past. The merchants all seem to know each other with a unique kind of intimacy communicated in nods and winks. But to us visitors they seldom say anything. Clive the bookseller is the only merchant we know by name. I drop by his stall whenever we pass through the market, and although we are not in the position to buy any books, it is satisfying to look at them sealed inside the plastic bags that Clive dusts every morning. Books still deserve respect, he said once, even in this hopeless world.

Today, Clive gave me permission to take some of the books out of their plastic coverings. When I smelled the distinctive scent of old books, I was reminded of how Julian had joked about founding a scent library. Imagine—he said to me one day in a bookshop—if, at the press of a button, you could enjoy a whiff of cedar, or this old train ticket—he held up a piece of ephemera he had discovered in a volume of Kafka's diary. Imagine, he continued, such an archive.

The sound of Clive typing on the typewriter pulled me out of that remembered scene. I sealed the books back in their bags and wondered where he was able to find ink ribbons. As I leaned over to place the book back on the shelf, I glanced at his typewriter and realized that there was no ink ribbon, only the keys hitting the blank page.

On our way out of the market, we passed by the co-op housing where many of the merchants live. Some of the people in the co-ops are long-term residents; others are visitors. There are also those who travel constantly, though it's never clear where it is they go with all their belongings strapped to their backs. Many have lost their employment, and now wander aimlessly in places that they would have hurried past on their way to the jobs that had regulated their days.

These prefab buildings are far better than the semi-permanent structures in the peripheral regions of the city, which are usually unfinished construction sites that will be cleared away at some indeterminate date. Worse still are the tent villages, built of found materials or parts of demolished structures.

Julian and I saw a series of photographs at a small gallery, on another one of our collecting trips, after I had accepted the position as librarian and archivist. The photos showed the early tent villages. All that were visible in the frames were the clothes, toys, blankets, books, pots and pans, and other miscellany that defined home for those who stayed in the temporary spaces. But even without the presence of people, the photos, for me, were charged with pathos.

While I had hoped to discuss ideas about absence and the meaning of home with Julian, he glanced at the photos and said, I don't get it. What am I supposed to be looking at?

His comment should have struck me as a warning, but at the time, I chose to focus on the photos instead. I wondered what these objects would say if they were able to speak. Would they describe the struggles they witnessed? The bonds that developed against the chorus of calamitous change? Would they describe how one day, the owners did not return, abandoning the things that they had handled with such care through their daily rituals?

DECEMBER 12

Heavy snow overnight. Aidan said there might not be any point in protecting the house, since it will be torn down in a few months anyway. But we cannot resist. We spent the morning shoveling snow and building barricades, strengthening windows, and bringing fresh logs inside. I also checked on the plants living in the Library wall. The flowers withered when the cold first set in, but there is still the possibility of new blossoms in the spring.

In the afternoon, I joined Miranda for another sewing session. The quilt is coming together beautifully. We listened to jazz, which Miranda is fond of. A calm end to the day.

DECEMBER 13

Have been sleeping better due to the pills. Earlier this evening, as I was leaving the Library, I saw that Alex has returned the copy of *Austerlitz*. The book has become creased, which irks me. Perhaps I should not have lent it to him. In any case, it is too late, as he has left a note—written in nearly indecipherable handwriting—next to *Austerlitz*, indicating that he has borrowed *To the Lighthouse* and Woolf's diaries. I worry that these will be returned in a similar condition. I feel a bit foolish about my concern for cheap paperbacks. But it isn't so much the monetary value of the books that lend them meaning. These exact copies were the ones I read at specific points in life, and those were the passages I underlined. To replace the books would mean the loss of a singular record.

But I cannot help picturing Alex with the books in his tent, and suddenly they seem to belong to him, covered with his scent and fingerprints. The image makes me feel sick. For the first time, I'm not sure I want the books back anymore.

DECEMBER 15

I helped Miranda with her quilt again today. I noticed her sewing box, with orange fabric on the outside and a cream lining on the inside. I was reminded of Degas's *Le Viol*, with the open sewing box at its center. I have not thought of that painting for a long time, not since I wrote about it all those years ago, in a frenzy of aloneness and rage.

The first time I set eyes on it, in a special exhibition at the National Gallery, a sensation of dread overwhelmed me. Nothing had as yet happened to me in the real world outside the painting, but when I looked at it, I felt an invisible mass weighing down on my chest. If the room were emptied of the figures depicted, if it were just the space with its floral wallpaper and the small bed pushed up against the wall, I could picture myself living there.

But the presence of the man and his shadow changes everything. The woman cowers in the corner, berating herself for having trusted such a man and inviting him in, perhaps for having loved him. As she turns away from him, she recalls their initial encounter at a dance. She remembers his dazzling eyes and the warmth of his hand on her waist. She sobs and makes no attempt to hide her tears. Perhaps the man has tried to comfort her. Perhaps he is saying, *It will be okay. I will take care of you. I will be responsible for what has happened.* She feels slightly consoled, but when she turns to face him, she is horrified by the look in his eyes, the eyes that say *You have once again been deceived.*

At least this was how I read the Degas at the time.

Miranda tapped my hand lightly as I made a few errors with the stitching. You need to focus, she said.

PICTURE POSTCARD
Single postcard, part of a series depicting the Paris flood of 1910, the "crue de la Seine." Postmarked March 29, 1912. Recto—Rue de Lyon transformed into a canal lined with Haussmannized buildings; small boats glide down the street. In the foreground, a man carries a woman on his back across a makeshift boardwalk. In fair condition.

DECEMBER 17
Last night, a vivid dream. I was in Julian's arms, naked under the covers. He appeared younger, happier, sharing with me a story about his mother. He looked at me with his bright green eyes. Then I was running down a grassy path in the rain, a path parallel to a fog-veiled marshland, desperate to get back to Julian. I awoke, drenched in sweat, with globular shapes still visible in my field of vision.

I cannot remember the last time I dreamt of him. In the first few years after he left, the dreams were collages of actual places we'd visited in the city or moments we had shared. As time passed, the dreams took on an uncanny quality, increasingly untethered from reality as we had experienced it together. His image pursued me into my unconscious, replicating itself a thousandfold so that my sleep was nothing but a vast sea of his face and his body spinning around me, leaving nausea and vertigo in its wake. Those dreams populated my nights for years until Julian faded into the background of my life. How shocking that a few months with someone could create so many strata of subconscious terrain.

I did consider telling Aidan about the dream, but decided not to.

DECEMBER 19

Time has been slipping through me, like water through a sieve. Entire decades seem to be swallowed up by an afternoon, a year fitting neatly into a single hour. I float in a haze, one minute standing before my work and the next minute walking down the streets with Julian. The images and objects before me, in the present, flit by unnoticed, like clouds.

I have given up on the archive for the day, and have come to the southeast pavilion in spite of the cold. This morning I had the sudden realization that perhaps Alex reminds me of Julian. Is that really the case? Maybe. Though they do not at all resemble each other in appearance or behavior.

Earlier today, I once again saw Alex sitting in the tent, utterly motionless. Later I found him sauntering around the perimeter of the Hall with a book in his hands, like a prisoner walking in the prison yard. Despite the fact that he was moving, I was struck by the feeling that he has remained in that state of motionlessness, enfolded in his thoughts or absence of thoughts. Like an immovable monolith, Alex puts me in mind of an uninhabited building with many voids. I have seen that building before, in Julian. But this time, I am not drawn into its depths. The repetitiveness of

Alex's walk, the endless circles he traced around the Hall, spoke of the same impenetrable mind. It's hard to picture the impact these books might have had on him. They are mere props; to what, I cannot imagine.

As I crept away from the Hall I felt the vessels in my temples swell up and my face became inflamed. I was desperate to get away, and had no idea why I was there in the first place.

DECEMBER 21

Fell asleep just past midnight; awoke in the middle of the night. Tossed in bed until sleep finally came, close to dawn. Then the short bout of rest brought a legion of termites like vengeful furies, scuttling over rotten wood and descending upon me with rage, to the accompaniment of cymbals and drums like a symphony from hell. That swarm was death itself. They drilled and scratched and bit. I could not move, pinned to the bed in a cage or a room that had locked doors on all sides and no view of the outside world. I awoke at the second when the swarm of termites began to surge like hot liquid under my skin. Felt sick and tremulous all day. Did very little work. Must force myself to go back into the Library first thing tomorrow morning.

SCRAPBOOK

Black, leather-bound scrapbook, belonging to a Helen Hardwick, of Greenwich. Pages contain personal documents, pasted in, dating from 1937 to 1963. Collection includes wedding invitations, congratulation cards, list of presents received, and newspaper clippings. Most pages water damaged; some torn. Blank section in the middle, followed by section containing a list of baby shower presents, and cards congratulating the recipient on the birth of a baby girl, Dottie, in 1938. Notebook ends with a newspaper article announcing the death of Dorothy Hardwick, aged twenty-five, in a motor vehicle collision.

DECEMBER 22

The sun is out but does not produce any warmth. I have been entirely dependent on sleeping pills in order to keep the nightmares of termites at bay. Have not been able to do much in the Library.

Yesterday, Aidan and I made another trip back to the city for the anniversary of Dad's death, which we do every year. To reach the memorial, we had to enter the urban core and the exclusive neighborhoods. Those whom disaster has not touched live in this core, a city parallel to the city of the outer rings. They build high-rises to retreat from the water, and plant rooftop gardens in glass cubes, like the hanging gardens of Babylon. We hear of cavernous subterranean havens where pools are lined with precious gems and filled with carp. There are also rumors of climate-controlled underground gardens with lush flora, cascading waterfalls, and rolling hills.

Aidan and I arrived in the city center shortly after midday. Cars without residents' permits cannot access the zone, so we parked the car and continued on foot. We passed through the checkpoint, guarded by an armed sentry, a young man who glanced at our IDs and resumed his state of boredom.

Inside the fenced-off core of the city, under the massive geodesic dome, the air—generated by machines—was the air of an earlier time. Children were playing in parks, adults sat outside cafés or ran errands in air-conditioned shops. From the checkpoint, we walked to the boundary of the submerged zone, near the river. Somewhere in that expanse of drowned streets and deserted houses sits my childhood home. A steel fence barred pedestrians from venturing into the zone, which was still in danger of flash floods as recently as four years ago, before the drought began.

In a small square, right in front of the barrier, sits the memorial to those who perished in the first floods. Aidan's studio designed the monument, one of the few public projects he has worked on.

Aidan and I had many late-night chats during the design process, and studied pictures of memorials around the world. Such monuments are supposed to perpetuate the memory of an event, Aidan explained, but stone is mutable. He spoke of the vertical drop into the darkness that he saw in New York City; the voids and concrete tower in Berlin; and the barred window at the tip of the Île de la Cité in Paris. Aidan learned through these memorials that one way to speak of disaster is through indirection.

The building he eventually designed had a cavernous underground space into which the visitor descended. A glass ceiling covered the dimly lit space, and water poured down on the transparent surface, so that when the visitor looks up, she might imagine the sensation of being engulfed by the waves. Nothing aside from light, shadows, and water exists in the concrete monument.

One afternoon fourteen years ago, I received the news of Dad's death over the phone while I was in the garden at Mornington. A neighbor witnessed him falling into the water from a heart attack; his body washed down the flooded street. I shed no tears. There was a sudden blinding light, followed by darkness. I woke up on the grass, my clothes and cheeks dampened by the wet soil. At least an hour must have passed, for the clouds had moved on and the shadows on the grass had lengthened.

In the immediate aftermath of loss, the outside world seemed far away. Existence was bearable only in a confined enclosure.

I stayed in the bedroom for weeks, and Aidan brought tea that turned cold and books that he returned to the shelves, unread.

Grief had a distinctive sound. An unrelenting noise, like the sound of machines drilling into concrete. At night, I could not sleep. Once, I woke up in a sweat in the night. Aidan was away for work. I got up and bumped into furniture in the dark, and went to stand by the window. The moon was an eerie crescent, the gardens patches of silvery gray, gently touched by the night wind. I should have been able to hear the movement of the branches, a sound that always comforted me. But instead, there was only the sound of the drilling in my head.

I did not want to picture Dad's death, but my imagination could not help but conjure the image of him choking on the muddy water of the overflowing river. He died by water—beside which he had grown up, on the western shores, where the waves crashed daily against the cliffs and daily carried out into its depths the detritus left on the shores. Dad once told me that he missed the salty smell of the sea and the residual grains of sand that were stuck under the nails and remained on his bed for days following a visit to the beach.

After the funeral, and after the flood water retreated, I returned to our drowned house. The electricity had stopped working, so I went into the dark building with a flashlight. And with the same rainboots I'd worn when last I visited the gardens with Dad, I stepped into our home.

I found, in the trail of the receded water, fox pawprints in the mud. Slugs and other riverbed insects clung to the walls and furnishings. The objects that survived intact were the metallic and plastic things. All other materials—wood, fabric, paper—were swollen with brown river water. All the plants had died. Dad's botanical prints and pressed leaves were beyond salvage, much like everything else in my lower-ground-floor studio, which remained submerged in water that reached my thighs.

I noticed, on the wall of my old room, a marbled pattern of deep-green mold that had begun to spread, fanning out like a map of rivers and tributaries, and I thought of all the places to which Dad and I would never travel together. I pressed the wall and my finger left a permanent indentation.

On the upper level of the house, some of Dad's belongings were still intact. His room smelled of the river. The floorboards creaked and the door was too swollen to close properly. I went through everything and collected some items in my rucksack: clothes covered in mildew; photo albums with pages that stuck to one another; a glasses case, a water bottle, and old CD cases, all caked in mud.

There was a wooden bench along one side of Dad's study, and two leather armchairs by the window, next to a desk that he cleared at the end of each day. Above the window frame, I had hung plastic toys on strings—a menagerie of zoo animals—so that he would have something to look at outside the window on dreary days when the view was disappointing. I placed these toys into the rucksack.

On a bookshelf, I saw the pebble with grey-and-white streaks, one of Dad's most treasured objects, a souvenir from the last trip that he took with my mother, before she left us for what he imagined to be a carefree life of music concerts and cocktail parties on the French Riviera, where she had always wanted to live. In his mind, she had remained in France and never returned home, for shortly after that trip to Nice, she packed another bag and disappeared without a word or a note, leaving behind an infant in a crib and a man who grew wary of travel, fearful that each trip meant the end of something important. When I visited southern France in my twenties, I kept an eye out for an older woman who resembled me, but all I found was a pebble much like the one Dad had. Both his pebble and mine survived the flood, and those I also placed into the bag.

After I'd collected everything I could rescue, I laid them out on the bed that had sunk under the weight of the absorbed water, and I photographed them. Then I lay down on the soggy wooden floorboards next to the bed, and cried for the first time since hearing the news of his death.

These annual visits to the memorial are as affecting for Aidan as they are for me. When we stand in that concrete space with the water pouring over the glass roof above us, I know he is mourning his mother as much as I'm mourning Dad, though she died under very different circumstances.

Julian's experience of loss, I recall, had been the opposite of mine. In a gallery, on one of our collecting trips, Julian considered purchasing a series of photographs by a Japanese photographer, taken with the camera half-submerged in water, resembling the perspective of one who is drowning.

She drowned herself, you know, my mum, Julian said when we stood in front of the photos.

I had no idea, I said. I'm so sorry.

So dramatic. Literary, even. Aidan was devastated. He dyed his hair soon afterward. Our mum was blond. It was like he wanted to carry on some part of her. He seemed less upset when our Dad died, but then Dad was never around much anyways.

Do you ever miss them? I asked Julian.

No. Why would I?

I paused. Because... isn't that what people do, we mourn and miss those whom we have lost?

Julian tilted his head to one side, and said, But that presumes their irreplaceability. If I lost everyone I loved, I'd just find new people. There's no reason to get upset about such things.

As he spoke, he waved to the gallery attendant and gestured to one of the photos on the walls, to start the transaction process.

In that moment, my vision suddenly weakened and I could no longer be sure of the person I saw in front of me. But I must have buried the shock I felt in response to what he'd said, and, in my foolishness, I must have hoped that I would be indispensable to him, that the loss of the fictive bond we were to develop would be the loss he could not survive.

Remembering all this now, I am astounded by my own choices, by the absurdity of my younger self, with its desires and obsessions mired in reasons that have been eroded by time, leaving the consequences, like scintillating shards of glass.

DECEMBER 25

Christmas Day. No snow, only the slippery, glistening ice. Woke up with a severe headache, after a difficult night's sleep filled with disquiet. The waning effectiveness of the sleeping pills led to upsetting dreams of which I could recall no more than splintered images. Nevertheless, had to get up and prepare everything.

We decorated the Long Gallery. Then we played card games in the afternoon. For dinner, Miranda and Aidan made a sculptural Christmas log using the chocolate ration that they've been saving up since October. I managed to convince everyone to have the vegan roast with us, instead of getting meat from the village. After dinner, we listened to music. I even drank a little. For at least one day, we lived as if nothing much had changed in the world, as if grief were not a constant.

Alex did not join us for any of the activities. I was glad not to have seen him for the entire day.

DECEMBER 29

On the news today: more people have drowned in the sea. We have canceled our plans for the New Year's Eve group dinner; it does not seem appropriate to be celebrating. Sometimes, after reading the news, my instinct is to cover my eyes and ears and shut myself from the world, because the stories demand too much of me. What is the adequate response to the affliction and death of so many living beings?

When I was a teenager, I read an article about a woman who had drowned herself in the Thames. For love, the reporter speculated. Dad reminded me again and again that nothing, no man, is ever worth dismantling my life for. He made me nod to signal I had understood. I nodded, though I had only a vague idea of what it meant to love and to die for love. The news never showed the corpse, just the outline of a body covered with a tarp. But even at that time, I knew that drowned bodies become pale and swollen. The sea or river seeps into the porous skin. The face is no longer recognizable, as though the water has erased identity, turning the flesh into a fluid mass.

You have been invited to visit an apartment. You arrive to find the door ajar. When you enter, you are confronted with a shocking tableau. A woman—the artist who sent you the invitation—is stripped from the waist down, bent over a table, and her hands are bound with rope. Her buttocks and legs are smeared with blood, and a pair of blood-stained underwear has fallen around her ankles. The room is gloomy and decrepit. On the floor are broken pieces of ceramic and a pool of blood. You—and the others who have been invited to witness this recreation of the rape and murder of a fellow student at the University of Iowa—are forced to look, to confront the reality of the female body stripped bare and brutalized. You walk away feeling that you were not merely a spectator, but a voyeur.

With this 1973 performance piece—documented in a photograph, Untitled (Rape Scene)—*the Cuban American artist Ana Mendieta contributed to the feminist art movement that arose in the late 1960s. Feminist performance artists (such as Suzanne Lacy and Yoko Ono) began to challenge the so-called heroic rape tradition in Western art, in which paintings and sculptures aestheticize sexual violence. Projects such as Lacy's influential* Ablutions *(begun in 1971), with its narratives of suffering and its use of blood and viscera, wrote over the eroticized, compliant bodies in the works of the Old Masters. Feminist art historians, also, began to question the celebratory and eroticized representations of rape which, in spite of their mythological or historical origin, seemed to glorify the act.*

In Rape Performance, *Mendieta was photographed sprawled out in a grassy area, naked from the waist down, with streaks of blood between her legs, her genitals exposed, and her body bent over a log, thus obscuring the face and upper torso. The image brings to mind a 1907 etching by Käthe Kollwitz, entitled* Vergewaltigt *("Raped"), part of the Peasants' War series, which depicted the cruelty of the German aristocrats in the sixteenth century. In Kollwitz's etching, the ravaged body blends into the fallen leaves and undergrowth. The partially covered torso is twisted, the hands bound behind the back or cut off. The woman's skirt is pulled up and spread across her body. Her head is tilted backward and, as in Mendieta's photo, her face is not visible.*

"My art," Mendieta once remarked, "comes out of rage and displacement... I think all art comes out of sublimated rage."

Six

Milan is as hot as Rome. The footsteps of the pedestrians have created a pall of dust that envelops the city center, trapped inside yet another gigantic dome. After depositing his luggage in a locker, Julian hails a taxi outside the train station and asks to be taken to the Duomo. He considers sightseeing a distasteful activity, but he does not want to meet his brother again without having seen the cathedral, one of the few monuments that remain largely intact.

Julian walks into the Duomo and a rush of cool air washes over him. There is a small group of students standing before the altar and a few people sitting in the pews. He finds a seat near the apse and rests his eyes briefly, before resuming his tour of the cathedral while listening to the Mahler symphony again on his headphones. Parts of the first movement strike him as discordant. Yet somehow the mess of interlocking notes works. It seems to him that the Gothic vaults and imposing columns of the cathedral share this quality of dissonance. He remembers vaguely something that Aidan once told him, that architecture could be likened to music; that music is, in turn, liquid architecture. And if music is a temporal art—the division and expansion of notes in time—that meant architecture, as petrified music, is frozen time.

That is an idea worth noting down, Julian thinks to himself. He takes out his notebook and pen, and places the traveling inkwell on the bench, from which he fills the pen and blots it using a cloth that is stained with ink. He writes a note about frozen music. The practice of keeping a notebook is one that he has planned to start for some time, and he is pleased with this opening fragment.

After the walk through the cathedral, Julian finds a restaurant inside the nearby Galleria. As he is settling into his seat, he sees a woman in a floral silk dress walking by outside. She catches his gaze through the window and smiles. Without warning, the memory of an unknown woman's body emerges, and a pang of desire passes through him. He has always had an eye for beauty. And because of his looks, he has been almost guaranteed to have anyone he desired. He cannot imagine living life without such a guarantee.

A few guests enter the restaurant for early dinner. Julian orders coffee and takes out his writing instruments and his copy of Kafka. Two elderly Italian women dine at the next table. He takes note of their jewelry—a pearl necklace, two silver bracelets, a brooch in the shape of a bird—and faded silk scarves. He cannot make out the content of their conversation, though he wonders whether they are from another part of Italy, for their accents sound different from the Italian he has heard in Milan. Julian writes down these observations in his notebook.

The cathedral is now lit. As evening approaches, the vagrants appear in greater numbers in the piazza outside. Julian assumed that the city center had been cleansed, like many other cities, but perhaps the authorities here have merely imposed a time limit for access to the heart of the city. An old beggar with a ragged hat, torn jacket, and a grocery bag filled with miscellany makes brief eye contact with him through the glass window. Julian shudders, pretending he could smell the sweat and urine through the glass.

He repositions his chair so that he faces the inside of the café. He orders some bread. A well-dressed middle-aged couple nod to him and the others as they sit down at the next table. Cafés and restaurants are never as crowded as they used to be, and the few who can still afford the luxury consider themselves members of the same clan. There are always silent nods or smiles, acknowledgement of the shared experience of survival.

When his bread arrives, he puts on his headphones and resumes the Mahler. Outside the window, the homeless man has moved on. A few shabbily dressed children play tag in the piazza. Julian recalls a phase when he and Aidan raced across the garden at Mornington after dinner every evening. Aidan was usually faster. The idea of being slow irritated Julian, and he longed for the chance to win, so that he might be able to boast to classmates at school. But time and time again, he would run out of breath or his legs would become too tired as he watched Aidan dash ahead. The only time he won was when Aidan stopped in the middle of the garden and stared at the house, its lights lit up and its façade made radiant by the deepening darkness. When Julian caught up to Aidan, he found him standing still on the grass. Julian did not bother to ask what he was doing and raced ahead toward the finish line. He still remembers how his shouts of "I won, I won" sent a flock of black birds spiraling into the evening sky.

Julian pauses the symphony and makes another attempt at Kafka, but he skips over most of the longer passages and the parts on self-loathing. He jumps ahead to the travel diary section of the book, and searches for Kafka's musings on Milan. He is surprised to learn that for Kafka, the beauty of the Galleria was sufficient consolation for his never having seen the Roman ruins. Kafka strikes him as someone who would have preferred ruins.

He puts the book aside and orders the rest of his dinner: *prosciutto di Parma* to start, followed by *bistecca alla Fiorentina* with truffled gnocchi. When he looks around the restaurant, he notices that the Italian women who'd arrived before him have left, and a new guest has taken their place, an American man no older than twenty-five. He is speaking to the couple and sharing an album, which, as Julian gathers while he starts his antipasto, is filled with wedding photos. The man enthuses about the sights in Florence and the many souvenirs he and his new wife have collected.

While the couple listens and smiles, Julian puts his headphones back on and turns on the white noise app. A low hum fills his ears. The fervor with which the man speaks of the wedding and the honeymoon irritates Julian more than the growing crowd of vagrants outside. He fails to understand the purpose of photo albums, of such records of places visited and things experienced, when all of it is in the past anyway.

When the steak arrives, he cuts into it and relishes the sight of the blood oozing out from the meat. By the time Julian finishes his meal, the couple and the American man have already left, leaving an elderly woman at the far end of the restaurant. It is eight o'clock, and he decides he will sit for one more hour before heading back to the train station. He orders coffee and dessert.

He suddenly wonders whether Turner had ever painted the Duomo. A quick search online leads him to a few pencil drawings in sketchbooks and illustrations for Walter Scott's *Prose Works*, but no major oil paintings such as those he had done for Rome and Venice.

Julian then goes through a series of Turner images online. He thinks of *A View on the Seine* and pulls up a digital copy on his tablet. He could not say why he bid on it at auction beyond the fact that he desired to own a Turner. Before he began collecting art, he had assumed that an artwork belonged to the artist, even posthumously, and that the act of creation was the ultimate act of possession. But when he saw his signature on the document, next to the title of the painting, he understood the true meaning of ownership.

Julian is, in fact, not very fond of *A View on the Seine*. He found it a little banal, but he had to enthuse over it in front of others, in order to justify the purchase. Since then, he has seen other Turners on sale, and while some of them were renowned pieces, he was not inspired to acquire any of them, except for *Rain, Steam, and Speed*, on which he was outbid.

When he first brought *A View on the Seine* back from the auction house, he spent hours staring at it, hoping that some truth would emerge from the prolonged viewing and shake him to the core. But the revelation never came. He read about the river confluence depicted in the landscape, and learned that the point at which the currents of one river meet the tidal zone of another river is a place where boats struggle against the bore waves, a natural phenomenon known locally as the *mascaret* or *barre*. He was disturbed by the possibility of shipwreck at the point of confluence, so he moved the painting from a prominent spot in the Library to the alcove. When he signed the ownership of Mornington Hall over to Aidan, he was happy to leave *A View on the Seine* as part of the package. But Julian was furious when it was sold. He was angry at Aidan for having driven the house into financial ruin, but also angry at himself for not having gone back to study the painting one final time, to try to understand it at last.

This present journey back to the house is, for Julian, a journey back to the Turner, even though it is no longer there and even though he never loved it in the first place. He would like to stand in front of the empty space on the wall and imagine that moment of complete comprehension, that moment when the veil is lifted.

He thinks of Penelope, sitting on the veranda at Mornington, her face lit by lamplight, telling him about Turner's use of color and light. He enjoyed looking at her when she described an artwork. He knew she was sensitive to his gaze and felt the weight of his eyes on her neck, her legs, her breasts. Could Penelope be considered beautiful? He was uncertain. In her youth, she had a softness in her features, grace in her movements, a charming smile, but she was not attractive in the conventional sense. Julian surprised himself in not caring.

The music playing through the headphones is approaching what Mahler referred to as "a cry of despair" or a "death-shriek"—a term that Julian recollects from his readings—the softer and softer notes that lead toward silence. Mornington Hall will soon face its own demise. The house, in his memory, is no longer a whole building, but is broken up within him, a staircase here or a nook there, scattered in remote corners of his mind. But Julian can still trace the hallways of the house, and he can picture the ornamental details of each room before him as clearly as he can see the lines on his own hands. He opens the old aerial photo of Mornington, silent and serene in the lost greenery of the English countryside. But he remembers the noise of renovation, the conversations in the Dining Hall, and the sound of cooking in the kitchen. Then, at the center, the column of books that he knows he might never see again.

A dramatic sequence in the symphony rouses him. The coffee has gone cold. Julian pays and tips the waiter generously for allowing him to sit undisturbed for many hours. He packs up his belongings in a hurry. These thoughts about Mornington compel him to move forward again.

The sleeper train to Gare de Lyon pulls out of Milano Centrale ten minutes past the scheduled 23:00 departure time. As soon as Julian settles into his compartment, he positions himself in the sitting area next to the window. Although it is first class, the compartment is still too narrow, and the bathroom has scarcely enough space for an adult. Once again, he wishes he had chosen the slower and cheaper train. He changes into his sleepwear and slippers, though he has no intention of sleeping.

At an event organized by a friend in New York, Julian learned of a practice that has become popular—induced sleeplessness. The practice involves a twenty-minute nap for every two hours of wakefulness throughout the night, so the mind receives regular rest while still being able to produce work. In the past, he has experimented with different patterns of sleeplessness, in an attempt to lengthen his workday; none of those methods increased productivity or prevented exhaustion during the day. But this new method has proven to be effective for him. The twenty-minute intervals send him into the deepest sleep. Most of the time, his sleep is devoid of dreams, and he wakes up feeling refreshed.

Before he sleeps, Julian takes a quick shower in the cramped bathroom. He then sets up a temporary workspace by the window. The laptop, notebook, and pen are laid out neatly, alongside the Kafka. He draws the curtain and sets the alarm for twenty minutes. Then he falls asleep on the narrow bed to the hum of the moving train.

When the alarm sounds at midnight, he gets up and starts working at the laptop, drafting a presentation for an upcoming conference. At certain points during the two-hour stretch, he cups his hands around his eyes and peers into the dark terrain outside. Soon, the train will enter the French countryside and pass by the Mediterranean coast of southern France. Staring out the window, he sees nothing save clusters of light from towns and cars.

After another twenty minutes of dreamless sleep, he completes his presentation and catches up on emails. During the third interval of sleep, he dreams of his mother, and after he wakes up, he finds it difficult to focus. The dream was composed of snapshots of his mother picking flowers in the garden at Mornington. Julian remembers how Charlotte often set off with a basket and came back from the garden with her clothes damp from the dew or stained with mud. After taking off her jacket, she would bring the basket of flowers into the Dining Hall and lay the stems out on the table. She would then cut the stems and arrange the flowers in the vases she had already prepared. She caressed the petals, cleaned away the mud, and pruned the dead leaves, which she placed in a bowl. If an insect were on a leaf, she would return it back onto the grass outside.

Julian would accompany his mother as she distributed the vases around the house, and during those wanders through the rooms, he understood how much she loved Mornington Hall. He was not surprised when she drowned herself in the lake. In hindsight, something about the way she tended to the flowers and insects suggested to Julian that her own life would be brief.

Thoughts of his mother overcome him like a sudden illness, and he is eager to shake off the feeling of feebleness. He gets out of bed and peers outside. He sees, in the distance, the surface of the Mediterranean reflecting the moonlight. The view pleases him, though he does not look at it for long, since looking out the train window at night means catching a reflection of himself. Sometimes, his own eyes staring back at him are all he can see.

He answers more emails, but his attention is wavering. At 5:20 a.m., he peeks outside the window again. He has no clue where the train is. He notices, near the tracks, numerous brilliantly lit greenhouses with rows of vegetables inside, like rectangles of light dotting the rural region. When the train leaves the greenhouses behind, nothing remains outside the window except the light of the train shining on the black shapes rushing past.

Julian closes the curtain and attempts to read Kafka again. As he scans the words, his mind drifts back to those days with Penelope. When he first saw her, her face framed by the leaves of the palm trees in the Conservatory, he was reminded of a passage he had read about the face of Mona Lisa, upon which all the thoughts of the world were etched. He examined Penelope more closely later, her weary eyes, the furrowed brows as she bent over a book or analyzed a painting, and he could indeed see so much of the world in her, though he could never articulate those feelings.

The train passes over a slight bump and Julian is shaken out of his memory. He checks his watch; it is almost 6 a.m. He puts on his headphones and plays the Mahler from the beginning, at a louder volume than before. What he appreciates about the first movement are the sudden shifts and the quick succession of notes that make it nearly impossible to doze off while listening to the piece. As soon as his mind starts to wander, the music shakes him and he returns to the present.

At 6:15, he pulls the curtains apart to find the morning light outside. His reflection is no longer visible on the glass, so he ties up the curtains. For a brief second, he glimpses a brown animal dash across a small opening between two shrubs.

Julian recalls how he once caught an animal in the gardens at Mornington. He and Aidan had been tracking a fox that lived nearby. But the trap he had set ended up catching a red squirrel instead. It was not quite dead when they found it, and its eyes were black orbs of fear as it gazed up at them. Its soft fur was speckled with blood, its tail squashed under the metallic bars of the trap. Aidan, who was maybe five at the time, cried and ran away. Left alone with the dying animal, Julian wondered what to do. He was uncertain whether he should muffle it to death or club it. He ended up taking the trap and the squirrel to a nearby pond and throwing it in the water, where it sank, still strapped to the wooden board. From time to time, he thinks about that tiny creature and wonders what it must feel like to dwell in a world full of predators.

At 6:30 a.m., Julian decides to start his last interval of sleep a bit earlier. He dreams of a string of disconnected words. Then he cuts his fingers on the sheets of paper, and licks the wound with the tip of his tongue. When he wakes up, he goes to the sink to wash his hands and rinse his mouth. A strange taste lingers, like the tang of blood.

The train compartment is filled with sunlight and Julian realizes that he has overslept. The watch indicates that it is almost 7:10, thirty minutes before the scheduled arrival in Paris. He brushes his teeth, changes into a fresh set of clothes, and sits down next to the window for the final stretch of the journey. The train is passing through the suburbs of Paris. Riot fires have blackened some of the walls. An old car is burning between two estate towers.

When the train enters the central rings of the city, through the opening in the impressive geodesic dome, everything is changed. The walls are free of graffiti, and the streets cleared of anything unsightly. Boulangeries and florist shops sit next to cafés and bistros. Before the train pulls into Gare de Lyon, Julian takes out the vintage ticket from his wallet and rubs it until the scent transfers onto his fingers.

Picture this: a woman whose face has been replaced by her torso. Her eyes have become breasts, the nose is substituted by a belly button, and her mouth has been transformed into a vulva, a voiceless orifice waiting to be filled. This is René Magritte's Le Viol *(1934), which was featured on the cover of André Breton's 1934 pamphlet* Qu'est-ce que le Surréalisme?.

This "face-body" belongs with her Surrealist sisters, who inhabit paintings, drawings, photographs, and sculptures: a voluptuous naked woman wrapped in a shimmering black fabric, her head unseen, her flesh offered up like a delectable gift (Man Ray, Torso (Lama [sic] Sheath), *1930); a woman cut up and disassembled, with the parts separated into five individual frames (Magritte,* L'Évidence eternelle, *1930); a female figure lying on the ground, her spine arched, her legs spread wide open, one arm thrown over her elongated neck, in which a small but deep cut is discernible (Giacometti,* Woman with Her Throat Cut, *1932); a monster with a woman's legs and a fish's head, like an inverse mermaid (Magritte,* L'Invention Collective, *1934); a painting of a woman showing nothing but her naked torso and genitalia (Magritte,* Representation, *1937); a man raping a woman with his baton-like penis while strangling her with his claw-like hands (Picasso,* Rape, *1937); a female body stuffed into a bottle (Magritte,* Femme-Bouteille, *ca. 1941); a woman fondling herself in the shower and licking her own shoulder (Magritte,* Le Galet, *1948). These are the Surrealist women. Frequently headless, as Mary Ann Caws writes, and therefore sightless and voiceless. Often limbless too. Fragments strewn across the masculinized space of the museums.*

Then there are the dolls. Life-size female mannequins composed of wood, plaster, and metal bits assembled haphazardly, like half-complete automata or a pile of body parts. Some are seated upright, but most lie on a mattress, as if in the aftermath of violent assault. All are naked and armless; some are headless. Hans Bellmer's Die Puppe *("The Doll," 1934) first appeared in the Surrealist magazine* Minotaure *as a series of eighteen photographs. In 1935, Bellmer constructed a second doll, with a spherical belly that acted as a ball joint, to which he attached four legs, sometimes multiple breasts and pelvises. Bellmer photographed the cephalopod-like doll over the course of three years. The photos mimicked macabre crime scenes. In one, the doll is flung down a flight of stairs; in another, she is suspended by her navel from a doorway. Other photos, taken in a forest, show the doll hanging from a tree like splayed meat, or thrown on the grass at night. The predator is absent from all the photos except one, where the dark form of a man lurks in the background, spying on the doll tied to a tree.*

It is true that the Surrealists aimed to liberate the conformist mind by disrupting the social and moral codes of the bourgeoisie. They urged viewers to question conventional thinking. Who says pornography is a form of violent misogyny? Who says the dolls are the products of a predatory mind? Maybe Die Puppe *is a response to de Sade, to Offenbach's opera, to the Nazis, to Freud. Maybe Bellmer's work is a way for him to deal with his own childhood trauma, or his fears of rejection and abandonment. And maybe his experience of trauma justifies his blindness to the suffering of others. Maybe.*

A note of interest: Die Puppe *was accompanied by an essay Bellmer wrote entitled "Memories of the Doll Theme." In the essay, he recounts his fantasies of little girls playing erotic games, his gaze fixed on "their bowed and especially knock-kneed legs," his mind bewitched by "the casual quiver of their pink pleats"—the "pink pleats" being Bellmer's motif for female genitalia. He ends "Memories of the Doll Theme" by lamenting how the "pink region"* was denied to him, and how he wishes to triumph over the girls who keep themselves aloof, with "wide eyes which turn away," by making the dolls in their image and "assault[ing] their plastic form" with "aggressive fingers." Enough said.

Let us return to Magritte's freakish face-body. This female thing is nothing but a body, robbed of her identity and subjectivity, unable to speak or cry out. We don't know what to make of her. But as she turns toward us with her dumb, uncomprehending face, we, in turn, must decide whether to stare back or look away in disgust.

SEVEN

JANUARY

JANUARY 1

The year began with headaches and backache. The snow continues. Aidan and I spent the first day of the year huddled next to
the fire in our room, reading the news. The house is incredibly
still. In winter, the rest of the world seems to recede further and
further away, as though viewed through the wrong end of a telescope. Behind closed eyes, all I see are images of the past that
violently thrust aside the images of the drowning on the news.
Perhaps it is me, and not the world, that is receding.

JANUARY 3

Aidan and I have decided to start packing our personal belongings, instead of leaving it to the last minute. The room we set
aside for storage has become chaotic, no matter how diligently
I have tried to organize the boxes. I fit smaller bundles into the
crevices between boxes, and a fortress of things emerges. My
arms and back ache from loading and unloading items. But I'm
glad I haven't seen Alex in a few days, and have resisted the
temptation to check on him in the Hall.

JANUARY 4

I fell while carrying an enormous pile of books today. Cried, out of frustration. With myself. With all that remains to be done. The archive has grown disorderly. My stomach feels sick even though I have not eaten anything out of the ordinary. I have become physically feeble, and the calm I had sustained for so many years has given way to this inner tumult that allows me no control and no recovery. The past resembles the invisible decay in a rotten tooth, slowly taking over, presaging nothing but pain.

A brief break in the evening, after seeing Celia; she returned to Mornington this afternoon. We joined Miranda for another sewing session, despite the fact that my hand still hurt from the fall earlier. The quilt is nearly finished, a beautiful collection of greens, pinks, and yellows.

OBJECT

Stereoscope, *ca.* 1901. Produced by Underwood & Underwood, New York. Made of wood, metal, and velvet. Measuring 32 cm long x 18 cm wide x 14 cm tall. Designed for stereoscopic photographs. Extremely fragile.

JANUARY 5

Saw Alex for the first time today after a short hiatus. He came to return the other books he borrowed last month. I have learned to overlook the creased spines and accept the imperfections as another kind of record.

Out of the blue, Alex asked me about the work I do in the Library. I stuttered as I told him about the items I've recently catalogued. He asked if he could visit the underground storage space. I hesitated, filled with a sense of dread at the thought of being in the space alone with him. His face was expressionless as I weighed my options. It would have been too awkward to refuse him, to have to lie. So I asked him to wait while I went and grabbed a few more lamps. The light brought some comfort as we descended the ladder and found ourselves among the archive items. Alex looked around as I prattled on about the history of the Library; he made no comments and asked no questions. I tried to keep some distance between myself and him, never allowing our bodies to touch in any way, which was by no means easy given the narrowness of the space. I showed him the stereoscopic cards I have been working on. He appeared interested in them. I demonstrated how the device works and he peered through the lenses to see a photo of a battlefield. This seems so familiar, he said. I proceeded to relate more about the stereoscope, but he turned around unexpectedly and went back up the ladder without a word. I was alarmed by the abruptness of his departure. Again, that silence, that inscrutability. I considered asking him why the view looked familiar, but I'm not sure I want to know the answer. When he stood close to me as we looked at the stereoscope, I could smell his scent, and I'm ashamed to admit I was disgusted. A bitter smell, overlaid with the artificial fragrance of cleaning solutions, like a hospital room.

JANUARY 5—LATE NIGHT

Headache and sleeplessness. The pills have lost their effect again. Cannot get Alex's odor out of my head. I gave up trying to fall asleep and have decided to spend some time with my notebook. I have tucked into its pages one of the stereoscopic views, of a building bisected by a bomb. The broken wooden planks that jut out into the air resemble the serrated edges of torn flesh. In the foreground: rubble and barbed wire fences, and miniscule human figures darting across the wounded terrain.

I slid the card into the antique stereoscope, and the flat images became three-dimensional. The two photos overlapped to create the illusion of depth, like a set of human eyes, and from two separate halves emerged one harmonized whole. Thus, the distant past is enlivened.

The sight of the semi-destroyed town somehow transported me to London, to that summer I spent with Julian. An unprecedented heat wave soaked the city in hot vapors that year. In the tunnels of the Tube, a suffocating combination of airlessness and stench. On the streets, burning tarmac and the glare of skyscrapers.

In spite of the heat, Julian and I acquired items for the collection—several sculptures, antique atlases, and oil paintings. In between the private sales and auction houses, we visited the Tate, after learning that a Turner—*Landscape with a River and a Bay in the Distance*—was on loan from the Louvre. But we wandered around the Clore Gallery and could not find it. We stopped in front of other Turners to admire them, and searched online for an image of the Louvre painting in order to remind ourselves what it looked like. But it was not there. After some time, we gave up.

At the end of each day, Julian would be eager to return to his apartment to review his notes, compare prices, and assess potential acquisitions. There were evenings when, exhausted from a long day, I would sit and watch him work, his eyes fixed on the screen, his hands fidgeting with a pen. At times he would grumble furiously to himself.

Though Julian seemed to sleep so rarely, he fell asleep instantly whenever he decided to take a break, whereas even then I would be kept awake by images and thoughts from the day. One night, as he slept on the floor beside the sofa, I lay down close to him, with a few inches between our bodies. That was the only kind of intimacy we shared. After those first two kisses, Julian and I did not kiss again. He never attempted to crawl into the bed or onto the sofa with me. He might squeeze my hand for a second or two, though we never embraced. The picture I once held in my head—of the satyr and the nymph—appeared ludicrous in the face of his reserve. We maintained the distance between us, without recourse to words.

JANUARY 9—LATE NIGHT

Could not help myself. This evening I stood at the entrance to the Hall and watched Alex's tent for about fifteen minutes. Such strange obsession! I heard the sound of shuffling. No lights were on; perhaps he was sleeping. I'm reminded of how Julian made tiny ticking noises in his sleep, an almost mechanical ticking. One night, in his apartment in London, I lay in the dark, listening to the rhythmic sound, insistent and steady, one click never louder than the one before. I wondered if Alex makes a similar sound, though I dared not go closer to the tent.

Checked the calendar. We are now approximately three months away from the demolition. Three months until Julian's return. Am I waiting? The fear of the waiting and the aching, the fear of the endless hours that yield nothing but closed doors and empty rooms. But no, I am not really waiting. I will no longer give him that power.

JANUARY 10

Unable to focus. Kept making mistakes with the archive and the catalogue entries. Misplaced items, mislabeled boxes, errors in documentation. I seem to have lost the rhythm and regularity that governed my days for so long.

Walked into Celia's studio feeling ill, but I did not want to cancel the session, for the portrait is almost done.

I struggled to stay still. My mind perturbed by a scene that has resurfaced unexpectedly: we were moving boxes one afternoon and Julian fell after losing his footing. A bruise bloomed on his right knee. Over the ensuing days, the bruise deepened into a stain of purple and burgundy, and spread across his skin.

One evening, he sat on the sofa, scrubbing the bruise with a dish scrubber. The skin became red and raw, with spots of blood. When I offered to bandage it, he stood up and shouted, It's fucking revolting. He then stormed off to the bathroom. As I was left standing in the hallway, holding the bandage and antiseptic cream, I wondered what he had meant by "it," the thing that was revolting.

At the end of the session, I told Celia I had a headache and could not stay for tea. I feel terrible for having lied to her. Really, I just wished to be alone and take a sleeping pill.

ARTIST'S POSTCARDS
Joni Murphy, *Weekness: One of Seven Nonstop Flights*. Published by Catch & Release Press, Toronto and Amsterdam, 2007. Collection of twenty-four reprints of popular touristic postcards, held inside torn paper folder. On the verso side of each card is either a short fragment written by the artist or a quote from a literary text. On the back of a few cards, a reader had crossed out parts of the text using a black marker.

JANUARY 11
During my tea break today, I came across Alex in the Long Gallery. I rarely see him anywhere outside the Hall. He was standing, with that strange stillness of his, in front of the wall. At first, I thought he was looking at a painting, but as I approached, I noticed he was staring at the wallpaper with an intense gaze as though he had seen something of great importance. I asked him what was the matter. To which he replied, Nothing. Just thinking.

JANUARY 12

Unable to sleep. Lay in the dark for three hours, uselessly charting the floating of shadows across the walls. Besieged by the past. These memories feel like a secret shame. Is the gravity of the world not enough to pull me away from myself? Why do I keep slipping back into the past, when so much in the present demands my attention? The longer I stay away from the archive, from the work around the house, the smaller I become, unable to help others, no more than a thing fit to hide in walls or under floorboards, sneaking out to grab what little sustenance is available, then sneaking back into the dark to wallow in misery.

JANUARY 13

Aidan and I have started packing the contents of his studio. On one section of the wall, there was a series of black-and-white copies of the Pompeii photos by the American photographer William Wylie, cut from the book that Aidan bought in preparation for the trip to Pompeii that we took over ten years ago. I remember walking through the ruins in the suffocating heat, mesmerized and perturbed by the plaster casts of once-living beings. Suspended in the instant of death, the rough-hewn stone figures embodied pathos. I recall seeing a dog curled in on itself, overcome by fear. A few of the humans lay on their sides; others raised their arms up in the attempt to delay, for a few seconds, the arrival of oblivion.

In one of the pictures, a group of plaster casts lie on massive metallic plates, perhaps awaiting transfer to the display cases. My eyes are drawn to a female figure in the background, frozen in the act of defiance, with one hand raised to the sky and the other protecting the child by her side. Next to this is a photo of the molds that the archaeologist Giuseppe Fiorelli used to make the plaster models. The human-shaped cases are bisected and opened, revealing the hollow halves. The night before our trip,

I read about the molten lava that enveloped the flesh, leaving shells of solidified volcanic ash that formed voids in the shape of the perished bodies and preserved the remaining bones. In these voids, the plaster set.

Remembering is akin to the process of pouring plaster into the lacunae made by time and catastrophe. We tip words and images into the molds of the past, but what emerges, when the container is cracked open, does not approximate the living thing that once existed. The reconstructed form can never be more than a petrified copy of the breathing, trembling whole.

Aidan no longer needs these pictures, so I took them off the walls and folded them into my notebook.

January 14

Woke up in a sweat, trembling. A million termites in my dream, crawling all over. They swirled in dark vortices that spiraled upward above me, suffocating all light out of the room. Then I felt as if they merged with me, became me, or I became them. For a second after I roused myself, my limbs were flailing wildly, as though I had innumerable little legs on which I could not walk. I had become one of them. An abject, unclean thing. I had to take a shower immediately, to wash off the slime I imagined on my skin. Then afterward, I took out my copy of *Norham Castle, Sunrise*, in which I had always found comfort. I taped the print onto the wall and stood in front of it, to calm the disturbance in my heart. But whatever strength I gained from the image quickly spent itself, and I wasted the day failing to concentrate on anything.

I must stop this inexorable fall into the past. But I cannot shrink these memories that grow larger and larger, pushing out everything else, including the self that I have constructed over the last twenty years. I am going to pieces. A layer of substance within me has begun to dissolve, and my entire interior is being reordered, messed up, torn asunder.

Perhaps what I need to do is to sink to the very bottom, to get to that day. But how does one get to that place and return, without being destroyed?

PICTURE POSTCARDS

Series of twenty cards, *ca.* 1900, showing buildings or sites in European cities that were demolished before the end of the twentieth century. Black-and-white photos, all postmarked and franked. Most in fair condition. Sites depicted include the Euston Arch in London, the Lothbury entrance to the Bank of England, La Jetée-Promenade in Nice, and L'ascenseur de Notre-Dame-de-la-Garde in Marseilles.

JANUARY 26

I do not want to see red and yet red is all I see. I wish I knew the exact name of that shade of red which is particular to the flesh. A haze of fevers and insomnia renders the event two weeks ago dreamlike and surreal, an event like a disease of the eye, painting everything blood red. It is only with distance that the details give themselves over to language.

A loud bang at night. A scream. We rushed downstairs to find Miranda on the floor outside the kitchen. That red, on her head and her body. The rug beneath dyed burgundy. Carlos in tears. Then the frantic calls to the police, the ambulance. The pressing of the wound.

Aidan accompanied them to the hospital. I stayed. Washed the rug and scrubbed the floorboards with help from others. The red turned pink, diluted by water. The floorboards stained dark brown. My fingernails dyed the color of rust.

An entire day of waiting. Then Miranda woke up. We rushed to the hospital. The police were there. She will be fine, according to the doctor.

Miranda and her bandaged body. I held her hands and we both cried.

It was Alex in the night. Knife in hand, rolled-up canvas under his arm. An unexpected encounter on his way out the kitchen door.

I just wanted some water, Miranda said. He first struck her across the head. Blood trickled through the wound. Her face swelled. Her temples throbbed. The blood tasted metallic, she said.

How could I not have known that Alex was gone? How could I not have noticed that a painting was missing? Back at the house, we went through all the rooms, Aidan and I. Looking for Alex. For what he had taken. Then I saw it. The empty space on the Library wall. The reproduction of the Turner. The wooden frame lay broken on the floor. I cried out.

We have to report the theft, I demanded. Aidan was less certain. It's not worth that much, he said. Alex probably did not know it was a copy. Aidan did not want to turn Alex into a fugitive, forced into hiding, unable to seek any kind of help.

The painting is important, I said. It must be returned.

Aidan held me as I wept. But it's not the original, Pen.

I called the police anyway. Don't expect anything, they said. He won't be able to get much for it in any case.

Everyone is obsessed with the reproduction's low monetary value, which is irrelevant.

In bed for days, choked with grief. Celia joined me in the bedroom and read to me while I stared out the window. All I could see was red.

Miranda came back after a week. Her movements slower. Her eyes scanning every corner. I stayed with her in her room for a while. She said she would never again go downstairs in the middle of the night for a cup of water.

JANUARY 26—LATE NIGHT

Have given up any attempt to sleep, held captive by my thoughts. Instead, I sit here listening to the sound of Aidan breathing in bed.

What I cannot admit even to Aidan is that the greatest disaster, for me, is not Miranda's suffering, though of course I care for her. The disaster is the loss of the Turner reproduction, the single connection I had left to the original.

It is partly my fault for not having anticipated this. Alex asked to borrow books, to go into the Library, he maintained his aloofness, all so he could commit this act. How could I not have guessed? I should have trusted the sense of anxiety that his presence induced. I should not have allowed my concern about sympathy—or the performance of sympathy—to deter me from taking action.

JANUARY 27

Cannot decide whether to forgive Alex or despise him for what he has done. How can I reject someone I was once committed to helping? I can almost hear Aidan's voice scolding me for the fragility of my compassion. He tried to reassure me that it is not my fault. Nor is it Alex's, for his judgment had been warped by difficult circumstances. Aidan's vision of the world is predicated on humans being basically good. Sometimes I wonder if his optimism is not a kind of inflexibility and his work an expression of guilt for having been so privileged.

Aidan said we could commission another reproduction. But the one that was taken, the one that was held by the original frame, is irreplaceable. Aidan's attachment to material things does not extend beyond his mother's glass flutes and bowls, which he keeps inside a specially designed box with soft lining and a shatter-proof exterior. I cannot convince him that a link exists between Turner, the original painting, and the frame that held both the original and, later, the reproduction. To touch that picture and that frame was, in some ways, to shake Turner's hand across time. In Aidan's eyes, Turner is a stranger to me, and such attachment is unjustified.

JANUARY 28

Snow has stopped. But the glittering ice remains. Still unable to work. Tormented by the thought that others might find me neglectful. The remaining items in the Library are collecting dust. Yet I feel paralyzed, an unclean thing pinned to the bed, staring at the walls and ceiling for hours on end. To move even an inch requires tremendous strength. I will remain here, motionless. Ironic how easy stillness is when one has fallen into an abyss.

JANUARY 29

Miranda spent some time with me today. Her wound is healing. At the behest of the hospital psychiatrist, she has started keeping a journal as a way of dealing with the event. She has also resumed her sewing.

I am ashamed by my initial response to her suffering, my fixation on the painting. I do feel her pain. Even though it is not mine. Except maybe it is also my pain. I do not want to return to that time when I was blind to everything but pain. The red-tinted pain that forced all else into the background. I came close to telling Miranda about the event twenty-two years ago, but could not bring myself to do so. It seems so indulgent, that self-exposure.

Since those essays I wrote over two decades ago, in the immediate aftermath, I have not revisited the event in written form, nor have I spoken to anyone except Dad and Aidan. I cannot even write his name in this notebook anymore. I have come to inhabit the silence, a realm beyond words. How can language ever be sufficient?

JANUARY 29—EVENING
I ought to be able to write about what happened.

JANUARY 30
The physical difficulty of writing and the inner need for it. I'm brought back to those days when I first attempted to write about *A View on the Seine*, when I stood mute and dumb in front of the painting, racking my brain, unable to compose a coherent sentence.

Aidan is the only person who has ever had faith in my ability to put words on the page. I have made unfair assumptions about him lately, assumptions wrapped up in resentment. I remember the trip we took to Pompeii, where we had an argument, one of the few we ever had. He insisted on staying longer in order to complete his sketches, but I was overcome by exhaustion and heat. I rambled through the ruins with bitterness, and by the end of our visit, I was no longer able to take in anything, save the sight of Aidan walking in front of me, sketchbook and camera in hand. On the train ride back to Rome, while he napped, I looked outside the window and saw a magnificent villa with a row of cypresses, through which the rays of the setting sun shone. Aidan had been meaning to photograph such a view, and he had searched everywhere for the right light, the right conditions. But out of a sense of vindictiveness, I did not wake him up. That evening, he apologized for his self-absorbedness. I, in turn, apologized, and described to him the sight that he had missed on the train ride. He said my description was as good as the view itself, which was one of the kindest, most improbable things anyone has ever said to me.

I can imagine Aidan's voice telling me that I should write, that writing is the only way by which I can hope to grapple with everything that has been festering within me, barring me from the present. Again, that feeling of having become some unnameable monster, burrowing deeper and deeper into the earth, quiet and darkness all around me.

January 31

Julian suggested returning to his apartment in the early afternoon, after we visited the Soane Museum. Heat baked the city and our clothes clung to our bodies. We longed for the cooling effect of the brushed concrete floor and walls, shaded from the sun by blackout blinds.

It is difficult to remember the day in sequence because what happened looms so large that it seems to be at the beginning, even though it was in fact in the middle, a center from which all else radiated.

Late in the night, after Julian left, I thought I could smell the rain. Somewhere, water was dripping. From my position on the floor, my eyes scanned the room and rested on the painting hanging on the wall, its white skeletal voids dimmed by the dark so that they were no longer distinguishable from the black, the total black that swallowed the bleached bones, leaving nothing behind save a fathomless hole, as unfaltering as the shrieking of the nocturnal bird outside the window.

Eight

April 8, morning

As Julian steps off the train onto the platform at Gare de Lyon, he sees the crowds barricaded behind fences and the police standing guard with rifles. The station has become more chaotic since his last visit. He takes the fast-track lane and heads to the VIP lounge on the upper level of the station, with large glass windows that overlook the platforms. The glass, however, does not keep out the noise, the shouts and swearing from those who have been denied entry.

He orders an English-style breakfast, then puts on his headphones and turns on the white noise. There are a few other travelers in the lounge, mostly businessmen in suits, each preoccupied with their electronic devices. An elderly man sits down at the table next to Julian's. The man nods in his direction, and it takes Julian a few seconds to realize that the man is blind. Julian removes his headphones.

"Bonjour," the man says to him.

At first Julian is uncertain whether the man is speaking to him. "Bonjour," he replies. "Morning."

"On your way to London?" the man replies in heavily accented, though eloquent, English. "I've just returned from a visit there. The wait to go through customs on this end will be long, so be mentally prepared."

"Yes, I plan to get to Gare du Nord in good time," Julian says.

"Good. Don't be alarmed by this," the man pointed to his sunglasses. "I was not born this way. This was something that just happened."

The man spoke of how he lost his eyesight one day, suddenly, upon waking. There was no cure. He had to learn to accept a life lived in darkness.

"Sometimes I think maybe eyesight is overrated," the man shrugs and says, "I see differently now. I continue to travel. Plus, I have many assistants. One of them is moving my luggage onto the train as we speak. And I don't have to work. Eyesight was not exactly essential to my business anyways. What is it that you do, if I may ask?"

Julian hesitates. "I'm an architect. I need to be able to draw, to see spaces and buildings."

"Ah, I understand. That is very interesting work."

Julian waits for a few seconds for the man to ask him more about architecture. But he does not, and instead begins to eat his breakfast.

Julian turns to his own breakfast and coffee. He closes his eyes temporarily, and reaches for the fork and knife. He turns toward the window, with his eyes still closed, and attempts to imagine what it would be like to lose the benefit of sight, to have to guess distance, colors, or the shapes of things. He tries to visualize how he would be able to run or walk down the street. But his imagination fails him. When he opens his eyes, he finds that the bits of bacon he has carved up with his eyes closed are uneven and messy.

The waiter goes over to the blind man and speaks to him in French. The man gathers up his belongings and prepares to leave.

"Wait," Julian calls after him. "I'd like to ask you something, if you don't mind? How do you know where you're going? I mean, aside from the walking stick that gives you a sense of the immediate environment. How do you know where you are headed if you cannot see what's around you?"

The man turns around and walks over to Julian's table. He smiles. "I rely on my other senses. I get by. But in another way, I'm not sure I ever knew where I was headed, not even when I had eyesight, you know what I mean? I doubt anyone really knows where they're going. But you walk ahead anyways, no? Bon voyage." The man pats Julian on the shoulder and walks off.

That comment bothers Julian in a way he does not quite understand. He finishes his breakfast and goes to the ground floor of the station, where he instructs a courier to send his luggage ahead to the hotel. He keeps with him in the satchel Kafka's diaries and the writing instruments.

The air outside is muggy, in spite of the temperature control inside the dome that stretches over this part of the city. A sweet scent lingers. From the station, Julian crosses the Seine and passes through the Jardin des Plantes, then begins weaving his way through the fifth arrondissement, an area he loves. The neighborhood is quiet. Or rather, the authorities have managed to keep the heart of the city free from the chaos of the outer rings. He takes a break in the Jardin du Luxembourg. The grass is parched and the pond does not have water, but otherwise the park, with the green benches and artificial flower beds, looks much the same as it did when he last visited.

From the garden, he wanders toward the river. He walks past a row of bookshops, a cinema, and a university campus, before pausing outside the Thermes de Cluny, which he habitually avoids, partly due to his dislike of ruins, and partly due to the fact that he shares a name with the Roman emperor with whom the baths are associated. He once read about the monumental vaulted room, the *frigidarium*, of the Thermes, and wondered why anyone bothered to preserve such ancient things that should have collapsed eons ago.

Julian proceeds to one of his favorite bookshops in the city, a place that has been frozen in time, almost like an amusement park. On the upper floor of the bookshop, by the open window, he hears the bells of the reconstructed Notre-Dame. Then someone begins to play the piano that is crammed between the bookshelves; the notes of the song offer a harmonious accompaniment to the tolling bells. It is a perfect moment, and Julian proceeds to record the details in his notebook.

As he sits down on a bench, he notices on the bookshelf next to him a slimy silvery thing dashing across the surface of the shelf. Without hesitation, he picks up a nearby book and crushes the silverfish. He loathes insects. On one occasion, Penelope read him a poem that Turner had written, about ephemerids. The painter attempted to describe the transience of insect lives and the splendor inherent in that transience. Julian found the concept ridiculous and the poem mediocre, though he did not say so to Penelope.

He removes the book to examine the grotesque residue of the bug. Then he takes out a tissue and wipes the book, ridding it of the offensive smudge. He kicks the soiled tissue into a corner beside the bookshelf and proceeds to browse, with the bells of Notre-Dame still tolling in the background. Near the back of the bookshop, there is a table of books by Rilke, a writer whom Julian has been meaning to read. He buys two volumes, Rilke's book on Rodin and *Rilke on Paris*.

After the tour of the bookshop, he wanders over to one of his favorite cafés for lunch. He attempts to read some Kafka, but cannot concentrate. The detail that appeals the most to him is the image of Kafka limping down the streets of Paris in pain, with a sprained toe and pus-filled abscesses on his back. In contrast, the scene in front of Julian is dappled with beauty and calm. He admires the red awning of the adjacent café and the well-dressed patrons sipping coffee; the cobalt blue of the street signs; and the creamy off-white and gray stones of the

Haussmannized façades that have survived catastrophe after catastrophe.

These Parisian streets have remained locked in time—or, rather, outside time. Over the years, Julian has come to find Paris tedious precisely because it is unchanging. The Paris of revolutions is gone. Even the Eiffel Tower, a structure that was meant to be temporary, has become a permanent fixture. Perhaps others find comfort in this changelessness. But for Julian the whole point of a city is change. He thinks about Baron Haussmann's transformation of Paris—the grand "cuttings" across whole neighborhoods that were tantamount to a form of killing, demolishing buildings, displacing populations, and disinfecting whole neighborhoods. He can picture Haussmann walking through the old Paris, drafting plans to rid the city of the vile, unsanitary crowds that clogged up its arteries. Haussmann no doubt wanted to transform the city in order to cleanse it. That's a sentiment with which Julian can sympathize.

A cloud passes overhead, and he observes a glint in the dome that covers this arrondissement, a reminder that change has occurred in the world outside. He writes down this observation in his notebook. He then takes out the books he has purchased and flips through them. *Rilke on Paris* consists of excerpts from the writing the poet completed during his stay in the city. To Tora Holmström, Rilke writes of how Paris is a kind of work that makes demands upon the visitor. Julian likes the sentences and copies them down in his notebook, though he wonders whether the city has made any demands on him.

The last time he was in Paris for business, he met an American girl who walked into the bar in a voluptuous way, unaware of how the tight skirt accentuated the grotesqueness of her body. She made eye contact with all the men in the bar, and even though Julian was not her first choice, she invited him back to her room. For the first thirty minutes, he regretted accepting the invitation, but he was too tired to go out and find someone else. So he stayed, even when he was repulsed by her body. He also learned that the girl's initial display of confidence in the bar was nothing but a performance, and that she harbored deep insecurities, which she unloaded in a drunken stupor. When he left her hotel room in the morning, he felt a vague sense of confusion, a soft voice demanding that he glean something meaningful from the encounter. But like so much of what he had experienced, he never fully grasped what it said about him or his life.

Julian continues flipping through the Rilke book and comes across another passage about the bookstalls along the Seine, which he copies down. He is happy that the pages of his notebook are gradually being filled. He enjoys the experience of collecting observations and quotes, though he has not yet come up with an appropriate title for the notebook.

After lunch, he strolls along the river, crosses the Pont de la Tournelle and wanders through Île Saint-Louis, where he purchases olive oil from a small shop, which he does every time he is in Paris. From there, he walks to the Île de la Cité to visit the Deportation Memorial, another tradition he has upheld. The narrow and subterranean space comforts him somehow, despite the fact that the monument is supposed to have the opposite effect on visitors. Julian also likes the way in which the city, beheld through the heavy iron gate at the tip of the island, appears imprisoned.

He walks by Notre-Dame, past a group of tourists waiting in line. He remembers the burning of the old cathedral. He obsessed over the photos and re-watched the video clips for days, almost elated when the flames engulfed the structure. The smoke bloomed, and the orange fire was dazzling against the pale city. That was a Paris that he would have liked to see. They rebuilt the cathedral to look almost exactly like the one that burnt down, albeit with updated materials. Julian felt that that was a wasted opportunity to create something new, and the costly, much-anticipated restoration only contributed to the banality of the city.

He crosses the Pont Neuf and heads to the Louvre. At the start of this journey, Julian had already decided on a visit to the museum, which he had not seen on his previous two trips to the city. As soon as he enters the Louvre, he starts speeding through the sculpture galleries. He finds statues disconcerting. They seem to glare back at him with empty eyes of stone. But a fragmentary statue of a male torso grabs his attention. He pauses and looks. The statue, being headless, does not have a gaze, so he is able to linger in front of it. He reads the exhibit label on the plinth, which quotes from Rilke's poem on the Archaic torso of Apollo. The poet's words enliven the statue, and after reading them, Julian is moved by the torso in a way that he cannot describe. "You must change your life." He shivers when he rereads that line. He understands that an encounter with art might be a life-changing experience. But he does not like the way in which Rilke frames the line as a command from a headless statue that is supposed to remain silent, one that is not supposed to stare and judge.

Julian wanders through the museum in a daze, with Rilke's line stuck in his mind. He walks past most of the artworks without stopping. Still life and botanical illustrations annoy him, as does Hubert Robert's *capriccio* of a ruinous Grande Galerie, with a young artist painting amidst the debris. Robert's message of hope strikes him as trite. In the Grande Galerie itself, he takes a break and reads with amusement Kafka's description of "the excitement and the knots of people, as if the *Mona Lisa* had just been stolen." According to the footnote, the Leonardo was in fact stolen shortly before Kafka's trip, and everyone stood staring at the blank space on the wall.

Julian records some thoughts on Kafka, then walks on. As he goes through the next room, an image catches his eye with its distinct blue and orange hues. He slows down and pauses in front of *L'enlèvement des Sabines* by Nicolas Poussin. He can guess how the pivotal word would be translated in English. He has always been puzzled by how a word that easily rhymes with innocuous words such as "shape," "tape," or "cape," could conjure up so much horror. Julian looks at the Poussin—the women's flinging arms, the muscular soldiers, the impressive architecture—and he cannot understand what any of this has to do with the experience of pleasure.

He does not want to waste any more time and rushes to the real reason for his visit to the Louvre: the Turner that he had tried to see years ago, at the Tate with Penelope. As soon as he enters the room, *Landscape with a River and a Bay in the Distance* catches his eye. It is difficult to grasp the painting, because there are no clear outlines, no pictorial objects, just shades of brown, beige, and gray, with a patch of blue sky in the upper right-hand corner. The tree, cut off by the frame, confirms that this is a landscape. There is a body of water in the background; in the foreground, a dark-brown blotch. Julian cannot make out whether there are human figures there, or maybe a boat. He takes out his notebook and attempts a sketch of the tree, the one part of the picture that he could replicate with confidence. He feels compelled to write some kind of analysis, but stops short, uncertain whether he has anything to say. He reminds himself that he is still learning how to see, and must not rush the process.

He walks to the other side of the room to study the painting from a distance. Penelope once told him about Turner's preparatory studies called "color beginnings," a term that he thought charming. Turner completed watercolor sketches in order to capture a transient scene or image before it melted away. The few brushstrokes of colors contained the potential of an entire painting. They were never meant to be exhibited, though they have come to be regarded as precursors to twentieth-century abstraction.

Julian saw one of these color beginnings at a special exhibition in New York seven years ago. As he stood there contemplating the misty bands of yellow and blue, he was seized by a sense of panic. No barrier stood between him and the picture. For a split second he felt an intense need to remove it from the wall, to either deface it or keep it in his own possession. In hindsight, he cannot be certain which path he would have chosen if he had successfully taken the watercolor. He reached out and held the gilt frame for about thirty seconds before the guards stopped him. He did not even remove it from the hook. But as he was led away, he felt deep down that the picture belonged to him. He recalls reading about thieves who took two Turners right in the middle of an exhibition; they must have felt as he did that day.

The museum administrators were not terribly upset. Julian made a frenzied explanation, muttered a few words about Stendhal syndrome, and proposed to donate a large sum of money. They dismissed him as an eccentric art lover, banned him from the museum for twelve months, all the while thanking him for his donation as they escorted him out. The incident was mentioned on a local news website. Julian later printed a high-resolution copy of the color beginning and framed it, where it now hangs in his office.

In the Louvre, he stands in front of *Landscape with a River and a Bay in the Distance* until the ache in his legs rouses him. Then he walks out of the labyrinth of the museum, through the sculpture gallery and past the fragment of the torso, which he does not pause to look at again.

Before going to the hotel, Julian wanders around the Tuileries gardens. Between the Jeu de Paume and the Orangerie, in a corridor lined with trees, he comes across a group of bronze sculptures of hands displayed atop six granite blocks: *The Welcoming Hands*, by Louise Bourgeois. Hands intertwined and holding onto one another. Hands that touch, that engage in the process of making something. He understands that the hands are meant to be about union or exchange. But to whom do they belong? he wonders. Why are the hands cut off from the body? Julian places his palm on top of one of the hands. The coldness of the bronze is soothing for a few seconds. But when he looks at the stump where the arm should have been, he is gripped by the fear of disembodied hands that reach toward him in the dark, hands that search for him, and never give up searching, no matter how strenuously he attempts to escape.

Julian pulls himself together. He hurries away from the garden and checks into his hotel in the Rue de Valois. After a short nap, he changes into a fresh suit before heading to the Palais Royal for dinner. He sits on the patio of a restaurant, with a view of the colonnade and the rows of artificial trees. A French family dines at the table next to his. The child is asleep in the stroller. The mother is enjoying her dessert in miniscule bites so as not to soil her pristine white blouse. The man is leaning back in his chair, reading a book. Julian watches them from behind his sunglasses. He begins to imagine the travels of this family, their train journeys, their holiday home in the countryside. He has an inexplicable longing to speak to them. He wants to know what consolation the man and the woman offer each other at the end of an ordinary day, what they say to each other before sleep, how they might hold each other. As Julian is imagining all this, the man finishes his espresso and waves to the waiter for the bill. The woman reapplies her lipstick and puts on her cream-colored blazer before walking toward the trees, pushing the stroller before her.

Julian realizes then that the only people with whom he has conversed over the last few days have been the scholar on the train en route to Milan and the man at Gare de Lyon.

Before returning to the hotel, he takes a detour and wanders through a less familiar part of the district. He passes by an arcade. With all the shops shuttered, the dimly lit corridor appears haunted, so he hurries away from it. On a street near the Opéra, he comes across a house, the upper floors of which are visible above the wire mesh fence. A streetlight is nearby, but most of the building lies in the shadows. The structure is half-demolished, with all its insides exposed. Julian is reminded of black-and-white photographs he once saw, of buildings with enormous circles cut into them, leaving gaping holes like the eyepiece of a gigantic telescope. He stands on the pavement and peers up at the rooms that bear traces of human habitation. The concrete-and-glass block is almost Brutalist, and looks out of place in the neighborhood. Julian speculates that it was social housing, and is now being razed to make way for luxury apartments. He imagines the air that circulated in these rooms—the stench of soiled clothes, breath exhaled by the ill, the stale smell of cigarettes, the scent left behind by children. Even though he has never lived in such a place, there is a sense of familiarity here. These smells enter his mind easily; they are at home in him. For a second, he feels like he is on the verge of retching. He leans over the curb and waits for the nausea to pass. As soon as he regains control, he rushes back in the direction he came.

In the hotel room, Julian attempts to relax on the balcony with a bottle of wine. The Eiffel Tower sparkles in the distance. He flips through Rilke's book on Rodin and comes across a description of all the moving hands in the sculptor's works, next to a photograph of a bronze hand twisted in pain or ecstasy. He likes this idea of "a history of hands," which erases that sense of the uncanny he felt in front of the sculptures in the Tuileries. He copies down the passage in his notebook.

Aside from his mother's hand, and Aidan's for a brief period of time, the only hands Julian has known have been the hands of women. He admits to himself that he does not know much about romance, in spite of the relationships he has had. Over the years, he has cultivated the habit of collecting commonplaces of love: "You are the love of my life"; "I am grateful to have met you." He references these phrases whenever the occasion calls upon him to express the appropriate emotions. Films have also furnished him with a set of indispensable gestures. The persona he presents is that of someone who listens without speaking, one who shares stories that mirror the experiences of the desired subject. In this manner, he told a woman who volunteered with the UN of his own experiences building housing for the poor, even though the information was gleaned from online videos.

Julian doubts that any of the women who claimed to have loved him actually understood love any more than he did. At university, there was a girl named Sophia, who put him in mind of a nymph in the woods. She moved through crowds with a calculated grace, conscious that all passersby marveled at her beauty. Sophia's love for Julian was rooted in his idolization of her, so in a sense she was enamored with the image of herself seen through his eyes.

Daphne, the one with whom he had considered marriage, loved him because he allowed her to demonstrate her capacity for kindness and selflessness. She tolerated his outbursts and never complained when he refused to see her or return her calls.

While he valued Sophia for her beauty and Daphne for her patience, others he had valued for their intelligence or the knowledge that they were able to impart. He kept meticulous notes from the time he spent with scholars, scientists, and journalists. Of all the gratification he felt in romantic entanglements, this collecting was the most important to him, and the random fact or reference formed the ideal memento that he archived with zeal.

Somewhere in the middle of all that, there was Penelope.

At the start of each relationship, Julian would be absolutely certain of the qualities he prized in the other person. But over time, the effect of those qualities wore off. A few years ago, he came close to loving Tessa, who managed a small gallery. He admired her dedication to art and her championing of young artists. But it was the same dedication that fueled her activist work as a feminist, and in spite of her beauty, her intelligence, and the way she made up humorous explanations for all of his scars, he woke up one day and concluded that he could never again listen to her talk about patriarchy and the rights of women to their own bodies.

With Daphne, during a trip they took to Iceland, Julian realized that her impulse to empathize with others infuriated him. A month after their trip, he sent her a dossier consisting of a report and a list of her character flaws that he had observed during their relationship. He was in the habit of documenting every detail. He took notes on arguments, activities, conversation topics, the quality of the sex; he graphed the fluctuations of his own emotions. He then used this information to compile a report, which he sent to the woman upon his decision to disengage from her. For Daphne, he had also enclosed a less-than-flattering photo he took of her while she slept in the hotel. He placed everything inside a beautiful box covered with decorative paper and tied with a ribbon.

When the news arrived months later that Daphne had been admitted into a hospital for depression, Julian was taken aback. He felt sure that he had done what he could and clarified the situation in his dossier. He remembers casually telling Aidan about the incident, during one of their weekend visits to Mornington when their father was still alive, and he remembers Aidan's outrage, which he also found surprising. Aidan told him, perhaps for the first time ever, that there was something wrong with him, and that he needed to change. Julian did not know how to respond to the outburst. He dismissed Aidan's accusation that he discarded the women in his life. Aidan asked, in a rather naïve way, what in their privileged life, the life that they had shared, could have caused Julian to become so cruel. In response, Julian went to the glass cabinet in the Long Gallery, took out a few

Venetian flutes that belonged to their mother, and smashed them to the floor beside Aidan's feet.

That episode resulted in a permanent rift between Julian and his brother. At least that was how he explained the widening distance between them. They never mentioned the incident. In fact, they rarely spoke after that point.

The sky is now completely dark. Julian moves everything inside and take a shower. He notices, during the shower, a mosquito with a half-broken wing, struggling away from the currents of water that could wash it down the drain. In the tight space, there is nothing between this thing and Julian's naked flesh. He feels a certain sadness for it and wonders whether it knows that with a broken wing it can never go anywhere, that all this flailing and twisting is useless. He decides to spare its life.

After the shower, he gets into bed with the Rodin book, ready to start his first twenty-minute interval of sleep. He intends to finish both books before morning. Reading Rilke makes him want to visit the Rodin Museum, to see whether Rodin can change his mind about sculpture, but there is no time. Perhaps he will go on the return journey, as he plans to fly back to New York from Paris, instead of from London.

After reading about Rodin's *The Age of Bronze*, he spends a few minutes studying images of the sculpture online. He had seen a bronze copy at the V&A, and found it unnecessarily sensual, effeminate even, and he felt embarrassed standing in front of the statue. But reading Rilke's description—of the body that has withstood great suffering—makes Julian wants to examine the sculpture again more closely. He proceeds to read about how the first plaster statue made by Rodin is almost certainly lost, but all the copies are exact replicas of the original, so that the statue never really changes regardless of who cast it, when it was made, or from what material.

Rilke also writes of the bronze figure's longing for awakening. Julian admits that he has often felt such a longing, though he is unclear from what he needs to be awakened. All he feels is something opaque forming within, a dark mass floating in the nebulous cesspool that he calls the self.

The reading has led down a path that he does not prefer, so Julian starts his sleep routine earlier than planned. He turns on the alarm and dims the lights. But five minutes into the first interval of sleep, he is still wide awake. He can hear doors slamming shut. Voices pass by in the hallway. Somewhere, a glass shatters on the floor, and muffled swearing is followed by laughter. In the silence of the room, the sound of his watch ticking is also amplified. He holds the watch up to the lamp and scrutinizes the sapphire crystal surface, underneath which a tiny moon made of gold is housed. That moon is the reason he purchased this watch, which has become one of his favorite possessions. He remembers how Penelope had marveled at a perpetual calendar he wore daily at the time when he knew her. That watch broke when Julian fell on the pavement during one of the panic attacks he had following his move to New York. The sapphire cracked; a web-like fracture spread across the surface of the watch. But he decided not to have it repaired.

The alarm sounds; he has not slept at all. He turns on the light and attempts to read more on Rodin. Rilke speaks of the way in which one sculpture turns inward, in a gesture that suggests it is listening to itself. Julian wonders what he would hear if he were to "bend inward," whatever that might mean. Then that line once again echoes in his mind: "You must change your life."

He turns the page and sees a photo of another one of Rodin's sculptures: a woman with her head cradled in her bent arm. It is entitled *Eve*. What Julian sees is a gesture of fear. It is a figure he has come across before. He feels a sudden surge of pain, as if an inner part of him were rending. He clutches at his chest and scrambles out of bed to grab the bottle of sleeping pills that he keeps as a last resort. As he stares at the capsules in his palm, for a brief moment he considers taking more than the prescribed dose. But the moment passes, and he takes the recommended dose of two pills and staggers back into bed.

The last thing he hears before he loses consciousness is the ticking of the watch.

When Julian wakes up the next morning, he is overcome with grogginess. It has been a long while since he has slept through the whole night. He checks his watch and realizes that he has only a few hours left before the train departs for London. He packs his belongings in a hurry. When he steps into the bathroom, he notices that the mosquito is still struggling in one corner of the shower. He turns on the showerhead and washes it down the drain.

After breakfast in the hotel restaurant, he calls a taxi, which takes him swiftly down the boulevards and side streets that he would have liked to experience on foot, if he had woken up on time. As the taxi approaches Gare du Nord, Julian sees a procession of protesters. They are mainly young people, though there are others close to his own age or even older, those who have recollections of a different world. Chants of "égalité" echo down the streets.

Because the vehicle cannot cut through the crowds, Julian is forced to get out of the taxi a few blocks from the station. Pulling his luggage behind him, he stays as close to the walls as possible and elbows others out of the way. As the chants grow louder, the crowd moves faster, buoyed on by a collective longing for change. Julian loses his grip on his luggage and becomes caught in the current of movement that sweeps him past the entrance to the station. In a panic, he shoves the people next to him. Then he feels a fist pummel into his face, followed by the taste of blood in his mouth. Someone grabs him by the arm and smashes him against a wall. A warm stream of blood trickles down one cheek and his vision blurs. Police sirens echo down the street, trailed by shouts and whistles. The current of bodies moves on, leaving Julian behind.

After the asphalt becomes visible again, he looks down to see cuts and scuff marks on his hands. He has no idea how much time has elapsed. In the scuffle, someone took his wallet, phone, watch, and, from his satchel, the tablet and headphones, leaving the books and notebook. His passport and credit card are still in the inner pocket of his jacket. He stumbles back a few blocks and finds his luggage by the side of the road, opened, with the remaining contents thrown across the pavement. The bottle of pills is gone, as is the olive oil he bought, and his designer clothes. The toiletries and underwear remain, and these Julian shoves back into the luggage before heading to the station.

By the time he cleans up in the washroom and puts on bandages, the train he was meant to catch has already departed. He chooses not to report the theft, as such incidents have become commonplace. He checks the schedule and waits for the next train, two hours after the original one. To ensure that he has quiet on the train, he books all the seats in one of the first-class cars, something he wishes he had done on the earlier trains.

Gare du Nord is chaotic. Bands of refugees camp inside and outside the station, filling every available spot, leaving a narrow path for the passengers boarding the trains. Armed guards are posted everywhere. Every few hours, a team of customs officers review the next round of applications, at which point, the crowds rush forth. Some people receive their papers; others are turned away. Those who become aggressive are dragged out of the station in restraints.

Julian purchases a new tablet, phone and headphones, a set of clothes, and rests in the Business Premier lounge, far from the commotion outside. He tries to ignore the pain in his body and the pounding in his head. When the train arrives at last, he is comforted by the emptiness of the first-class carriage. He feels a great sense of relief when the train starts moving. He takes out his books and notebook and places them on the small table. The cover of Kafka's diaries was torn during the scuffle, which irritates him. He flips through the pages he has already written in the notebook—the quotes, the random observations, the sketch of Turner's tree—and he decides that "Landscape" is an appropriate title for the notebook, which he writes on the flyleaf.

Julian feels keenly the loss of his watch, and searches online for a replacement. He scrolls through images of chronographs, perpetual calendars, annual calendars, moon phases, time-only watches, world-timers, and minute-repeaters. He remains so engrossed in the pictures and detailed specifications that he does not notice when the train emerges on the other side of the tunnel. When he looks outside the window and sees the fields of England, Julian feels as though he is hurtling through the unknown. He rushes to the washroom and splashes cold water on his face, which temporarily calms him.

When he returns to the seat, he closes all the blinds, so that the view does not intrude into his consciousness. He knows that the train is moving toward London, but he remembers what the blind man at the station said, about never knowing where one is going, with or without eyesight.

When you walk into the first of the interlinked cage-like chambers, you see children's chairs and school desks. You walk further and you're surprised by an electric chair, an instrument of torture and punishment. In the third chamber you find wooden chairs suspended over a bed, like an invisible committee sitting in judgment over a scene of copulation. You discover scraps of tapestry dispersed throughout the enclosure, representing the mother, the one who weaves and mends. A sense of disquiet descends on you as you exit the space.

Like the other Cells *Louise Bourgeois constructed throughout her career,* Passage Dangereux *(1997) is at once an installation, prison, theater set, diorama, and personal reliquary filled with sculptural forms and found objects. We cannot speak of Bourgeois's* oeuvre *without speaking of the biographical and psychological roots of her art-making. Memories contain the seeds of art. Bourgeois the ragpicker selects fragments from her past and assembles them into brand new wholes in the* Cells. *The recollected past is rooted in childhood, perhaps one marked by trauma. Many of the elements in* Passage Dangereux—*the children's furniture, the starched linen cuffs signifying the father, the wooden chairs from her father's attic—all point to the fragile and intractable bonds of family. In* Cell (Choisy), *an architectural model of Bourgeois's childhood home is placed in the center of the cage, and hanging above the house is a guillotine, which threatens to cut the self off from the past.*

Looking at Bourgeois's works, reading her diaries, and watching her in video footage, we sense helplessness, rage, loneliness, and the fear of abandonment. In a documentary, an elderly Bourgeois is driven to tears when recounting the story of her father carving a piece of tangerine. In another documentary, we watch as Bourgeois smashes a ceramic vase and stomps on the shards in a fit of rage. "The subject of pain," Bourgeois writes, "is the business I am in... The Cells *represent different types of pain: the physical, the emotional and psychological, and the mental and intellectual. When does the emotional become physical? When does the physical become emotional? It's a circle going round and round."*

To walk through Passage Dangereux *is thus to walk through an archive of memories. The past, reconstructed through art, might be defeated. It might even be forgotten. But sometimes the pain returns, and the remembering self—in the form of a child—walks down the corridor of the past, oppressed by the electric chair, and searches desperately for the mother-weaver, fearful of being left behind.*

NINE

FEBRUARY

FEBRUARY 15

Aidan has already fallen asleep. I remain at the desk, with the irrepressible desire to write, to return to that day.

When I woke up on the floor of Julian's apartment, with dust and dried sweat matted on my cheek, I heard the sounds of morning in the city outside. Intermittent laughter, which echoed down the streets at night, was replaced by the cacophony of cars and construction work. I got up, after great struggle, and went to the window. The world appeared unchanged.

I was overcome by the need to walk, to keep moving, without a second's delay. So I grabbed my bag and started walking, away from Julian's building.

The heat had not yet settled on the city. In front of a garden sprinkler, I cleaned my limbs and face as best as I could, shielded by a large shrub. I walked on. Down streets lined with concrete blocks and old housing projects, past glass towers and neighborhood parks, past a segment of the multi-layered London Wall. In the grand lobby of an office building, I saw a large photograph showing an aerial view of the city. I stood outside the window and stared at this image of the city with its domes and spires, its glass monuments and brick terraces. The photograph reminded me of a novel I'd read, in which a character walks from Goodge

Street all the way to Putney Hill, where he kills himself at a look-out with a panoramic view of London. The cityscape is the last thing he sees. As I turned and continued walking west, I considered making a similar journey to a high vantage point, from which I would be able to behold the city one last time.

I walked against the tide of well-dressed office workers. There were some stares as I walked down the street. I have always dreaded appearing different. But after the event, difference was indelibly etched on my body, and the thought of being marked out in the crowd was unbearable. I thus purchased a cap to hide the wound on my head, and long-sleeved jacket and trousers, in spite of the heat, to cover the bruises that had grown and darkened. I kept my head down, hoping that others were too preoccupied with their day to notice me at all. When my phone died, I bought a burner phone in one of the nondescript convenience shops. I ate readymade food from supermarkets and sat in alleyways away from the gaze of others.

That first evening, I chose an unremarkable hotel, clean and sparsely furnished. In the dim light of the bathroom, I cleaned away the grime on my flesh, the dried layers of blood and fluids that were caked on my skin, and bandaged the wound on my head. I double-checked the lock on the door and pushed a chair up against the doorknob. Time splintered that night. I looked at my watch every ten minutes, every thirty minutes, every hour, until the counting ceased to have any meaning. I half-slept in a chair, with shoes on, ready for daylight, ready to keep walking. I wondered if I would ever be able to read a book in the same way again, to study a painting and know that it is beautiful, without thinking of what had happened, what had been lost. I visualized again that walk up to a hill, that view of the city, though I had no idea what method I might use to take my own life.

I fell asleep in the middle of the night, and woke up close to midday, having lost all sense of time. My sleep was feverish, filled with nightmares I forgot upon waking. Not wanting to stay in the hotel room for another night, I checked out and continued walking toward the city center, with my cap pulled over my forehead and my sleeves unrolled all the way down my arms. The movement generated a rhythm by which I could keep certain thoughts at bay.

By nightfall, I reached one of the busiest hubs in the city. I found a spot in front of a locked door, with a view of the crowds, and there I rested for the evening. A few pedestrians noticed me. Some of the glances were sympathetic; others, less kind. There were a few other individuals who sat down against the walls or closed doors in the same alleyway: an old man with a shaggy dog, a young couple with many rucksacks, who may have been on a lengthy trek, and another person whose entire body was covered with a blanket. None of them seemed to notice anything out of the ordinary as I removed my jacket. Amongst this small community of travelers, I could at least find some acceptance. As the night deepened, we each settled into our niches. The residual heat from the day kept us warm.

I continued to observe the passersby throughout most of the night. The nightclub crowd followed the dinner and theater crowd. There were shouts and laughter, the honking of cars, loud conversation and music on speakers. The sounds formed a kind of enclosure in which I could escape the thoughts in my own head. I fell asleep not long after the nightclubs closed. When I woke up, vans were loading supplies into restaurants and cafés, and the early commuters were headed to work in the pale morning light. The young couple had already left, and the person under the blanket was still sleeping. The man with the dog was eating biscuits. When he saw that I had woken up, he walked over and offered me a biscuit and a can of Coke. My cap had fallen during the night, and my wound must have been visible, but he said nothing and smiled as I took the biscuit and drink from him. That was one of the few acts of kindness I had experienced in a long time.

The city is a large mnemonic device. The past seeps through the cracks in the walls and bleeds out of the stones. It would be dishonest to claim that I did not think of the days I spent with Julian. My mind gravitated to the places where I had strolled with him. A short ten-minute walk might take me to a spot laden with moments of togetherness. But those memories were landmines. In the attempt to evade them, I erased those places and drew a new map of the city. This revised London no longer had his street, his entire neighborhood, or the galleries we had frequented. It was a city torn and pockmarked, like the spectral double of a war-torn citadel.

One of the few places free from landmines was the British Museum, which I visited on my third day of wandering. I went through the security check, past the tourists, and walked through all the galleries without any set plan until I covered every inch of the exhibition rooms. Then I repeated the process and went through all the rooms again. The museum was overcrowded; no one paid me any attention. Eventually, my legs tiring, I stopped in the gallery with the Elgin Marbles.

Most of the figures in the frieze were missing heads and limbs, with some of the fragments held in other museums. In one corner of the gallery, part of the South Metopes of the Parthenon, there was a frieze showing a centaur abducting a headless Lapith woman. This was a part of the museum I had never paid much attention to on previous visits. The centaur, bald and bearded, gazed into the distance with blank eyes, his mind already on the next conquest. With her left hand, the woman struggles to loosen his grip. But she fails. The centaur lifts her off the ground and carries her away, in this moment of triumph captured in marble.

I stood closer to the frieze and tried to imagine what went through the head of the Lapith woman as she was abducted by the beast. Seeing her gesture of resistance, I realized that in all the galleries and museums, in all the books, there were images of violence that had hitherto passed me by.

I purchased a notebook in the museum shop and made a rough sketch of the frieze, then sat on the steps outside the museum, watching the crowd in the plaza from under the rim of my cap. I wondered how many people paused in front of that frieze, and if they did, I wondered what they would have made of the fate of this stone woman, shrouded in mythology. I spent most of the day there, on the steps of the British Museum, thinking about the act of violence preserved in stone. The panoramic view of the city from atop a hill intruded into my mind several times.

In the evening, I resumed my walk, notebook in hand, and continued walking west, toward the neighborhood where I grew up. When I reached Dad's house, the lights on the upper floors were lit. I did not knock or go in the front door. Instead, I climbed the fence that divided our garden from the communal garden, and crept in through the conservatory door, which I unlocked with the key I had hidden under a pot long ago. I sank into the wicker chair in the conservatory and slept until dawn, when the sound of the front door closing signaled that Dad had left for work. I took a shower in my old bathroom, grabbed a fresh set of clothes, and exchanged the blood-stained cap for an old straw hat. I then snuck out of the house the same way I came. I texted Aidan to say that I was back in London temporarily due to a family emergency, and would not return to Mornington for some time. I texted Dad, saying that I intended to go on research leave. It was impossible to stay there; it was impossible to return to life as it existed before.

From the house, I walked to the river, then along the embankment until I arrived at the Tate, which I could only look at from outside. I rented a room on the top floor of a small bed and breakfast nearby. A Victorian writing desk sat in front of the window, and a single bed was tucked underneath the sloping attic ceiling. I bought takeout and ate next to the open window, watching the lights of the city overtake the fading light of the sun. The Gothic spire of a nearby church appeared like thin metal filing etched upon the deep-blue paper of the sky.

In the small bathroom, I washed myself again and again, using the hottest setting for the water, scrubbing until the skin turned red. I changed the bandage on my head, and put on yet another set of clothes; more blood had stained the fabric. When the steam evaporated, I caught my reflection in the small oval mirror: the creases on the forehead, the dark circles under the eyes, the dull skin. I had forgotten how old I was, for it seemed I had aged rapidly, and had taken on the face of someone who was approaching death.

The next morning, after waking up from the first full night of sleep I'd had for days, I wandered around the neighborhood, retracing the same routes over and over again until I could recite the names of the streets, the colors of the buildings, and the shapes of the trees. I was careful to take the side streets in order to avoid the crowds. By then my feet had already become blistered and swollen from the walking. My legs weakened and regular breaks were necessary.

While resting on a bench near Tate Britain, I saw someone I recognized. I referred to her as "the Mapplethorpe Woman," because I did not know her name, and because whenever I had seen her in the reading rooms at the British Library during my research days, she always had with her a collection of Robert Mapplethorpe photos spread out on the desk in front of her. I wanted to speak to her, but never found the right opportunity. I was curious about her interest in Mapplethorpe and wished to know her thoughts on his sensual calla lilies, with their sinewy veins and the undulating petals that arch upward.

When I saw her coming out of the Tate that day, I impulsively decided to follow her, without any intention of speaking to her. I walked a few paces behind her to the nearest Tube station. I hesitated outside the entrance, reluctant to walk into the crowd. But I was overpowered by the desire to see more of her, so I pulled down my hat and walked into the station. I temporarily lost sight of her, but caught up with her again on the northbound platform. On the train, I sat at the opposite end of the same car. She was absorbed in whatever she was listening to through her headphones for the duration of the fifteen-minute journey, after which she transferred at a major station. I followed her down the corridors and onto an eastbound train. She disembarked at Angel, and there I could not follow, that area having been erased in my revised map of the city. I remained in my seat, and as the train departed the station, I watched as the Mapplethorpe Woman, in her red dress, disappeared up the stairs.

For the rest of that day, and for the subsequent weeks, I spent hours on the Underground, roaming the subterranean city, traveling on different lines, from station to station. Beneath the surface, the city was without boundaries. Zones that were fraught with memories became indistinguishable from all other zones.

My time was occupied with observations of the other passengers. I imagined the origin and destination of their journeys. I perceived the fatigue in their bodies, the way some people slumped over the bags held in their laps. There were those with an unmoving gaze fixed on their screens, contrasted with the shifting eyes of those eager to be distracted. Most people withdrew to an inner world and paid little attention to their surroundings.

I became accustomed to the presence of other people. During rush hour, as I stood on the train, buffered by the bodies of strangers, I felt a sense of security. My appearance started improving; there were no longer any stares. I felt I could perform the role of a woman on her way to work—like everyone else, wrapped up in the plans for the day.

In the evenings, I returned to the bed and breakfast near the Tate and took long, hot showers, and slept. At dawn, I got up before the morning rush and started another day on the Tube. By then, the summer heat had died down, and the warmth of the Underground was welcome.

There were a few people I learned to recognize on the daily commute. A young man who had a book in hand every day, who progressed from the beginning of *In Search of Lost Time* to its end. A woman who looked unspeakably sad every day. One morning, when she got on the train in tears, most people pretended not to see her, save for one couple who offered her a tissue and said, It will be all right.

I also glimpsed the lives of others through overheard conversations. One time, a woman spoke loudly on her phone as she accused a lover of infidelity; everyone pretended to be reading or listening to music, but the tenseness in their bodies suggested that they were all eavesdropping as she shouted, It's over, you fucking piece of shit. It's over. After she disembarked, shouting more obscenities as she went, there was a marked relaxing in everyone's postures.

Another time, two well-dressed young men were discussing an exhibition, with the self-consciously loud voices of those who were eager for others to take note of their opinions. One said, I'm surprised that they gave him this entire exhibition. I've always thought of him as rather... well, mediocre.

The other replied, Yeah, I'm not sure about the painting from memory technique. If you try to reconstruct something over the span of years, or if you try to reconstruct an event that happened a long time ago, how accurate can it be?

I did not catch the name of the artist whose work they deemed mediocre, but the concept of painting from memory seemed to me a compelling one. I wished I had the courage to go up to them and converse with them about the artist, but at that point, I still could not bear to speak to strangers for long, to have them look into my eyes, fearful that if they were to do so, they would intuit all that I had struggled through.

My use of the Tube became more erratic. Sometimes I disembarked at a random station and switched lines, going up stairs or escalators, down long tunnels. I disregarded signs or directions until the end of the day, when I needed to go back to the bed and breakfast. Other times, I allowed myself to be buoyed by the current of the crowd, carried down the paths taken by the majority of commuters.

When I tired of the Tube, I switched over to the DLR and the Overground. I traveled to stations with bizarre-sounding names that I recited to myself, as though they formed a litany. The further the train moved from the city center the more murals and graffiti I saw, the colors and images that seemed to compose the true face of the city, revealed upon arrival or departure. From the train window, I was also able to peek into the houses closest to the tracks, rooms in which people worked, lived, passed in and out of the episodes in their lives. I tried to imagine what they had gone through, yet I was unable to envision anything that was not corroded by grief or violence.

On one of the Overground lines furthest from city center, I reached the end of the line and wandered around the outer zones of the city. I had expected to find desolate streets lined with factories or wind-flattened meadows. But instead, there were signs of the city encroaching on its periphery. Giant diggers, paused in mid-lift, stood in front of mounds of dirt. The cranes and scaffolding were decked with lights, and the forklifts hummed gently beside the rubble, ready to build upon the ruins. Cement mixers churned endlessly, and down the orange chutes came the debris of dying buildings.

In a vacant lot cleared for construction, a lone, sculptural tree stood. Small flowers traced a border around the lot. My mind drifted back to one of the garden tours I went on with Dad.

En route to the garden, we'd passed by a mound of dirt, left over from a construction project that had been put on hold. It's a brownfield site, Dad told me. But amongst the garbage and abandoned building materials, wildflowers and grasses had sprouted. Ruderal species, these plants are called, from the Latin *rudera*, meaning "rubble." They were not attractive botanical specimens, and they would not have been welcome in the garden to which we were headed, where even the appearance of wildness would have been deliberately cultivated. But there was something reassuring about the rebirth of the natural after the disturbances of the land. Dad spoke of how the delicate blades of grass also evoked a sense of forgetting, like the grass that grows over battlefields. But maybe this kind of forgetting is necessary. Perfect recollection, even if it were possible, would be another form of destruction.

I walked further from the Overground station and chanced upon a community living in makeshift shelters cobbled together from plywood and sheets of corrugated iron. I slowed my pace as I approached. Three individuals were sitting around a fire, their heads bent together in conversation. About five others were sitting very still and looking in the direction of the river, as if they expected someone or something to arrive imminently. Observing them, I was reminded of an entire literature of waiting, starting with Penelope waiting by the loom. I read somewhere that the state of waiting is like the state of dreaming. One is never certain of what one sees. Events fuse together and time expands.

In retrospect, I realize that in spite of all the movement across the city, I was in some ways standing still and waiting for Julian's return. His image was superimposed on every sight. I searched for him on the trains, on the streets, inside cars stopped at traffic lights, at tables outside cafés. At night, right before I fell asleep, I traced the cadence of his voice when all other voices had receded into the background. I imagined listening to him speak of the things he loved or desired, but never about the things he feared or regretted. Those words were not a part of Julian's vocabulary.

I have often wondered why Penelope, my namesake, waits for Odysseus, never gives up waiting. And how throughout all that waiting, she weaves her tapestry. Waiting gives power to the other; the one who waits is wholly dependent. Maybe Penelope weaves and unweaves her tapestry as a way of allaying both the fear of losing Odysseus and the anxiety about never being free from this dependence on him. Never being free from the memory of him.

That night, after the walk in the edgelands of the city, I returned to the little room near the Tate and cried for the first time since what had happened. I trembled in the bed and cried until my body lost all strength. Then I fell into a deep, dreamless sleep.

After a month of daily journeys on the train, I moved back into Dad's house, having sent Aidan a message requesting extended leave from the Library. I did not say anything to Dad until much later, and in those first few weeks back at home, I evaded conversations, left the house early each morning, and returned late. Dad believed that I was doing research somewhere, but I continued to walk in the city every day, in our neighborhood or further west. The calluses on my feet hardened, and my legs stopped aching in the night. The head wound healed. The bruises turned deep purple then moss green, before fading into pinkish-brown blotches.

Three months or so passed. By late autumn, I had charted familiar routes for my walks. One of my favorite routes was by the river, which took me past the Tate. One day, I did not pass the building, as I usually did, but went inside. It was a place freighted with memories. But I did not want Turner to belong to a past from which I had been severed. That space, those paintings, needed to be reclaimed.

I walked straight into the Clore Gallery and sat on one of the benches. Beheld in a single view, the Turners blended together, a variegated collection of blue, gray, and pale yellow. Directly in front of me were two works. The first was *A Disaster at Sea*, portraying the drowning of 108 women who were abandoned by their captain. Some of the figures were bent over in despair, their contorted bodies in danger of being swallowed by the white waves. A child lay on its back in the mother's arms, appearing almost peaceful. The dying women and children formed the nucleus of the painting, around which the storm raged.

The second painting was *The Rape of Proserpine*, on loan from another gallery. It brought me back to the metope of the Lapith woman in the British Museum. I was also reminded of a statue of Proserpine I had seen, capturing the moment when she was dragged into the underworld, where her body would be entombed in darkness as winter ravaged the outside world. But in the Turner, there was springtime and sunlight. The resin varnish had discolored the painting, and the unnatural amber hue accentuated the brightness of the rays of light that pierced the clouds. The vast landscape, against which the act of violence occurred, was almost serene. The viewer's gaze might even glide over Proserpine's pale body in the lower left-hand corner of the scene, her arms reaching toward her powerless, lamenting companions.

But there were two easily overlooked parts of the painting that echoed the violent act: the pile of ruins on top of the hill in the distance and the bare branches of the tree, their lines mirroring Proserpine's outstretched arms as she was dragged away by the god of the underworld.

Facing *The Rape of Proserpine*, I felt I was seeing, for the first time, an artist I have always known.

After some time in front of the painting, I took out the note-book I had started at the British Museum. I settled on a seat in a V-shaped alcove by a window, with a view of the courtyard outside and the paintings in the gallery. I began to write. About the pictures on the wall, about decay and darkness.

Elsewhere in the Tate, there were more portrayals of female bodies, displayed and exposed. Seated in front of those art-works, I continued writing. When the first notebook was filled, I purchased another one from the shop and continued writing. At home, I went online and collected images that echoed the ones I encountered in the gallery. Many of them, once seen, cannot be unseen. Some of the pornographic *shunga* drawings, or erotic art, from the Edo era in Japan, I could only glance at with squinted eyes, so horrific was their effect. In one picture, a crematorium worker violated the corpse of a woman he had dressed, her limbs dangling lifelessly over his grotesque body. In another, a woman was gagged and bound, her ankles tied to the ends of a pole so that her legs could remain spread wide apart while the man, with his genitalia distended and engorged, plunged into her. In the background, there was a scythe-like crescent moon above a twisted pine tree.

I consulted academic studies on the subject and added to the notebook, weaving the scholarly references into my own ekphrastic fragments. The result was a haphazard tapestry of images and words that my academic colleagues would have scoffed at. Language broke free, and I was no longer constrained by the strict discourse that had bound me throughout my educa-tion. The concern for argument, for clarity even, fell away. There remained only the art and the eyes that see.

I moved from paintings to sculpture and photography; I moved across eras. There were times when rage swelled within me as I analyzed the artworks, times when my feelings were con-firmed by Artemisia Gentileschi's *Judith Slaying Holofernes*, by that act of cutting. But most days, the images gave a mysterious coherence to things. I have never known the lasting truth of any work of art—I do not even know if such a truth exists—but while studying those pieces, I reached a new understanding, one that tied together all the analyses I had read of the female nude and the male gaze in Western art. Because for once, I stood in front of the artworks as the figurative body depicted.

Between the fragments, I interleaved literary passages that address the same subject. One passage that I reread multiple times was by Kafka, about an anthropomorphized bridge that stretched across an abyss. One day a man came along and jumped onto the bridge, right in the middle of its body, until the bridge shook with unbearable pain and, torn in half, plunged down into the abyss where it was pierced by the sharp stones beneath. The shocking and inexplicable violence of the scene resonated with an image I had in my mind, of my body being broken up from within, shattered into countless shards thrown down a dark and immeasurable ravine.

I wrote every day, swiftly and instinctively, at the desk, in the gallery, on park benches. It was as though this ritualistic writing was purging me of the self I was when I had walked through the city earlier that year. Never again did I consider walking up a hill and taking my own life while looking at the panorama of the city. Through the writing, the waiting ended, and a new experience of time began. Waiting was oriented to a future endpoint, the point of longed-for return. But writing spoke of the past and the present, of their hold on the future. Through writing, I accepted that there would be no return. At one point, it was only a month since what had happened with Julian; then it was six months; then a year; two years; a decade; two decades. Mere seconds in geologic time.

Since that day at the Tate, I have continued to keep a notebook. From the fragments on art and the passages extracted from books, I moved on to other images and ideas. This present notebook, the forty-second, is the successor to all the preceding ones. At times it seems as if everything that happened with Julian led to the creation of these notebooks, as if what matters is not the event itself, but what I chose to do with it.

That winter, I photocopied pages from the notebooks and gave them to Dad before I told him the truth. We spoke of the assault without using the actual word, and for a time, there was a lacuna between us where the word ought to have been.

You should never have gone to that house, Dad would say almost every day. He asked repeatedly, Why? How could he have done such a thing? I need to understand why. To which I replied, Does it matter why? It doesn't matter.

Dad fell ill for a period of time, then started calling lawyers and doctors. It took tremendous effort to persuade him not to pursue the matter further. I had heard stories of other women and men, in circumstances resembling or not resembling mine, who had had their experiences taken from them, rewritten in legal jargon, reinterpreted by others, and lost in the labyrinth of proceedings. I did not want to go through any of that. What happened to me, I told Dad, is a private matter. The event is mine alone. He cried even more; we argued. In the end, he gave in, though I could never tell whether he really understood my reasons. He continued to compile a collection of articles on trauma, court cases, news clippings, even photos of Mornington Hall, creating a bizarre scrapbook.

I stayed at home with Dad for a few months. During that time, Aidan sent me multiple messages. I did not respond. And one day, he showed up at our house in London. He explained how Julian had signed over Mornington to him before moving to New York, how the Library was still in need of a librarian and archivist, and how he missed my presence.

We took a walk that day, when Aidan visited me, and some-where by the river, I told him what happened. He, too, cried, one of the few instances when I have ever seen him cry.

I had the feeling, Aidan said, that Julian is like brittle glass. If you touch him, he will shatter into a thousand pieces. It's ironic that he enjoys smashing things. He destroys things in his path, so nothing can touch him.

What do you think happened to him? I asked Aidan. Something must have happened to him.

I have no idea, Aidan said. Nothing happened when we were young except our mother passed away, but Julian didn't even seem that upset. I don't think I really know him, even though we grew up together. It's a weird feeling, to have spent so much time with someone and not know them at all. Maybe nothing can explain how a person becomes like that. Maybe an explanation is not even necessary. It won't change what happened.

I was intrigued by his mysteriousness, I said. I thought it concealed something deeper within, something that might resonate with what's in myself. But now I wonder if there was anything there at all.

Julian shrank back from all those relationships, Aidan said. And the things he did. I could never understand why. I am not suggesting that anything could justify what he has done.

No. I know.

There was silence between us for a few minutes, punctuated by the sound of the traffic and the river in front of us.

Then Aidan said, I can't say I will ever fully understand what you've been through, how you feel, but I will try.

He looked at me as I continued gazing at the buildings across the river, and he placed his hand on my shoulder. I turned to him and smiled, the first time I had smiled at anyone in a long while.

A few months later, in yet another unbearable summer when insects thrived and melting ice flooded into the sea, I moved back to Mornington Hall with Aidan and resumed my role as librarian and archivist. The house, too, was a place I needed to reclaim.

At first, when you step into the empty gallery space, the silhouettes on the wall appear innocent enough. Come closer, and the shadow figures seem to thaw and jump into a dance of violence and eroticism. Gone: An Historical Romance of a Civil War as it Occurred b'tween the Dusky Thighs of One Young Negress and Her Heart *(1994) is one of Kara Walker's earliest cut-paper panoramas, which use racially charged images mined from the antebellum South to critique racist stereotypes and expose the horrors of slavery.*

On the far-left side of Gone, *a young genteel couple lean in for a kiss. Upon closer inspection, the viewer detects another pair of legs under the lady's skirt. As the legs are shoeless, they most likely belong to a slave, who is engaged in something unspeakable with the white mistress. Meanwhile, the gentleman's sword is about to stab a Black girl who stands behind him. On the far-right side of the panorama, there is another couple, a white man—as indicated by his outfit—who holds a Black woman on his shoulders. His head vanishes into her voluminous skirt, so that his actions are unseen. But judging from the woman's vomit, it is an act of violation.*

Gone *is incendiary, like Walker's other black-paper silhouettes which include acts such as rape, bestiality, defecation, and lynching. Walker reinvented the benign decorative craft to establish a radical type of history painting, one where the gruesome and the obscene are deliberately juxtaposed to the delicacy of the paper medium.*

These transgressive tableaux also resist a simple opposition between oppressor and oppressed—an aspect of Walker's work that has attracted criticism. In Gone *and other pieces, there is complicity between the slaves and white plantation owners, even instances in which the slaves turn on their masters—as suggested by the pair of legs under the mistress's skirt. The roles of slave and slave master are reversed and re-enacted ad infinitum; everyone takes turns brutalizing one another in a whirlwind of abjection and rage. In Walker's world, no one is free from degradation and no one really triumphs.*

TEN

APRIL 9, LATE AFTERNOON

Even with the blinds drawn, Julian can picture in his mind the scenery passing by outside the train window, unraveling like a documentary of the country. He raises the blinds. In the distance, high-tension pylons stretch across barren fields in an unbroken succession. The train passes by a junkyard with a gigantic sign that reads, "The Future is Waiting." The phrase strikes Julian as ironic, for he cannot imagine what future awaits a place such as this.

There are as yet no signs of the city.

He draws the blinds closed again and resumes his reading. But Kafka never engages his attention for long. He is annoyed by the writer's fixations on the body and his relentless self-consciousness. He switches to the Rilke books. Next to a photo from the Rodin Museum, of a cabinet filled with sculpted hands and limbs, there is a passage from Rilke's letter describing the plaster models in Rodin's Paris studio, with the torso of one figure lying next to the arm of another. But instead of seeing these fragments as separate atoms that need to be combined into wholes, Rilke regards each as complete in itself, without any need of being united with other pieces. Julian likes this idea, so he copies down the passage in his notebook.

The image of the sculptor surrounded by fragments reminds Julian of Sir John Soane's Museum in London, which he had first visited with Penelope all those years ago, on one of their collecting trips. He walked through the museum, looking at the collection of antiquities and paintings while stealing glances at Penelope. Sometimes she caught his gaze and smiled back at him. She seemed wholly content in that bizarre place, which was at once a house, a museum, and a mausoleum. The gloomy, crammed spaces depressed Julian. But as he watched Penelope—the only living thing in a room of stones—standing next to the marble sarcophagus beneath the dome and the pantheon of busts, he felt that he had discovered something hitherto unknown to him.

He remembers the way that she absorbed everything in museums and galleries, like one who was voracious after a bout of starvation. In bookshops, she had the habit of running her hands down the spines in order to browse the titles. And she would stand and read the first few pages of a given book, her finger tracking the progression of each sentence, allowing time for the words to sink in.

There are other images that remain with him. He sees Penelope standing still in the middle of the Millennium Bridge as the crowd flowed by. He sees her hand that he held in his as they stood above the rushing river, and he can trace the lifeline on her palm, the only line that can be followed through the chaos and clamor of the city, the line that has remained clear and true in his memory for more than twenty years, amidst the untold alleyways, intersections, and dense network of streets through which he has traveled.

In those days with Penelope, Julian observed how she was developing an attachment to him. He embraced it at times. But at other times, he could not bear the suffocation. The longing and tenderness could be replaced so quickly by the impulse to lock her image away in a vault from which it might never escape.

In all those nights they spent together, he was terrified—of those hands and legs, of the power she had accrued over a short span of months.

That afternoon, back in the apartment, after their visit to the Soane Museum, Julian rested in an armchair as exhaustion crept over him. Penelope was standing at the kitchen counter, making a cup of tea and buttering a slice of toast. He listened to the clinking of the spoon against the side of the mug, the knife scraping against the toast; he smelled the tea and butter. At that instant, not for the first time, he felt the impulse to kiss her, and felt the desire weigh on him more and more as the hands on the clock inched forward, as she sat down at the desk with her tea, as she asked him what was the matter, to which he responded by pulling her toward him.

The train enters the darkness of a tunnel and Julian is drawn back to Turner's *Rain, Steam, and Speed*. He imagines the early days of the railway, around the period when the painting was completed, when the passengers were equally shocked and amazed by the speed of the train, which carried them across land at a fraction of the time it would have taken before. But the train also hurtled them toward an unknowable future, when the individual's experience of *durée* would be replaced by the measurable chunks of time imposed by the clock, when accidents could occur at any given moment, jolting spines out of place or reducing bodies to crimson pulp. Even if the body survived, the mind might be injured irreparably, and the memory of seeing red would re-emerge at the most unexpected moments to haunt the consciousness.

It strikes Julian that one's perception of time is never reliable. One lives through many slices of time, in each of which one performs a different role. In one, he is an art historian; in another, an architect. A lover. A victim. A killer. A rapist. Entire lives might rise up from the depths and intermingle with the real. Other lives remain submerged, like heavy chests sunken at the bottom of the sea, unacknowledged by the self and unseen by others.

Julian can never tell how much time he spends within each role. Sometimes, the role is fleeting, a matter of hours. Other times, days, even months, might go by without his paying much attention. Time slips away from him as the train proceeds from the countryside to the outskirts of the city. Time slips away as he stands over the sink in the suffocating bathroom of the train, splashing water on his face so that his reflection, when he looks up in the mirror, is shrouded with water. His vision only clears when he emerges from the bathroom and sees before him, on the wall, a poster advertising an upcoming exhibition on Francis Bacon, featuring part of the triptych *Three Studies for a Crucifixion*. A mangled body—which might be human—lies in agony on what appears to be a divan, after molestation or butchering, unable to escape or cry for help, reduced to a thing in the slaughterhouse. No beauty of the nude here, no promise of redemption. Just flesh punctured and slashed. It is an image that Julian has always felt in tune with, and he has long admired Bacon, even though he can only tolerate the works in black and white. This direct confrontation with a lurid print that enlarges the details of the gashed body floods Julian's mind with thoughts of pain. He wonders what Bacon had seen and felt to have his imagination so consumed by images of meat.

The painting's mess of red, black, and orange fills Julian's field of vision as he staggers back to his seat. He has beheld that same red in real life, in one of the many roles he has inhabited. He wonders what he would find if he were to peel back time, layer by layer, like peeling the skin off of a carcass: peel back his last twenty years of wandering; his time of togetherness with Penelope; peel back that afternoon when he was overcome by the need to consume her, when he imagined her as the most beautiful possession he had ever held in his hands; peel back the time in adolescence when he yearned to leave his childhood home; peel back the first time he learned the infinitesimal delay between a cut and the subsequent surge of pain, the absolute pain that shrinks a whole life to a tiny point in the flesh, pain without end that threatens to blot out consciousness and obliterate the experience, as though the cut never occurred at all. If he were to peel back all these layers, to a time before he knew the line "you must change your life," before he first saw blood pouring forth from a wound, he does not know what he would find at the center of it all.

Perhaps he would unearth a fragment of childhood shrouded in dense fog, an event he had seen, or half-seen, when he hid in the tree house in the park at Mornington, concealed by the foliage of the ash trees, an image that is now impossible to anchor in time, impossible to define, and impossible to distinguish from fear-infested reveries. In the tree house that night, Julian learned how easy it was to sever a limb from the body, with two swings of an axe, how the body of the unknown person—male, female, or child—became doll-like, lying limp at the feet of the axe-wielder, whose face remained in the shadows, whose large movements demonstrated the dynamism of the living body that cut, lugged, dug, pulled, and pushed the inert doll inside a hole in the ground before going off with a small object wrapped in cloth, which must have been a severed hand, or so Julian thought. He wanted to meet this person who trespassed on his family's land, he wanted to ask the axe-wielder why he kept the hand, whether the hand meant something to him, if it brought him the same comfort that the teddy bear brought Julian, which he kept in secret and which he hugged to his chest that night after the axe-wielder was long gone and he snuck back into his room, terrified of the twilit shape in the woods. Yet the next day, in the sunlight, Julian still returned to the spot where the act he witnessed took place, with his teddy bear in his rucksack, to find no blood anywhere, only disturbed earth, where bluebells continued to grow year after year, on that spot in the woods where he knew death to exist. Julian did not understand how there could be no blood, so perhaps he had imagined it after all, perhaps there was no man in the shadows, nothing other than his own fears that had taken the shape of an axe-wielder. Perhaps he no longer needed the teddy bear now that he was seven years old, and could put it back in its hiding place, lest anyone should find it and throw it away because it had become so ragged, even though it was the thing he loved best. Sometimes, at night, he held the teddy's soft paw the way someone might hold a hand.

Julian goes back into the corridor to look at the Francis Bacon poster again. He suddenly smells a putrid scent. It is the irrepressible stench of death, like the rotting corpse of an animal slaughtered at the height of fear and panic. He is uncertain whether the poster has somehow caused the smell. He tries to open a window, but they are all sealed shut. The stench swells. He rushes down the aisle of the train carriage in search of its source. But there is nothing.

He peeks outside: the train is approaching the city center. Open fields and derelict warehouses have given way to new developments. Close to the station, beyond the parapet, there are ring-like gasholders that have been converted into luxury properties, glowing under the clouded sky.

Julian also glimpses a faint reflection of himself in the dark gleam of the train window, superimposed on the cityscape. His posture is worse than he had feared, and he resembles something else out of a Francis Bacon painting, a grotesque grayish-white creature with an absurdly elongated neck that ends in an open mouth lined with sharp teeth. Julian recognizes himself as this monstrous, frightful thing, and even as he attempts to shorten his neck and keep his mouth firmly shut, he sees the sickly pale creature climbing out of him, its teeth biting into the side of his face, its hiss declaring to him that perhaps he has done wrong.

An announcement informs passengers that the train has arrived at St. Pancras International. Julian looks back at the reflection, but the creature is no longer visible. Passengers begin to disembark. He grabs his luggage and hurries off the train, except he does not go toward the exit like the other passengers. Instead, he goes to the end of an adjacent platform, with the feeling of the monster's teeth still in his flesh. He sees the head of the inbound train in the distance. He stares at the tracks and thinks about how easy it would be, how tempting it is, to jump at the second when the train enters the station, before the engine slows down. Death has been on his mind before. Once on the Tube, right after he left Penelope; twice in New York; and another time on a train out of Mexico City. He takes a step past the yellow line.

Julian leaves his luggage to the side and puts on his head-phones. He begins playing the Mahler. He skips to the final movement of the symphony, which he normally avoids because he considers the notes of transcendence and the religious mes-sage ludicrous, but such a message might prove useful at this juncture. After the tremor of the last judgment and the end of days comes the final flourish of trumpets. Then silence. A dis-tant nightingale. And softly, the chorus of saints. *O glaube, mein Herz, o glaube: / Es geht dir nichts verloren!* Although Julian feels the unease that the Mahler inspires in him, his mind is filled with calm as he hears the words that he half-understands, words that spell out to him a different mode of being. *Dein ist, was du gesehnt! / Dein, was du geliebt, was du gestritten!* He takes one step back from the edge of the platform. Julian senses that all the bits and pieces of his own self that were spilling out into the open are being slowly stowed back within him. The fanfare and the pealing bells evoke the magnificent space of a concert hall with red velvet curtains framing the proscenium arch. He closes his eyes and imagines standing alone in front of the orchestra, the music washing over him like the caress of a breeze. He takes another step away from the edge. *Bereite dich zu leben!* The long-necked monster loosens its grip.

When Julian opens his eyes, he sees on the concrete platform a white blotch that indicates something had been spray-painted over, possibly graffiti or a sign that is no longer relevant. He remembers a note in the introductory section of the Rodin book, about how the original plaster cast of *The Gates of Hell* at Meudon contains numerous voids where the figures had either been removed or were not yet added. *Aufersteh'n, ja aufersteh'n wirst du.* As the symphony approaches its finale, Julian closes his eyes again and pictures the gates filled with many gaps, resplendent in their incompleteness.

The inbound train rolls into the station. He looks at his reflection in the train window. The pale monster has receded into the dark void. He removes the headphones, picks up his bags, and walks toward the exit with the other passengers.

St. Pancras International remains largely unchanged, despite the time that has elapsed since Julian lived in London. The crowds are less unruly than at the Paris stations, though there are groups of travelers who are confined behind a transparent plexiglass partition, where they are told to wait indefinitely for permission to enter the country.

Julian passes through the border control and enters the station, lined with many of the same shops and restaurants he remembers. He crosses the street to the other side of the transport hub, where he is supposed to catch a train to Oxfordshire.

He stands for a few minutes under the atrium of the western concourse of King's Cross station, with the latticed steel ceiling that fans out like the branches of a large tree. Just as he debates whether to find a chair and take a break, he hears cheers and claps coming from outside. He follows the crowd into the plaza and sees the rain.

All around him, people are rejoicing. The station and surrounding area lie in the opening between two geodesic domes, so the rain hits the ground unhindered. A couple begins dancing. Others cup rainwater in their hands and drink it. A toddler jumps into a small puddle with glee. Julian stands in the middle of the plaza and gazes up at the sky, straining to keep his eyes open as the rain obscures his vision. He holds out his hands and collects water in his palms. Notes from the final movement of Mahler's symphony reverberate in his mind. The rain comes down more heavily, and most people retreat to the awning outside the station. Julian continues standing in the plaza. The rain seeps through his clothes. It falls on the glass, steel, and bricks of the station. It falls on the desiccated parks of the city, on the temporary structures and geodesic domes alike. The rain falls on the ruins new and old, on the living and the dead, and on all that refuses to die.

Perhaps the rain is falling on Penelope and on Mornington Hall, which, Julian recalls, is to be demolished the next day.

As he squints his eyes to survey the scene around him, he sees a woman who resembles Penelope run into the station. An unexpected pang spreads across his chest. He reminds himself that he does not know what she looks like these days, since his only reference point is from two decades ago. The woman is soon out of view. For a second, he considers running after her, but he decides he cannot take that risk.

Julian returns to the station—not to the national rail side, but back to the Eurostar. He purchases a ticket for Paris. When he takes out his wallet, he realizes that the vintage train ticket he kept in his old wallet for so long was lost during the scuffle outside Gare du Nord.

After he passes through the border control and security checks, Julian lingers on the platform. He closes his eyes and listens to the sounds of the station. Nothing seems to have changed in the world. Travelers still wheel suitcases around;

the speakers still announce arrivals, departures, and last-minute calls. He looks around him. People still embrace to say goodbye. Nearby, two teenage girls run toward each other and hug while jumping up and down. A mother is yelling at a child for dropping his ice cream on the floor.

In the transparent door of the train, Julian sees his entire body reflected. It puts him in mind of a sculpture. The rain can still be heard beating down on the roof of the station. The clock reads 7 p.m.

He boards the first-class car and finds his seat. After doing some research online, he decides that he will go to the Patek Philippe Salons in Paris for a new watch, after he visits the Rodin Museum.

As the train departs from St. Pancras, he looks outside at the buildings in the early evening light, shrouded in raindrops. On a road parallel to the train tracks, a truck draws near, rushing alongside the train briefly, moves away, and comes back for an instant before disappearing behind a row of houses. Another train looms up, blocking the view, then vanishes. As the city re-emerges in the wake of the passing train, Julian concludes that it is far better to see the city at the speed of the train than on foot, at street level.

He puts on his headphones and begins Mahler's symphony once again from the start. As the music glides into the softer second movement, Julian falls asleep, and the train rolls on toward a different city.

Imagine seeing from the far end of the gallery unremarkable dining tables around which families gather. But as you approach, you realize that the wooden tables, though they retain their outward shape, are in fact composed of manifold shards of splintered wood that have been glued together meticulously. The fragile tables might topple over at the slightest touch. You move closer, and notice that the dried, fractured surface of the wood resembles skin that has been cracked by the cold.

Doris Salcedo's Tabula Rasa (2018) is the result of interviews conducted with hundreds of victims of sexual violence (mostly women, but men and teenage boys too). On the outside, life continues (the table form is still recognizable); but inside, everything is broken (the wood has been shattered).

Salcedo's sculptures and installations are frequently read as elegies to the victims of political violence and civil conflicts. But direct representations of the brutalized or lifeless body are absent from her plain, somber works. Instead, we see chairs corroded by acid; furnishing encased in poured concrete; scarred animal tissue punctured and sewn with rough stitches. In La Casa Viuda ("The Widowed House"), doors are detached from buildings; articles of clothing melt into wood and concrete; metallic chairs evoke pain rather than comfort. The viewer contemplates the wounding of these inanimate objects of the domestic sphere, and her imagination conjures up the dismembered bodies and the homes torn apart by dehumanizing acts of violence.

By hiding, erasing, and suggesting, rather than revealing, Salcedo pushes back against centuries of Western art that reproduces, even fetishizes, the figurative body in pain. "I believe," Salcedo writes, "that the major possibilities of art are not in showing the spectacle of violence but instead in hiding it." Silence, she suggests, is the only appropriate response to violence and its aftermath. The silence of the material. The silence of the void left by those who have disappeared. And the silence that envelops the viewer as she stands before the artwork, wrapped in a solemn moment that exposes the inadequacies of language.

In silence, the mind also reflects on the work of repair. Plegaria Muda ("Silent Prayer," 2008–10), a piece that responds to gang violence in Los Angeles, features a series of tomb-like sculptures, each composed of two wooden tables, with one inverted and placed on top of the other. In between the two tables is a layer of earth from which tiny blades of grass grow and reach upward through the cracks in the upper table—a tremulous sign of renewal.

In Tabula Rasa, though the scarred surfaces of the tables bear evidence of mutilation, the rebuilt forms still speak of the need to piece together the fragments of a fractured life. Salcedo has commented on how the victims of assault live with the constant balance between destruction and mending, the unrelenting effort to overcome disintegration. There must be some attempt at a regenerated sense of self. That the tables will never be exactly the same as they were before the splintering is precisely the point, just as Salcedo's Shibboleth (2007), the gigantic crack down the monumental Turbine Hall in Tate Modern, leaves a permanent mark on the restored concrete floor.

ELEVEN

MARCH

MARCH 1

I have been thinking about Turner's studio again, about his habit of hoarding canvases then allowing them to deteriorate in decrepit corners. Ruskin was captivated by the fragility of the paintings, even though he despaired of the conservation challenge that they posed. He spoke of how the colors were in a state of "perpetual revolution," as though the fading and blackening were part of a work in progress.

I wonder if Turner welcomed the decay in order to witness, in the confines of his studio, the changes wrought by time. Perhaps he did not believe in permanence, and instead, valued the effects of the dust, soot, and rain. Or perhaps he simply wanted to see whether time took something away from the work of art or added to it.

MARCH 3

Today was my final session of sitting for Celia. After writing in my notebook in February—or walking through London in the pages of my notebook—I am finally able to attain stillness. For the first time, I observed Celia as she painted—her cautious movements from brush to palette, then brush to canvas; her eyes darting between me and the picture. She stood with her feet slightly apart and her arms stretched out; the brush seemed an extension of her body. At times she would move her shoulders or massage her neck to alleviate the pain of the physical labor of painting.

This final session was longer than the previous ones, but Celia appeared content at the end. Now we wait for it to dry, she said.

We had our usual tea and biscuits, and we chatted about everything except the portrait. We talked about our days at the Slade. We shared our plans for the future. Celia will leave Mornington at the start of next month, a few days after Miranda is scheduled to leave, to join her son for a period. She can't bear to see the house torn down, she said. She has become attached to it even though she told herself never to become attached to a physical place. We aim to spend as much time together as we can in this final month.

BOOK
Leitch Ritchie, *Heath's Picturesque Annual for 1832. Travelling Sketches in the North of Italy, the Tyrol, and on the Rhine.* Published by Longman, Rees, Orme, Brown & Green, London, 1823. Octavo. Blind-stamped red morocco, with gilt motifs on covers. Rear hinge paper cracked. Twenty-six engravings. Extra-illustrated or grangerized by previous owner, with a watercolor of the duomo di Milano pasted in. On another page, a row of early twentieth-century postage stamps glued in the margins.

MARCH 4
Five of the travelers left in February. We had a quiet farewell dinner. We did not play music as we usually do, and everyone spoke in soft voices. What happened in January, with Alex, was a kind of cut that severed the time before from these end days. I feel as though I have woken up from an illness, and that something

has burned away in the feverish dreams, some old attachment to things and places, to a particular notion of dwelling. In some ways, the house has already been demolished, as it is no longer the home we once knew.

Only Celia, Miranda, and Carlos remain. The hallways and the Long Gallery are quiet. There is no more need to oversee the management of the house, so I spend most of my days either in the Library or here in the room, packing and scribbling. I sometimes still see termites behind closed eyes, but from a distance, so that I am no longer amongst them, no longer one of them, digging furiously in the dark.

MARCH 9

Yesterday, Celia told me that the portrait has dried; and after some finishing touches, it is ready to be viewed. She invited me over to the studio today, and I saw it as soon as I walked in, sitting on the easel by the window.

It was unmistakably me, but me as I exist in different times. Even though the image is static, it in fact records in its many layers the dynamic subject that dwells in both past and present. It was me, with my asymmetrical face expressed by the thick impasto, the lines on the pale skin, the hunched-over shoulders, like an animal trying to hide in the forest. There is also, in the glimmer that Celia has painted in my eyes, a hint of what I might become in the future—eyes open, undaunted—so that as I go on living, I might grow into the image painted.

We sat down in front of the easel. Celia said that she had a feeling that throughout the sessions, I was thinking about someone I lost.

I disclosed that I was thinking about a man I once loved, but I left it at that.

There was such sadness in you, she said. But then, during these last two sittings, I saw a change. After so many hours of looking, I feel that I understand the subject sitting in front of me. But of course, much remains unknown. And that too becomes a part of the painting. When the viewer studies the portrait, they will be replicating my process of attempting to understand the subject depicted.

Celia offered me the painting as a gift, as a gesture of gratitude for her time at Mornington. I said I'd like to pay for it but truthfully, I do not have the money. I told her I could not accept something so precious, a project that has taken her months to complete.

We went back and forth for some time. Eventually, embarrassed by my own obstinacy and grateful for her patience, I accepted the gift and brought it back to our bedroom. I covered it with a cloth, self-conscious about the mere existence of a portrait of myself. What I could not tell Celia—and this is the second reason for my initial refusal—is that the possession of such a portrait seems to me a rather narcissistic act. I was debating what to do with the painting when Aidan came in and saw it. He loved the portrait and offered to keep it with his collection of prints and drawings. He said it captures how he sees me, a little timid, but nevertheless looking forward. It achieves what a camera cannot, he said.

BOOK
Virginia Woolf, *A Letter to a Young Poet*. Published by Leonard and Virginia Woolf at the Hogarth Press, 1932. First edition, one of six thousand copies. Stiff paper wrapper, with black-and-green illustration by John Banting, showing a hand holding a pen over a writing pad. Light toning to edges, but otherwise a fine copy.

MARCH 10

I took a walk by myself this afternoon, the familiar route through what remains of the woodland, to check on the remaining trees. All of them are disease-free and have survived the winter. Sometimes, the angle at which one tree leans toward another, or the lines of golden light that fall between the shadows of the trees close to sunset—sometimes these convince me that beauty is still possible.

On the way back through the commons, I noticed the vestiges of a bonfire that someone had started. The patch of charred earth and the remnants of burnt leaves assumed a peculiar shape, resembling that of a human figure. I was reminded of Ana Mendieta, whose work I had written about so long ago. I used to pay more attention to her early pieces, those photographs with explicit violence and goriness. But in recent years, I've been more captivated by her *Siluetas* series, where she portrayed female figures covered in flowers, molded in clay, scorched into the earth, floating on water, or melding with a tree. I find these images strange and sublime; in them, the female body converses with the landscape. Mendieta used earth, fire, and smoke to mark out the body that has suffered. But there is no victimhood there. Instead, the body, vanishing into nature where everything changes and shifts, is a reminder of impermanence and its promise of liberation.

MARCH 11

Approximately one month left until the demolition. One month until Julian's return. For the first time in nearly twenty years, I searched for a photo of him online. It was easy to find one through his company's website. In truth, he does not appear as aged as I thought he would. His gaze remains unchanged. He looks unburdened, tranquil even.

I can picture this face coming toward me, but I cannot guess what he might say to me, nor what I might say to him. It will not be a homecoming for him, because this is no longer his home. Nor will it be a reunion for us, because we will meet as strangers who will not move beyond polite acquaintanceship. We will watch the dismantling of Mornington Hall together. And that will be all. I hope we will be able to look each other in the eyes. For a brief time, we shared a single passion, a fascination with one another. We held between us an intense burst of light that heralded, not the birth of something new, but an ending. I hope we can both acknowledge that much, now that we have lived beyond that death.

In the photo, nothing in Julian's expression betrays what he might be thinking or feeling in the present. But I am no longer seduced by the inscrutability. In hindsight, perhaps I longed to decipher Julian as though he were a painting, observing him inch by inch, hoping to arrive at a conclusive understanding that would mean total possession. But in the end, there was only misreading and incomprehension.

When I was writing that lengthy entry in February, I thought of Louise Bourgeois, sculpting in her studio and transmuting emotions into physical form. Each sculpture was the chaos of memory made tangible. Art as a way of nullifying the past, of moving the self beyond pain. Once the work is done, it has served its purpose. Writing, too, is an exorcism. The past is negated through the act of transcribing words on the page, and the self re-emerges, alive in the here and now.

I fell ill for a few days after writing that entry. In the clouded interstices between waking and sleeping, I had expected to see Julian's shadow, but, instead, I saw Aidan, Celia, and Miranda, and many others whom I've met here at Mornington. When I recovered fully, my gaze was once again fixed on the present. At least until some day in the future, when another image, another event, might bring back the flood of memories. I cannot deny the possibility of that flood. But if that were to happen, I will return to the notebook and write my way out again.

March 14

Without warning, a windstorm swept through the land. The row of beech and pine windbreak trees disappeared years ago, so we are exposed and unprotected. It is impossible to go outside, and even staying indoors has become difficult, as we are constantly distracted by the thunderous roar of the gales and the quivering of windowpanes.

March 15

The wind has become fiercer. I barely slept, worrying about the trees. Peered through the crack in between the wooden planks that Aidan used to barricade the windows, which were strained almost to the point of breaking. I looked toward the woodland and could see nothing save branches and dead leaves blowing past the window. A white shape flickered by, possibly a plastic bag. Against the din of the storm, all I could picture in my mind were the fragile, mangled trees pushed to an early demise. Nevertheless, I hope—against all the evidence of devastation—that the trees survive.

March 17

Just as mysteriously as it arrived, the windstorm passed. We stepped into the parkland, went beyond the ha-has, and looked in the direction of the trees. There was nothing but the empty horizon. The woodland, forced down by the gusts, lay like a cornfield flattened by a harvester. I could not bear to even walk over there. Aidan and Carlos went to inspect the damage with a few of the neighbors, while I stayed close to the house with Miranda and Celia, clearing the debris from the gardens and cleaning the rain gutters. For the whole day, I was inundated by grief. The southeast pavilion is damaged irreparably after a tree fell onto the roof and into the middle of the room where I write in my notebook. I will never be able to write there again.

Before sleep last night, Aidan asked me if I wanted him to describe the extent of the damage in the woods. I said no, I would not be able to bear it. I had not expected to feel this grief for the trees. Now that they are gone, there is not much left for me in this place. I am ready to leave.

BOOK
Ideas for Rustic Furniture Proper For Garden Seats, Summer Houses, Hermitages, Cottages, Etc. Published by I. & J. Taylor, London, *ca.* 1790. Attributed to William Wrighte (unsubstantiated). Quarto. Contemporary cream wrappers; corners worn. Moderate spotting throughout. Twenty-five engraved plates illustrating eighteenth-century furniture designs, with chairs, tables, and garden gates made of delicate branches woven or tied together by ropes.

MARCH 18
Took sleeping pills, yet still restless throughout most of the night. I'm rushing to finish my work on the archive before the demolition. Trying not to look outside the window, trying not to picture the barren space where the trees once stood, the space through which the revving of chainsaws now echoes.

MARCH 24
The mobile home is almost complete—Aidan still needs to install the solar panels and the railing for the rooftop deck.

Today was the first time I've seen the finished interior. The living space—approximately forty square meters—appears much larger than I expected, with an elevated ceiling and a bedroom on the mezzanine level. A wood stove stands in one corner of the main sitting area, and the walls are lined with bookshelves made using salvaged logs. The fragrance of cedar suffuses the room. Sunlight comes in through the large glazed windows and skylights.

This is where we will be able to replicate the corner we had carved out for ourselves at Mornington. I must find some way to continue doing the work that has been so important to me here, though I do not know how just yet.

MARCH 25

We never heard back from the police regarding Alex's theft, nor do we know what happened to him. Aidan was right not to pursue the matter. My resentment toward Alex has faded—not completely, but enough so that I do not tremble at the thought of him anymore. I wonder if he managed to sell the reproduction. Or maybe he has retreated to a hiding spot where he simply lives with the painting. Perhaps its low monetary value is as irrelevant to him as it was to me.

We do not know where the original *A View on the Seine* is. Perhaps it's locked in a vault, along with all the other artworks that will forever be held as important investments. Perhaps it was lost in a disaster. But the fate of the original does not really matter at the end of the day.

I have in front of me the postcard version of the painting. When I look at it, the sadness I felt upon losing the oil reproduction returns, but not in its full force. I have accepted that the painting—both in its original and reproduced form—is gone. But I no longer need the reproduction that Alex stole, for the Turnerian colors and the luminous core at the center of the darkness are lodged in my mind. These details have taken root in my imagination, entangled with the image of Mornington, with those days in the city with Julian, so that I often find myself picturing *A View on the Seine* as if I had painted it. I realize now that perhaps what I meant to say about the painting when I first encountered it had something to do with the *relation* between the waves, the clouds, and the town in the middle. It was a mistake to focus on each separate section, part by part, as I had done. That led to confusion and defeat.

I have seen a photograph of the town Quillebeuf-sur-Seine, taken at the start of the twenty-first century, almost two hundred years after Turner painted the view. The grove of trees had grown and the town had expanded since the early 1800s. The church was there, though it had been renovated. And the same lighthouse still stood on the riverbank.

MARCH 26

Aidan and I are the only ones left in this corner of the house. At night, we are cocooned in the silence. I thought I heard a noise in the walls last night, a faint scrabbling or scratching against wood, somewhere deep in the house. Have the termites returned? Aidan said there is no longer any need to worry, for the house will soon be gone. My fear is that the termites will follow us.

Right before the demolition, Aidan plans to recycle the planks of wood, the marble from the Hall, the fabric from the carpets and curtains, and all the metal parts. His colleagues will join him and the team members from the demolition company to go through the house, removing all the installed fixtures, knocking the glass out of the window frames, sorting materials into piles, and salvaging what they can for future building projects. Afterward, the excavators will move in.

Soon, we too will become bodies on the move.

MANUSCRIPT

Travel diary of Mary Ashworth, from May 7 to June 15, 1847. Duodecimo. Burgundy polished calf notebook, with marbled endpapers. Eighty pages, written in a tidy hand, documenting Mary's journey through Alexandria and Cairo. Severely damaged by pests.

MARCH 28

This morning, I finished my work on the archive. It is as complete as it could ever be. I feel a tremendous sense of relief.

After I packed the final item, I sat down by the window of the Library. A sharp jolt of pain passed through me when I looked in the direction of the destroyed woodland. I turned to my book on Turner. My eyes were arrested by *Ehrenbreitstein, or The Bright Stone of Honour and the Tomb of Marceau, from Byron's Childe Harold*, a painting I saw at an exhibition, right before it was sold to a private collector.

From the lower right-hand corner of the painting, the Mosel runs up to meet the Rhine. In the distance is the town of Koblenz, lost in the blue mist. The viewer's eye follows the line of trees in the foreground, up the curve of the river, and into the depths of the picture.

I imagine a young woman who lives in the town, one of the blue-eyed peasant girls in Byron's poem. Every morning, she crosses the bridge from the old town in the south to the vineyards on the northern bank of the Mosel. There she fills her basket with grapes. Occasionally, she looks up and sees the ruins of the Ehrenbreitstein Fortress. She recalls the nighttime excursion she and her friends once took to an abandoned fortress by the Rhine. They found yellow groundsel flowers growing next to the blood-stained, bullet-riddled walls, and lace-like lichens flourishing on the wooden beams. After a game of hide-and-seek, they rested on the carpet of feathery moss and gazed up through the hollowed-out floors to admire the starry sky. She wonders if Ehrenbreitstein is a suitable spot for such excursions.

At the end of the work day, the girl climbs the hill with her companions, and they sit down near a fountain. There they enjoy the late afternoon sun that bathes the land in a golden haze. As the group chats, the girl notices a man with a sketchbook a few meters away from her. She waves to him, as she has seen him here before, but he remains engrossed in his drawing. She then turns in the other direction and sees the illumined Tomb of Marceau, the "small and simple Pyramid" described by Byron, "crowning the summit of the verdant mound." In school, she had learned that the monument is a memorial to the French revolutionary hero General François Séverin Marceau-Desgraviers, who died in battle. Marceau's bravery was such that friend and foe alike came to the pyramid to pay their respect.

The girl thinks of the brother she has lost in the war. Like Marceau, he too died at the age of twenty-seven. She remembers sailing a boat down the Mosel with him and braving the hazardous waters of the confluence together. She remembers the way he laughed and sang when he drank with friends, much like how the soldiers from opposite sides of the enemy line are drinking by the monument. Every evening, at sunset, the girl has a secret ritual: she whispers to herself a short prayer and a farewell to her brother. After this evening's prayer, she feels the warmth of the sun close in around her, the way skin closes around a wound.

She lies down on her stomach and contemplates the scenery. The moon is visible above the jagged battlements of Ehrenbreitstein. A small fox is sitting on the far side of the field, observing the humans. The girl wonders if the artist who is still sketching will return to this scene, to this moment of repose before the rebuilding begins.

As the rays of the setting sun lengthen, the girl perceives that all solid forms seem to be blurring at the edges. She squints her eyes and observes how the separate elements—the pyramid, the trees, the rivers, the ruinous fortress—blend together in a shimmering pool of vapor and light, from which new images might spring. The landscape she beholds is ever changing, ever shifting, robbed of certainty and predictability. But the girl is fine with that. After all, she has finished her day's work and can look forward to an evening of calm with her loved ones, who wait for her at home.

NOTES

The Louise Bourgeois epigraph is from an interview with Paulo Herkenhoff, in *Louise Bourgeois*, eds. Robert Storr, Paulo Herkenhoff, and Allan Schwartzman (New York: Phaidon, 2003), 22.

Page 3: Ideas and information on Turner's *Ehrenbreitstein* are drawn from the following sources: Peter Aspden, "Ehrenbreitstein, A Painting Outside Time," Sotheby's website (Jun 19, 2017); "Light and Landscape: J. M. W. Turner's Ehrenbreitstein," Sotheby's website (Apr 4, 2017); and the Frick Collection's webpage on *Ehrenbreitstein*. I also consulted Matthew Imms's 2018 and Alice Rylance-Watson's 2013 catalogue entries for *J. M. W. Turner: Sketchbooks, Drawings and Watercolours*, Tate Research Publication.

Page 4: "mouse-eaten or worm-eaten": John Ruskin, *The Works of John Ruskin*, eds. E. T. Cook and Alexander Wedderburn, 39 vols. (London: George Allen, 1903-12), 7:4-5. The state of Turner's studio is also described by Ruskin and his father, as quoted in Andrew Wilton, *Turner in His Time* (London: Thames & Hudson, 2006), 222.

I am further indebted to the following sources for my research on Turner's life and works: Martin Butlin and Evelyn Joll, *The Paintings of J. M. W. Turner* (London: Tate Gallery, 1984); Jonathan Hill, "The Weather in Architecture: Soane, Turner, and the 'Big Smoke'." *Journal of Architecture* 14, no. 3 (2009): 370-2; Jack Lindsay, *Turner: His Life and Work* (St. Albans, Herts: Panther Books, 1973); Franny Moyle, *Turner: The Extraordinary Life and Momentous Times of J. M. W. Turner* (New York: Penguin Press, 2016); Ian Warrell, *Turner on the Seine* (London: The Tate Gallery, 1999); Andrew

Wilton, *Turner in His Time* (London: Thames & Hudson, 2006). Equally important were the Tate website and *Tate Papers*.

Page 4: "millimetre by millimetre...": W. G. Sebald, *The Emigrants*, trans. Michael Hulse (New York: New Directions Books, 1996), 160–1.

Page 11: Information on the provenance of the Poussin painting is from the website of the Metropolitan Museum of Art.

Page 16: The character Celia is partly inspired by the British painter Celia Paul and her book *Self-Portrait* (New York: New York Review of Books, 2019).

Page 20: "sliding slowly into memories": this passage, and the image of the water tank, alludes to Sebald's *Vertigo*, trans. Michael Hulse (New York: New Directions Books, 1999), 82.

Pages 24–5: I am grateful for Catherine McCormack's *Women in the Picture: What Culture Does with Female Bodies* (New York: W. W. Norton & Company, 2021), which was invaluable to this section on the Loggia dei Lanzi, and to all subsequent sections on art. Yael Even's work on Renaissance Italian art was also central to this section, especially her articles for *Woman's Art Journal* (Spring-Summer 1991) and *Notes in the History of Art* (Summer 2004).

Pages 37–8: My description of tree disease and mortality owes much to Sebald's *The Rings of Saturn*, trans. Michael Hulse (New York: New Directions Books, 1999), as well as to the website of the National Trust. Corinne's Fowler's *Green Unpleasant Land* (Leeds: Peepal Tree Press, 2020) was also crucial for ideas on the history of the country house and the English countryside. Additional details have been selected from Ellen Meiksins Wood's *The Origin of Capitalism* (London: Verso Books, 2017).

Page 54: "Perhaps she will struggle at first and cry": Ovid, *The Art of Love and Other Poems*, trans. J. H. Mozley (Cambridge, MA: Loeb Classical Library, 1939), 59; first encountered in Margaret D. Carroll, "The Erotics of Absolutism: Rubens and the Mystification of Sexual Violence." *Representations*, no. 25 (Winter 1989), 4.

Page 55: "Raptus": McCormack, 134; John F. Moffitt, "Another Look at Michelangelo's 'Centauromachia'." *Notes in the History of Art* 25, no. 4 (Summer 2006), 21.

Pages 68–9: For this section on Titian, I consulted the following sources: Emmelyn Butterfield-Rosen for *Artforum* (2022); A. W. Eaton for *Hypatia* (2003); and McCormack, 123-133.

Page 70: "What is the use of them, but together?": quoted in Lindsay, 119.

Page 70: The Soane Museum's website was crucial for my writings on Soane.

Page 73: "expert[s] in longing": John Berger, *Photocopies* (New York: Vintage Books, 1996), 112.

Pages 79–80: For this section on *The Fall of Anarchy*, I consulted Sam Smiles's essay in *Tate Papers* (Spring 2016).

Page 81: "I realize that I am afraid of the physical strain of remembering": this sentence paraphrases a line from Franz Kafka's *Diaries*, trans. Joseph Kresh and Martin Greenberg (New York: Schocken Books, 1976), 233–4. Numerous allusions to or paraphrases of Kafka's diaries are threaded throughout Penelope's chapters.

Page 83: "Yet they lived among forgotten things": this line references V. S. Naipaul's *The Enigma of Arrival* (London: Picador, 2005), 13.

Page 89: The mallard drawing is found in *Collected Correspondence of J. M. W. Turner*, ed. John Gage (Oxford: Clarendon Press, 1980), 231.

Page 94: "a creature tied around the neck with a rope": this image is drawn from Kafka, *Diaries*, 224.

Pages 98–9: Ideas and information on Degas are mainly drawn from Nancy Princenthal's discussion in *Unspeakable Acts: Women, Art, and Sexual Violence in the 1970s* (New York: Thames & Hudson, 2019), 191–3. I also consulted Felix Krämer's article for *The Burlington Magazine* (2007).

Page 100: Information on Turner's Sandycombe Lodge is from Patrick Youngblood's article for *Turner Studies* (1982). Other relevant details were found in Moyle, *Turner*, 247, 281–2.

Page 104: The list in the December 6th entry is inspired by Louise Bourgeois's diary, in *Destruction of the Father/Reconstruction of the Father: Writings and Interviews, 1923–1997* (Cambridge, MA: MIT Press, 1998), 131.

Pages 107–8: These photographs refer to the "Refuge" series of French photographer Bruno Fert, published in *Granta* 149, *Europe: Strangers in the Land* (Autumn 2019).

Page 112: The December 21st entry is in dialogue with Kafka, *Diaries*, 363.

Pages 120–1: For this section on Ana Mendieta, I consulted Nancy Princenthal's *Unspeakable Acts*, 81–9, as well as Olivia Laing's writings on the artist, in *Everybody* (New York: W. W. Norton & Company, 2021) and in an essay for *Frieze* magazine (Aug 13, 2018). Elizabeth Manchester's 2009 catalogue entry for the Tate, on Mendieta's *Untitled (Rape Scene),* was equally important.

Page 121: The details on Kollwitz are drawn from Princenthal, 194.

Page 121: "My art comes out of rage and displacement": this quote was encountered in an article by Emily Labarge, *The Paris Review*, Mar 8, 2019, https://www.theparisreview.org/blog/2019/03/08/ana-mendieta-emotional-artist/.

Page 127: "The house, in his memory": this section alludes to Rainer Maria Rilke's *The Notebooks of Malte Laurids Brigge*, trans. Robert Vilain (Oxford: Oxford University Press, 2016), 15. References to Rilke's novel (henceforth abbreviated as *Notebooks*) are embedded throughout Julian's chapters.

Page 132: "Often limbless too": Mary Ann Caws, *The Surrealist Look: An Erotics of Encounter* (Cambridge, MA: MIT Press, 1997), 53.

Pages 132–4: In addition to Caw's monograph, I am grateful for the work of other art historians, whose research has been vital to this section on the Surrealists, and to the novel as a whole: Carol Duncan on MoMA, for *Art*

Journal (1989); Robin Adèle Greeley on Magritte, for *Oxford Art Journal* (1992); Susan Gubar on pornographic representations, for *Critical Inquiry* (1987); and Hannah J. Wetzel on Hans Bellmer, for *Inquiries Journal* (2021).

Pages 133–4: All excerpts from Bellmer's "Memories of the Doll Theme" are from Sue Taylor's *Hans Bellmer: The Anatomy of Anxiety* (Cambridge, MA: MIT Press, 2000): 28, 45, 53, 84-5. Reprinted by permission of MIT Press.

Page 156: "the excitement and the knots of people": Kafka, *Diaries*, 457.

Page 157: The part in which Julian pauses in front of Poussin's painting is meant to be an homage to J. M. Coetzee's *Disgrace* (New York: Penguin Books, 1999).

Page 157: "learning how to see": Rilke, *Notebooks*, 4.

Page 160: "they are at home in him": this part paraphrases a line from Rilke's *Notebooks*, 28.

Pages 168–9: For the section on Bourgeois, I'm indebted to the following authors and sources: Bourgeois's selected diary notes published in *Grand Street* (Summer 1998); Phaidon's *Louise Bourgeois* (2003); Linda Nochlin for *The London Review of Books* (2002); Anna Souter, *Women's Work: Representing the hysterical body in the late works of Louise Bourgeois* (MA thesis, Courtauld Institute of Art, 2014); and Nancy Spector, "Resentment Demands a Story." *Louise Bourgeois, Structures of Existence: The Cells*, ed. Julienne Lorz (Munich: Prestel, 2015), 73–9.

Page 169: The "subject of pain" passage by Louise Bourgeois was first published in 1991 by the Carnegie Museum of Art, Pittsburgh, in the exhibition catalogue for Carnegie International; it was excerpted in *Destruction of the Father/Reconstruction of the Father: Writings and Interviews, 1923–1997* (Cambridge, MA: MIT Press, 1998), 205. Reprinted by permission of MIT Press.

Page 180: "Waiting gives power to the other": this passage was inspired by a section in Bourgeois's interview in *Louise Bourgeois*, 13.

Page 183: "my body being broken up from within": this sentence alludes to Sebald's *Austerlitz*, trans. Anthea Bell (New York, Random House, 2001), 230.

Pages 183–4: "what matters is not the event itself": Annie Ernaux, *A Girl's Story*, trans. Alison L. Strayer (New York: Seven Stories Press, 2020), 149.

Pages 186–7: For the section on Kara Walker, I consulted Vivien Green Fryd's *Against Our Will: Sexual Trauma in American Art Since 1970* (University Park, PA: The Pennsylvania State University Press, 2019). Equally important were the following articles: Hilton Als and Andrea K. Scott for *The New Yorker* (2007, 2017); Dan Cameron for *On Paper* (1997); Roberta Smith and Julia Szabo for *The New York Times* (2006, 1997); Zadie Smith for *The New York Review of Books* (2020); David Wall for *Oxford Art Journal* (2010); and Marina Warner for *The London Review of Books* (2013).

Page 190: "A lover. A victim. A killer. A rapist": this list is inspired by a similar list in Gabriel Josipovici's *The Cemetery in Barnes* (Manchester: Carcanet, 2018), 41, 101.

Pages 198–9: I'm indebted to the scholars whose essays appear in *Doris Salcedo*, eds. Julie Rodrigues Widholm and Madeleine Grynsztejn (Chicago: University of Chicago Press/Museum of Contemporary Art Chicago, 2015). Additionally, the following sources have been vital to the section on Doris Salcedo: Tanya Barson for *Tate Papers* (Spring 2004); Madeleine Grynsztejn for *Tate Etc.* (Autumn 2007); Cathy Park Hong for *Poetry Foundation* (2015); Andreas Huyssen, "Doris Salcedo's Memory Sculpture: *Unland: The Orphan's Tunic*." *Present Pasts: Urban Palimpsests and the Politics of Memory* (Stanford: Stanford University Press, 2003), 110–121; Claudette Lauzon, "Unhomely Archives." *The Unmaking of Home in Contemporary Art* (Toronto: University of Toronto Press, 2017), 104–136; and Emily Spicer on *Tabula Rasa,* for *studio international* (2018).

Page 199: The Doris Salcedo quote is from Santiago Villaveces-Izquierdo, "Art and Mediations: Reflections on Violence and Representation." *Cultural Producers in Perilous States: Editing Events, Documenting Change*, ed. George E. Marcus (Chicago & London: University of Chicago Press, 1997), 238. Reprinted by permission of University of Chicago Press.

Page 205: "Once the work is done, it has served its purpose. Writing, too, is an exorcism": the language and ideas here are drawn from Louise Bourgeois's writings, *Destruction of the Father*, 142, 257.

In addition to the sources listed above, I am indebted to the following books, which have been foundational to my thinking and writing: Chloe Aridjis, *Asunder* (London: Chatto & Windus, 2013); John Berger, *Landscapes: John Berger on Art* (London: Verso, 2018); Michel Butor, *Changing Track* (1957), trans. Jean Stewart (Richmond, Surrey: Calder, 2018); Amina Cain, *Indelicacy* (New York: Farrar, Straus and Giroux, 2020); Italo Calvino, *Invisible Cities* (1972), trans. William Weaver (London: Vintage, 1997), and *Difficult Loves,* trans. William Weaver, Ann Goldstein, and Archibald Colquhoun (Boston & New York: Mariner Books); Teju Cole, *Open City* (New York: Random House, 2011); Lauren Elkin, *Flâneuse* (London: Chatto & Windus, 2016); Jenny Erpenbeck, *Go, Went, Gone*, trans. Susan Bernofsky (New York: New Directions Books, 2017); Maria Gainza, *Optic Nerve*, trans. Thomas Bunstead (New York: Catapult, 2019); Eric Hazan, *A Walk Through Paris: A Radical Exploration,* trans. David Fernbach (London: Verso, 2019); Linda Nochlin, *Representing Women* (New York: Thames & Hudson, 2019); Rainer Maria Rilke, *Selected Letters of Rainer Maria Rilke, 1902–1926*, trans. R. F. C. Hull (London: Macmillan & Co., 1947); Mithu Sanyal, *Rape: From Lucretia to #MeToo* (London: Verso, 2019); Ayşegül Savaş, *Walking on the Ceiling* (New York: Riverhead Books, 2019); Olga Tokarczuk, *Flights*, trans. Jennifer Croft (New York: Riverhead Books, 2017); and Kate Zambreno, *Drifts* (New York: Riverhead Books, 2020).

ACKNOWLEDGEMENTS

I would like to express my immense gratitude to all the people who have helped *Landscapes* come into being. Thank you, first and foremost, to Eric and Eliza, for your astute editorial feedback and stellar copyediting, and for giving this novel the perfect home. You have built something truly marvelous in Columbus, Ohio, and I feel incredibly fortunate and proud to be a part of the Two Dollar Radio community. Thanks, also, to Brett, for all your support.

That this book exists at all is due to the wonderful Stephanie Sinclair, who was the first to believe in me. Thank you.

For friendship and conversation, I wish to thank Amy, Nicole, Samantha, Jasmine, Craig, Anita, and Byron. I'm grateful for your kindness, and for your wisdom and encouragement in times of uncertainty.

My gratitude and admiration to my dear friend Eunkyung, whose paintings catalyzed my own thinking on art, and whose insights on the creative life guided me through the most challenging period.

To Mark, who sadly cannot be here to see the publication of this book; you will always be in my thoughts.

To my parents, for their steady, patient support. To my sister Vicky, whose invaluable companionship has sustained me through everything. And to our beloved animals (Boo, Hazelnut, Willowby, and Beaxy), whose mere presence is an everyday joy and a balm in difficult times.

Above all, my infinite love and gratitude to Diccon, guardian of my solitude, and my lighthouse at the end of the pier.